# "LA FORGE TO *ENTERPRISE*— MEDICAL EMERGENCY!

"Notify sickbay to prepare for emergency limb graft immediately!"

Geordi closed the channel to the ship and pushed his way through to the injured man's side, where Dren was examining his crew mate. "I sent for help," he said. "I have a med team on the way from the *Enterprise*. You're gonna be okay—"

He stopped suddenly and looked closely at the wound.

Instead of blood and bone and torn muscle tissue he saw trailing wires, torn muscle actuators and broken metal. He looked back and forth from the injured man to the *Freedom's* chief engineer, and asked quietly, "Could someone please tell me what's going on?"

## Look for STAR TREK Fiction from Pocket Books

Star Trek: The Original Series

## Star Trek: The Next Generation

#20

# STAR TREK®
## THE NEXT GENERATION™

---

# SPARTACUS

---

## T. L. MANCOUR

**POCKET BOOKS**

New York   London   Toronto   Sydney   Tokyo   Singapore

An *Original* Publication of POCKET BOOKS

POCKET BOOKS, a division of Simon & Schuster Inc.
1230 Avenue of the Americas, New York, NY 10020

This book is published by Pocket Books, a division of
Simon & Schuster Inc., under exclusive license from
Paramount Pictures.

ISBN: 0-671-76051-3

First Pocket Books printing February 1992

10 9 8 7 6 5 4 3 2 1

POCKET and colophon are registered trademarks of
Simon & Schuster Inc.

Printed in the U.S.A.

# SPARTACUS

# Chapter One

THE *ENTERPRISE* WAS coming apart all around him.

"Steady," Captain Jean-Luc Picard called out, gritting his teeth, even as he wrestled with the armrests of his chair to hold himself in place. The red alert strip throbbed at eye level on the bulkheads, bathing the bridge in a nightmarish, bloody glow. Behind him, he heard the sounds of his crew struggling to stay at their posts in the face of the terrible pounding the ship was taking.

Picard wondered how much more his ship could take—and as he wondered, he couldn't help but remember that in the last century, seven ships had been destroyed by storms like the one raging on the other side of the hull. A hull that was a mere two meters thick.

Another shock wave hit them—and out of the corner of his eye, Picard watched Will Riker, his first officer, scramble for a foothold, wincing when he halfway collapsed against the gently sloping rail that separated the lower bridge from the upper. Simultaneously, a low, almost inaudible growl from the tactical station behind him told him that Worf, his Klingon security officer, had also gotten tossed around.

Picard felt for both of them. He knew they were as exhausted as he was by the shakes and shivers that had irregularly punctuated the last three days. Exhausted and frustrated—not being able to walk across the room without being knocked unexpectedly to the deck could drive you half crazy.

It was a maddening situation. The *Enterprise,* the flagship of the Federation, was the culmination of over four hundred years of spaceflight technology. Built to explore all but the most deadly reaches of the galaxy, she could weather with near impunity the interstellar storms that had damaged and destroyed earlier vessels. Her hull's tritanium/duranium alloys and powerful deflector shields kept the ravages of the worst magnetic and radiation storms at bay, while the crew carried on its business blissfully unaware of the turmoil around them.

But a Gabriel Effect was dangerously different.

"Captain," called Worf, apparently having regained his composure. "Damage control reports that the port warp nacelle has been totally destroyed, with major damage to the secondary hull."

"Again?" sighed Picard. "Number One, verify, please." Riker hoisted himself to his feet and straightened his uniform. He briskly continued his way up the gentle ramp, this time using the handrail, to the tactical station, where Worf was studiously examining the damage report.

For some reason the computer favored the port

warp nacelle. Over the last three days it had been reported destroyed five times by the storm compared to the starboard nacelle's three times. The primary hull—where the computer core itself, as well as the bridge, was located—had been reported destroyed only twice.

"Spotters say that there's been no serious damage to the port nacelle," Riker said. "Or anywhere else. We reset the damage control programs—again."

"Of course not," Picard nodded. Another low growl told him Worf agreed with him.

On the forward viewscreen, the laser-pink lightning characteristic of the Effect arced jaggedly out of the murky cloud of gas that dominated the screen to touch an asteroid drifting by. The resulting impact created a spectacular explosion and light show that drew the worried attention of everyone on the bridge. Though it was a hauntingly beautiful sight, Picard would have been more appreciative if it didn't present such a grave danger to his ship. Secondary waves spilled out from the explosion and rocked the ship for a moment. As the shuddering of the deck beneath him ceased, he shook his head and waited for the automatic systems and the breathing of his crew to return to normal. So far the "lightning" had passed them by. He could only hope it would continue.

The last Picard had heard, most astrophysicists now thought that the Gabriel Effect was a reaction of certain electromagnetic energies with a very specific kind of gravitational field such as that caused by a cosmic string, perhaps, or even a naturally occurring space warp. Reality mechanics had something to do with it, they hypothesized, but both fields of study were still so new and theoretical that there was no language, let alone rules or laws, to describe the theory.

Gabriels were named not for the ancient Hebrew archangel, but for the captain of the first starship to encounter one and survive. Very little was known about the storms themselves, because a Gabriel had incredibly disturbing and disruptive influences on all kinds of electronic systems. Instruments and sensors could not be trusted to show correct measurements, solid-state computer circuitry went crazy, even simple electronic devices could malfunction or cease working entirely for no apparent reason. There were even instances of highly charged reality-changing waves erupting from the fringes of the storm like lightning, disrupting any field generating devices, such as the ones used to propel the starship faster than light. The storms were of indeterminate duration and could cover huge areas of space—and could conceivably cause almost anything to happen.

Of the list of ships that were listed destroyed, the USS *Francis Drake* was the most famous of the fatalities. Her hull, interior, and all hands had been transformed at the atomic level by some strange and unknown electromagnetic process into pure silica during a particularly violent Gabriel. Seventy-six men and women had lost their lives before they knew what was happening. The effect now in progress could have done the same to the *Enterprise* any millisecond since it began. Or worse. From the captain's point of view, besides their capacity for instant destruction, the most maddening thing about Gabriels was their disruptive effect on electronic equipment—especially computers, which ran nearly everything on board the ship.

Picard had weathered a Gabriel once in the *Star-*

*gazer,* and had hoped never to do so again. When the first indications of the storm sprang up as they made their way across the frontier to Starbase 112, he had stopped them immediately, and had shut down all nonessential electronic systems. Every system that could be was put on manual to keep the computer from accidentally killing them all, and the personnel that watched the controls were changed as frequently as possible. It frustrated him, but the only proven way to deal with a Gabriel was to sit tight and hope it went away.

He had been on the bridge continuously for hours now. He had grabbed only a few short hours of sleep in the last few days. There was nothing he, as captain, could really do, of course; the Effect didn't care if he was here or in his cabin, and could wipe them out either way. But he had a responsibility to his crew that demanded he provide at least one visible stable factor in the whirling chaos.

"Status report, Number One," he said, turning in his chair to face his first officer.

"All decks starting to report in," Will called back, standing next to Worf at tactical. "One minute, Captain."

Picard placed his head in one hand, and sighed again. Patience, he chided himself—the storm couldn't last forever, unless it affected the temporal dimension, as well as the spatial ones.

"Crusher here," a voice sounded. "Is it an emergency?"

"Is what an emergency, Doctor?" inquired Picard, frowning.

"Didn't you call me?" came the exasperated reply. "I heard you myself." Beverly Crusher was the ship's chief medical officer, and had been flooded, in the past few days, with minor injuries caused by the storm. Normally, this wouldn't be a problem. However, the advanced medical equipment and diagnostic computers that would usually have aided her had been deactivated, lest they misdiagnose, mistreat, or cause havoc on their own. Not even the simple medical scanners could be trusted in the storm. Beverly had been treating everyone with archaic instruments and common-sense medicine. She had even unearthed her stethoscope—a simple listening device used for diagnosis before the advent of medical scanners, a gift from her parents upon entering medical school—to help out. Although the crisis had allowed her and her staff to brush up on some old techniques, Dr. Crusher was not very happy with the way she was forced to run her sickbay, and it showed in her voice.

"No, Doctor. No one on the bridge called you. It must have been a communications error."

"That's the third time in the last twelve hours, Jean-Luc! I sent a trauma team to Engineering to deal with a coolant contamination, only to find everyone there perfectly healthy. On the way back, they got stuck in a turbolift," she said. "Geordi's people are still trying to get them out. And this stupid records computer keeps lecturing from *Gray's Anatomy* at me!"

Picard almost smiled. "I apologize for the inconvenience, Doctor. Really, there's nothing I can do. You'll just have to turn the volume down—"

"It won't go down!"

"—and wait until the storm is over," he finished.

"Crusher out," came the chilly reply. Lt. Commander Data, a pale-skinned android, and Ensign Wesley Crusher were at Ops and Conn, respectively;

the latter turned to the former and made an exasperated face.

"Mom's in a bad mood," Wesley whispered to the android.

"Apparently so," Picard murmured, quietly. Though he hadn't been meant to overhear, the boy—young man—was correct. Beverly Crusher had all the patience in the universe when it came to dealing with the health of her patients, but on more mundane matters she could—and did—get frustrated. After three days of frustrations, everyone's temper was wearing a little thin.

Truth be told, the overall level of tension on the ship was as high as Picard had ever seen it. That had been having an effect on the entire crew's performance; Deanna had told him as much a few short hours ago.

His ship's counselor, being half-Betazoid and able to read emotions, had warned him of the potential danger when people were placed under such continual stress. She had been seeing almost the entire bridge crew—save Data, of course—since the storm's second day. And many other personnel in critical areas of operation as well.

Deanna had told him that she was uncertain how much longer the crew could continue operating at even minimum efficiency. Not that Picard had needed all that much convincing—his own exhaustion, and the bags underneath her eyes were enough evidence for him.

The near total lack of diversions/amusements didn't help, either. Ten-Forward, the ship's main lounge and social club, was closed, the holodecks were turned off, the computer libraries were deactivated, and even the food slots had been powered down. He thought about the prepackaged emergency ration laying unopened on his desk even now. He just couldn't bring himself to eat another of those things.

And as the crew's patience wore thin, he was using up replacements at horrid rates. Data, of course, had not vacated his post since the ship had gone to yellow alert. Apparently the howling chaos that disrupted electronics had no effect on the more advanced positronic systems of Data's computers. Picard stared at his paler-than-death android with admiration. Data was built for this sort of thing, of course, and Picard wondered briefly if his second officer secretly reveled in the chance to show off his superior abilities. Doubtful, if not impossible, he decided—the android had no emotions, and therefore no ego to flatter. Sometimes Picard wished that Data would be less modest about his nature, learn to relax and enjoy instead of studying and worrying. But Data was Data, and Picard doubted if he would or even could change. In fact, he was certain that he didn't want him to.

"Captain," Wesley said, "sensors indicate that asteroid the Gabriel hit has become a seven-kilometer-wide chunk of nickel, iron, and . . . felsium."

"If it is felsium, sir," Riker began, taking his seat in the command area next to the captain, "it's of no danger to us."

"Not unless the Gabriel Effect emits a directed stream of highly charged phased particles in the lower electromagnetic range," Data said, pushing the rotating Ops panel away and turning towards the command area. "However, the chances of the storm producing such a stream in the first place are low;

and the chances that such a stream, once produced, would impact on the same body are significantly smaller."

"About the same chance of lightning striking in the same place twice," said Picard. "Which is just the sort of thing these storms are good at. Data, could the hull of the *Enterprise* withstand such an explosion?"

"Certainly, Captain. With standard deflector shields, we would take no damage at all—and only superficial damage to the unprotected hull. But there is no certainty that the cometary material is, indeed, what the sensors say it is. I would suggest launching a probe."

"Just to be safe," agreed Picard with a nod of his head. "Make it so."

Data returned his attention to the Ops console, and a few seconds later, a tiny shooting star erupted from the hull and onto the screen, soon lost in the turbulence of the storm.

"Probe away. Sensor data on the asteroid will be available in . . . two minutes."

Picard turned to his first officer. "How's the ship, Will?"

"The port nacelle is still there, and the secondary hull is undamaged, but the ship insists that there is a massive antimatter leak, compounded by a coolant leak. Apparently, it's gotten hold of one of the damage control drill routines and thinks it's real, and nothing we say is convincing it otherwise. At last report, the coolant leaks were approaching main engineering, and have been flooding sickbay with casualties. The computer is trying to alert sickbay now."

"Dr. Crusher will no doubt enjoy that," Picard

said, ruefully. "I can't be derelict in duty by assuming that they don't exist if the ship insists they do. Bridge to engineering."

"La Forge here," came the voice of the *Enterprise*'s chief engineer.

"Geordi, look around you very carefully. Is there a large antimatter leak or other malevolent contamination in your section?"

"Uh . . . negative, Captain. I wouldn't be talking to you if there was. Howard is looking a little ill-tempered, but I think that's those emergency rations we've been eating."

"Tell him I empathize," Picard said with a smile. "Fine. No need to abandon ship. How are your people holding out?"

Picard could picture Geordi's characteristic shrug. "Fine, Captain. A little tired of poking around with a flashlight and looking for imaginary problems, but they won't mutiny for a few days yet."

"Hopefully, the storm will be over before then. Keep me appraised of any difficulties. Picard out."

"Captain," Wesley said, suddenly, his fingers flying across his console. "Sensors seem to indicate that the background energy level is dropping. If it does, then it's possible that the secondary and the tertiary effects of the storm should recede or diminish. Of course, this may just be a temporary dip, but this could also be the end of it."

"Data, verify," Picard ordered. If what Crusher reported was true, then he wanted to know as soon as possible.

"Verified, Captain. Background energy level has fallen 7.254 percent in the last thirty minutes. There is the possibility of sensor error, however."

"Is there any way to double-check the readings?"

"Not without going outside of the system," Data replied.

"We can use the probe we just launched," Wesley interjected. "Once the probe is done scanning the asteroid, I can use it to sample storm levels in a number of planes, charting a graph—"

Picard cut him off. "Yes, yes, you don't need to explain it to me, Ensign. Just do it."

"Aye, aye, Captain," Wesley said, as he began preparing his console.

A minute or so went by in blissful silence, as the tiny probe the *Enterprise* had launched swept by the asteroid, pelting it with all manner of scanning waves. The information poured into its little brain, which processed and organized it before it spat it back to its mother.

"The probe corroborates our sensors' readings," Wesley said, "both of the asteroid's composition and of a lessening in storm activity."

"Confirmed, sir," Data said. "Estimating 23.5 minutes till the Gabriel's secondary and tertiary effects—including most of the electronic disturbances—will be noticeably diminished. However, the primary effects, as well as continued e-m emissions, will continue for some time. In any case, there will need to be a step-by-step diagnostic refit of every ship's system before we can safely be on our way."

"Excellent," Picard said. In his mind, there was a rising chorus of hallelujahs as he realized that he could get some sleep soon. So might, he reasoned, some other people. Perhaps he could take some of the pressure off Beverly and Deanna for a while.

"Attention all decks," he called out. "Sensors are indicating that the storm level is decreasing. The worst of it should be over in less than a half hour. We will then proceed to do a first level diagnostic run to repair any damage. Until then, however, I would like to remind everyone not to use any equipment until it has been checked out by one of the engineering staff. Once the ship has been thoroughly checked out and everything is in working order, we will proceed to Starbase 112 for personnel transfer—and a healthy dose of shore leave. Picard out."

Even through the soundproof decks he thought he could hear the cheers. The *Enterprise* had been in space for some time, and everyone needed to blow off a little steam. The ship had become quite a pressure cooker, too, since the holodecks and other amusements had to be shut down because of the storm. He wouldn't mind a little jaunt into fantasyland, himself, he decided. Another case as Dixon Hill, perhaps—

"Captain," Wesley said. "The probe we launched is picking up some sort of signal. Pretty regular. It could be another ship; it's hard to tell. It's probably just the storm, but . . ."

". . . but better safe than sorry," he said. "Start a passive sensor search. Open hailing frequencies as soon as the storm permits. If there's another ship in the area, it might not have been as lucky as we were."

"The storm's intensity is falling off logarithmically, Captain," Data said. "It should be possible to transmit on subspace frequencies immediately."

Picard turned his attention to the viewscreen. It was true. The murky cloud that had been the epicenter of the Gabriel had almost entirely dissipated as quickly as it had begun.

"Stand down from red alert," the captain ordered. "Mr. Worf, try and isolate Mr. Crusher's signal."

The Klingon nodded, and turned his attention to

his console. While Worf worked, Picard mentally reviewed the list of spacefaring races native to this sector—and came up empty.

They were well past the borders of Federation space at this point—had been, in fact, for the last week. Stars, and therefore habitable planets, were few and far between out here. It was light-years to the nearest inhabited world. This far out in the sector, he would not expect to run into any of "the usual suspects"—the Romulans, Catellox, or Cardassians. More likely, it was an exploratory vessel of some sort—which could mean a Ferengi trading ship, or simply a nonaligned vessel.

"I have isolated the signal," Worf said. "It is definitely another ship—minimal energy output. No matches with any known ship configurations."

"Hmm," Riker said, turning to face him. "I would have bet on the Ferengi."

Picard nodded. "We'll soon find out who they are, Number One." He stood, turning to Worf as he did so. "Open hailing frequencies."

"This is Captain Jean-Luc Picard of the USS *Enterprise*. We are an exploratory vessel on a peaceful mission in this sector of the galaxy. Please identify yourself." He turned to Worf again. "Put them on screen when they respond."

"Aye, sir." The Klingon hesitated. "Their signal is very weak, Captain. The image will be fuzzy," he warned.

True to his words, a vaguely humanoid image replaced the contracting dust cloud that surrounded the ship. There was a slight pause as the translators picked up the alien signal and transformed it into something he could understand.

"This is Captain Jared of the *Freedom*. Where are

you from, *Enterprise?* Are you in need of assistance?"

Picard smiled. Thank God they were friendly—the last thing his ship needed right now was a confrontation.

"We are from the Federation. And I think we have things under control," Picard assured the alien captain. The low energy readings Worf was getting from the alien ship—the *Freedom*—made him wonder if they'd been damaged themselves by the storm. "And yourselves? Are you in need of assistance?"

There was an extended pause. Picard thought he could see the other captain consulting with someone offscreen, but the disruption made it unclear.

"The Federation—I don't believe I've heard of it," Jared said. Though relayed almost at a monotone, Picard felt he detected a trace of suspicion in the other man's voice. Or maybe it was the translator . . .

"The formal name is the United Federation of Planets. We're an interplanetary organization made up of several hundred cultures. Starfleet is the exploratory arm of the Federation, and the *Enterprise* is a Starfleet vessel. Where are you from, *Freedom?*"

There was more hesitation, and perhaps more offscreen discussion—the image was so distorted that Picard couldn't tell for certain. "Worf, get them clearer," he said with quiet urgency.

"Aye, Captain," Worf returned in a low growl. The picture did become clearer, though whether because of Worf's fiddling or the slacking storm, Picard couldn't tell. Now he got his first look at Captain Jared, and the *Freedom*'s crew.

They were human—perfectly human.

Jared was seated in the middle of an area that looked shockingly like their own bridge—a handsome young man with longish dark hair, probably a few years younger than Riker—flanked by an extraordinarily beautiful woman on his right. Both were wearing nondescript tan coveralls. Picard also noted the machinery in the background was archaic and bulky by Federation standards.

"We have some significant damage to our ship, *Enterprise*," Jared said. "Three out of seven of our reactors are shut down, and we believe we have a lot of external damage. The storm we encountered played havoc with our internal electronic systems. The readings were so wild we thought we were under attack when it first began. We aren't going very far very fast unless we get them fixed."

"Acknowledged, *Freedom*," said Picard. He exchanged a quick glance with his first officer—Jared had neatly dodged the question he'd just asked by responding to his previous one. "We call the phenomenon we have mutually encountered a Gabriel Effect—they are very rare, but very dangerous. We are both lucky to survive intact." He paused. "Perhaps we can assist you in repairs. If you let us know what kind of drive you're using—"

"Condorite fusion reactors, *Enterprise*," the alien captain said. "State of the art."

"Condorite?" Riker said quietly, coming up behind his captain. "Sounds like an old ship. Nothing Geordi couldn't handle in his sleep."

Picard nodded. "Captain Jared, I think we might be able to spare an engineer or two."

There was a long pause, as Jared spoke again offscreen. In only seconds, he was back. "That would be very much appreciated, Captain. We are short of manpower and supplies. I haven't even properly assessed how badly we were damaged."

"Do you need medical help? My medical staff—"

"No, we have an excellent medical staff," Jared interrupted. "And no one was seriously injured. No problem there. But our reactors are damaged severely."

"I'm curious," Picard began carefully. "What brings you this far out in the middle of nowhere?"

"Exploring," Jared explained after a moment's hesitation. "We're looking for a place to settle. Our world was devastated by war, and my ship was one of the few to get away."

"Devastated?" That would certainly explain the youth of the *Freedom*'s commander. Emergency situations often called for emergency measures, and less experienced men might be pressed into service. "I'm sorry to hear that. I assume you are carrying refugees?"

The younger man paused, then nodded, his face stretched by the now only occasional static. "Refugees. Yes. Over four hundred, Captain."

Picard nodded. "Captain, I didn't get the name of the planet you were from."

Jared nodded, tight-lipped. "That's because I didn't say it."

Beside him, Picard felt Riker tense. Again, he hoped there was nothing more to Jared and his ship than met the eye.

"We're from Vemla, *Enterprise*. A small planet at the other end of this sector. Have you heard of it?"

"Data?" Picard prompted, turning to his second officer, thankful again that one of Data's more useful abilities was his enormous and accurate storehouse of information. While he had nowhere near the capacity of the *Enterprise*'s powerful computer library, he had the capability to pull at least basic information on many billions of subjects and present it in a form more digestible—and therefore more useful—to his human companions.

"Vemla," he said, almost instantly, his eyes seeming to read the information his brain retrieved. "Some small references in the logs of the Saren Trading Corps, several centuries ago. Due to Vemla's isolated position and lack of noteworthy or valuable merchandise, visits have been sporadic. Class M planet, humanoid race, technologically underdeveloped culture. Little else is known about the inhabitants or culture of the planet."

Picard noted Jared and the woman by his side watching Data with frank interest, and wondered if they had ever seen an android before. "Captain Jared—what happened to your world? Were you invaded?"

Jared paused, then shook his head. "No. I am distressed to say that internal warfare destroyed us. There just wasn't enough left to salvage after the last battle, so we thought we'd start over."

A sad tale, but one Picard had heard all too often. That at least partially explained his initial evasive behavior. Hard times often bred suspicion. "I wish you luck, Captain. I'll have a party sent over to begin repairs as soon as we're within range."

"Perhaps you'd like to come yourself, Captain. I'd be honored to give you a tour of my ship, battered though she is."

"Another time, *Freedom*. I shall send my first

officer in my place, however. Any courtesy extended
to him will reflect on me."

Jared nodded. "Shall I send a shuttle for your
party, or do you have one of your own?"

"Shuttles?" Picard smiled tiredly. Jared had a lot
to learn about real state-of-the-art technology. "We
don't need shuttles."

# Chapter Two

ON ANOTHER SHIP, quite far away, Force Commander Sawliru sat in his cabin, examining telemetry reports from the last few reconnaissance missions. His head ached tremendously, but he bore the pain with great fortitude, just as he bore the reason for his headache, Mission Commander Alkirg. She was constantly calling him on the ship's intercom to ask for an update on the status of the mission that she was commanding.

Each time she had called, Sawliru had told her the same thing: Nothing yet, I'll call you when I have something. He had repeated the litany once each half-hour for the last five days. Yet she persisted in disturbing him for the most trivial of reasons. This last one, something about disciplining two young officers for speaking out against the mission and "spreading general dissatisfaction" while off-duty, was typical of the inane drivel that he had been subjected to in the last few weeks. Unfortunately, he would have to give them some summary discipline to appease her, which would just add to his troubles. As the mission dragged on longer and longer, the men under his command had time to think, always the bane of any military organization. They grew more and more restless and anxious about the Objective, with a capital *O* (as Alkirg was constantly reminding all of them) and the purpose of the whole mission. Now they just wanted to go back home. Where, he reminded himself, there was an even bigger mess.

He couldn't blame the two young men for speaking out. He wanted to get rid of the entire thing and go back home, too. But he was a military man, and military men followed orders. It was quite possible that the success of the entire mission might come down to his ability to follow orders, for if he had his druthers, Alkirg's Objective would be destroyed, saving a considerable amount of useless and self-serving energy.

But Alkirg didn't see it like that. She wanted a relatively peaceful conclusion to the mission. He could see her point, of course; if she could pull this off, she would be assuring her political future. Failure would condemn her to obscurity—and he was sure he would go down with her. The friends she had left would ruin his military career. The issue was just too valuable to trust to a civilian, in Sawliru's opinion. It should have been a purely military matter from the beginning.

On top of his problems of mediating between his crew and his commander, one of the recon scouts had reported a slight aberration in the spectrographic analysis of one sector. It might have been the Objective. On the other hand, given the freak storm conditions the region had been experiencing, it was probably a chunk of cometary matter or a leftover probability whirl from the storm. But Alkirg would insist on close inspection, just as she had everything else. That could be dangerous—two of their recon craft had been found totally destroyed in that area, with large pieces of them, including their unfortunate pilots, turned to mercury by the demonic storm. If she insisted on searching the area, none of them would ever see home again. If they survived the aftereffects of the storm, they would just keep flitting from one node of junk to the other, until even their home star was invisible against the rest of the galaxy. His crew might mutiny, aliens might attack, any number of bad things might happen. And they were running out of food, water, fuel, and other supplies.

Force Commander Sawliru sighed, and reached into the top drawer of his desk for an aspirin.

They were running out of those, too.

Riker shimmered back into existence, and the interior of the *Freedom* took shape before him. The lighting here was dimmer than on their own ship, the air colder, with a sweetish odor to it. Not unpleasant, just a little cloying. He waited for his eyes to adjust to the lesser illumination, and in a few seconds he could see normally. He couldn't do anything about the odor. It wasn't like a Klingon ship, but still . . .

They had materialized in a large, comfortable-looking chamber. Several padded seats and tables were arranged in an efficient fashion. Alien works of what he guessed was art, and a detailed model of the *Freedom*, hung from the surrounding walls. Four Vemlans—two men, two women—stood in a loose reception line before them.

Captain Picard had instructed him to find out as

much as possible about the Vemlans. There was something about them that made Picard wary—and a man who had sat in the big chair as long as Jean-Luc Picard had learned to trust his hunches. Will devoutly wished ship's counselor Deanna Troi could have come with them—she was an expert on alien/human relations and was well versed in reading the subtle body language that often gave away what a person thought. In the Gabriel's aftermath, though, she was still needed back on the ship, and he would have to muddle through as best he could.

The Vemlans looked as human in person as they had on the viewscreen. Each was wearing a simple tan coverall garment, and a wide fabric belt with several pockets attached to it. The only symbol of rank or insignia he could see on their uniforms seemed to be different colored sashes running from left shoulder to right hip.

Jared was the tallest of the four facing them. Up close, his well-chiseled chin and a slightly hooked nose gave him the appearance of long-lost nobility, and the bright green sash he wore set him apart from the others. He stepped forward and held out his hands, and, in the second before he spoke, Will saw his eyes were filled with a strange, unforgiving intensity, very different from the calm eyes of their own captain. He'd seen the look before: It was the look of someone who thought that there was nothing that could frighten him, or remain in his way very long.

"I am Jared, captain of the *Freedom,*" he said, as if his name were a title of nobility. His voice was deep and throaty. "I thank you for your offered assistance. We did not think anyone was going to find us. While you are here please consider my people at your disposal; do not hesitate to ask for anything you need." His speech, his manner, his attitude seemed designed to impress them, as if he were doing them a favor by letting them on his vessel.

Riker remained unaffected. He'd led countless away teams and diplomatic missions, and had been greeted in as many different ways by as many different kinds of leaders as there were worlds in the galaxy.

He took a step forward and gave the universal gesture for peace—empty, outstretched arms.

"I greet you in the name of the United Federation of Planets, Captain. I am Commander William Riker, first officer of the USS *Enterprise*. Captain Picard would have been here himself, but his shipboard duties prevented that."

Jared nodded knowingly. "I quite understand, Commander. Running a ship is not easy even when you have the best of crews. This is my executive officer, Kurta. We do not utilize rank as such," he added, informatively.

The woman who had stood by Jared's side during their initial contact now stepped forward from the reception line as she was introduced. She wore a blue sash, and a matching blue band tied back her long brown hair. A light smile, so much in contrast to Jared's stern manner, played around her face. She bowed her head slightly, her eyes taking Will's measure as he took hers.

"She actually runs this ship. She is my right arm. More importantly," continued Jared, with obvious pride, "she is my wife."

"You are very fortunate, on all accounts," Riker said, bowing.

"It is good to meet you, Commander," said Kurta. "I hope we can speak about the rigors of being the captain's right arm, sometime."

Riker smiled his best in return. He sensed a kindred soul, yet something here was putting him on edge. "I look forward to it; I'd love to talk shop."

Jared indicated a smaller man to his left. "This is Dren, my chief engineer. Without him, we would never have survived the storm. We all owe him our lives."

Dren looked slight but able. His eyes were piercing and touched everything as if he were trying to figure out how the visitors worked. He stepped forward and smiled warmly. "He says that now, but he howls like a demon when the comm system goes awry."

"And this is my librarian, Maran," Jared continued. The other woman stepped forward and bowed. She was not as beautiful as Kurta, by Riker's admittedly biased standards, but she was every bit as striking. Regal, he decided. Like a high priestess meeting a nonbeliever. He made a conscious effort to bow just as graciously as he had with Kurta.

"Maran keeps our records, gathers information, and maintains a storehouse of data on any conceivable subject," Jared explained. "She is also my adviser on alien relations, which is why she is present. No offense, meant, of course."

"None taken," Riker responded. "We're all aliens to someone." He turned to his right. "This is my away team. Lieutenant Commander La Forge is our own chief engineer. He will be directly assisting you in repairs, and I think you'll find his knowledge useful. To my left is Commander Data, our operations officer and—"

"An android?" finished Maran, an indefinable

edge in her voice. "How intriguing. You permit androids to serve in a command capacity in your military?"

Riker shook his head. "Starfleet is the exploratory and service arm of the Federation, Maran," he explained. "We are not a military force. Mr. Data holds a full commission in Starfleet, and is an invaluable officer on our ship. Is there a problem with his presence? A religious objection, perhaps?" He tried to keep any hint of conflict out of his voice. He did not want to proceed without Data.

"Not at all, Commander," assured Jared, smoothly. "If Mr. Data is considered an officer by your crew, than he will receive no less treatment by mine."

"It is just . . . intriguing, that is all," finished Maran, quietly. Her eyes seemed to caress Data as they might a precious work of art. "I'm very interested in cybernetics. I always tried to keep up with the latest research on Vemla."

"Did you have androids?" Riker asked.

"Our scientists had created a few crude prototypes, which were used in laboratories on remote research stations, but then the wars intervened and most of their work was lost."

"Enough, Maren," interrupted Jared abruptly. "We must not waste these people's time with idle chatter, as pleasant as it may be. Dren, if you will escort Mr. La Forge to the engines so that you might begin repairs, I will ask Kurta to show these gentlemen around our ship. Unfortunately, Maran and I have much work to do. We are still in the process of finding a safe haven, and a planet to colonize. We have a veritable mountain of research yet to do."

"As you command, Captain," said Dren. He went

to Geordi's side and picked up the diagnostic kit the engineer had brought from the *Enterprise*. Riker exchanged a smile with La Forge. That kit was heavy. If Dren wanted to carry it, then he knew Geordi wouldn't object. In fact, Geordi would probably have to give him a hand.

Dren bent and lifted the diagnostic kit as if it were made of paper.

"If you'll follow me, Engineer, I'll introduce you to the engine crew," the Vemlan said.

Riker tried to hide his surprise as the two engineers left the room. Dren must have the muscles of a gorilla under that tan coverall, Will thought. A wiry gorilla.

"Dren will soon be spouting some completely unintelligible technical jargon," Kurta remarked. "I hope your Mr. La Forge will be able to keep up."

"No need to worry," said Riker. "I haven't met the man that can outtalk Geordi when he gets going about warp mechanics."

"Dren is considered mad by many of the crew," commented Maran, solemnly. "They say he spends so much time with the drives that the condorite reactors have addled his wits."

Data cocked his head in a way that meant that he did not understand. "Really? I have never heard that condorite could interfere with biological processes, though the unshielded waves can gradually erode electronic pathways."

"She just meant he spends too much time alone, on an obsessive subject, Data," Riker explained with a smile. "It's a joke."

"Yes, Dren spends most of his time with the drives," Kurta said, flashing Riker a nervous smile. Strange. "Now about that tour, Jared; I'm anxious to see your ship," Riker continued, sensing an awkward moment. He didn't understand the confusion, but he noted it.

"Certainly, Commander. Kurta, if you will do the honors? Gentlemen, I have a ship to attend to." With a slight, stately bow, the captain left the room, Maran faithfully on his heels. As he left, Kurta turned to her guests. "If you will follow me, please . . ."

The doors on the *Freedom* were not the automatic sliding type, as they were on the *Enterprise*. The entire ship, in fact, was more primitive in design than the Federation starship. Yet Kurta was as proud of the vessel as if she had built it herself. She talked of nothing else as she led Riker and Data through the narrow corridors of the ship toward its center.

"It's amazing that the *Freedom* was built at all," she explained. "Our governing council had decided that military needs were more important than scientific ones. The basic plans and technology were purchased from the Sarens long ago. Yet it took a major appeal by the scientific community for the ship to even be started. The project ran out of resources many times, but the designers and builders were stubborn and never gave up. She was finished three years ago. She's bigger than any military vessel in the Vemlan system, which was a major coup in itself."

"From our ship, it looks like the *Freedom* was based on a modular design, rather than a single hull," Riker said.

Kurta nodded. "The design allowed many sections of the ship to be worked on at once. The *Freedom* was actually the prototype of an entire class of exploration and colonization vessels. We were going to build an entire fleet along her lines. Unfortunately, the wars ended any further development. A real pity. We learned enough during her construction to be able to streamline the process, though. Once we establish a colony and can get it on its feet, we'll build a hundred like her—or better."

"Your experience is similar to the earliest attempts at interstellar exploration in the first half of the twenty-first century in Earth history. The military forces of several nations preempted scientific advances as a threat to national security or turned their discoveries into military technology. It wasn't until after the Eugenics Wars that any major attempt was made at constructing interstellar vessels. As a matter of fact, the *Freedom* is similar in many ways to those early vessels," commented Data.

"Are most of the crew scientists, then?" asked Riker.

Kurta frowned and shook her head. "No. There is quite a mix. We're really a cross section of Vemlan society. When things looked their worst during the wars, we grabbed as many as we could and left the system."

"A Noah's ark, of sorts," said Riker. Though come to think of it, Noah's ark had animals and children, and he had yet to see either on the *Freedom.*

"I don't understand the literary reference, but I think I grasp your meaning. Yes, we are a preservation of . . . what was."

She paused at a door and took a small card from her belt, which she inserted in a slot next to the entrance. The door clicked and she opened it. Interesting, noted Riker. A need for personally secure areas. Perhaps a carryover from the Vemlans' military past.

"My people brought three treasures from Vemla, Commander. This is the first." The room was huge and circular in shape. There were several cubicles along the walls in which tan-clad crew members, displaying various colors of sashes or none at all, were seated, reading from scrolls in machines or looking at pictures on terminal screens. In the center was a large holographic display module, ringed with seats for viewers, where two women were examining and discussing a piece of sculpture.

"This is our cultural heritage," Kurta explained as they surveyed the vast room, "as much as we were able to salvage. There are seven thousand years of history, philosophy, literature, poetry, mechanics, engineering, and science here. We also retrieved countless works of art. Most of the actual pieces were lost in the war, but we salvaged replicas of almost everything. With this library, we can remember where we are from and who we are, no matter where we settle."

Data and Riker followed Kurta around the huge room, observing the people and the material they were studying. Riker glanced over one woman's shoulder, and stopped dead in his tracks. The text on the screen was moving so fast that he could not make out the individual characters.

"The speed at which they absorb information is most impressive," Data offered.

"Impressive?" Riker raised an eyebrow. "That's an understatement."

Kurta seemed startled at their interest. "The machines can be adjusted to display information at varied rates. The people that use them most often, the technicians and scientists, can read very quickly, while the rest of us tend to muddle along at slower speeds. Since this is her department, Maran uses the facilities the most. She can absorb data faster than anyone I've ever seen."

"You don't know Commander Data, then," Riker said, smiling at his android comrade. "I'd be willing to put him up against anyone when it comes to absorbing information. He doesn't have the name he does for nothing."

Kurta considered, and shrugged. "It would be an interesting challenge. Maran is demonically fast."

The tour of the library was short, and ended with Data requesting a copy of a summary of Vemlan history to update the library of the *Enterprise.* Kurta agreed and left word with Maran's assistant to provide an adequate source. The tour continued on to the crew's lounge.

As they entered the lounge Riker could see that the area was quite crowded with young, good-looking Vemlans enjoying themselves in various ways. Come to think of it, Riker noticed, all of the Vemlans they had met so far had been young and good-looking. He still found the lack of children on a colony ship odd, and had yet to find a good way to bring it up. Perhaps the Vemlans had cultural taboos against introducing their children to strangers.

In one half of the largish room, people relaxed with game boards and card games, and there were several ports being used for interactive electronic games. On the other side there were crewmen involved with more physical games, from something resembling darts to a ball-toss game that looked very boisterous. The participants seemed to play with few mistakes and moved with a startling precision and efficiency, Riker noticed. Certainly the healthiest refugees he had ever seen in his life. This was nothing compared to the holodeck when it came to amusements, of course, but it had a certain rustic charm.

But Riker's nose was drawing him to one corner of the room.

A small kitchen with a bar separating it from the rest of the room was sending a wonderful, exotic, aroma into the air, making his stomach growl. Will suddenly remembered he'd been living on tasteless emergency rations for the last three days.

"Smells delicious doesn't it?" Kurta asked.

He nodded.

"You must try some, then," she urged. "It will take but a moment."

"Thank you," said Riker. He was somewhat of a gourmand and was always interested in trying other cultures' specialties. Besides, the food slots back on the *Enterprise* were nearly at the bottom of the list of equipment to be checked out and reactivated.

Kurta inclined her head questioningly toward Data.

"No thank you. My system does not require organic sustenance in this form."

"You don't eat?"

"Not as a rule. I absorb an organic compound on a monthly basis, and use a direct power tap to charge my systems when necessary. I do not, however, need to eat, though I can utilize the sensors in my oral cavity to simulate human responses to culinary matter."

"You can taste, then."

"Yes. I have even found several foods to be of an interesting composition, though I do not possess the ability to truly distinguish between aesthetically pleasing foods and those considered—less desirable."

"Data is many things, but he's no gourmand," Riker explained.

"It was not included in my programming," the android said, simply.

"Well, nonetheless," Kurta continued, "I would highly recommend that you try Porupt's creations, anyway. If nothing else, you can store the sensations for reference at a future time."

"Very well," Data said. Kurta led them over to the kitchen area, and introduced them to the chef, Porupt, who was chopping and slicing the alien-looking ingredients on the board in front of him with the dexterity of a juggler. He smiled a hello and, without taking his eyes off Kurta and her guests, deftly lifted the cutting board and scraped the contents swiftly into a pan where they sizzled delightfully. Damn good, Riker thought. This guy knows how to swing a knife. It reminded him of his own cooking attempts, and he noted that he needed to have another of his infrequent dinner parties soon. The cook gave the pan a quick stir, and began cutting up more ingredients.

"Kurta. I heard we have visitors," Porupt said. "I see you brought them to the most important part of the ship first. Would you care for a bite?"

"It certainly smells good," Riker said, his mouth watering. "What is it, exactly?"

The chef's eyes twinkled mischievously. "Old family recipe. A secret."

He plucked a container from a rack below the bar and added a small amount to the pan. As he stirred the flavors together, a fine shower of hot oil rained upon his arms, though he didn't seem to notice it. Riker found that strange, but supposed that the man might be used to it.

Kurta slipped behind the kitchen and poured three glasses of a bright green beverage. "This is, I believe, the proper vintage for the dish?"

Porupt scowled. "Yes, it will do; but it's supposed to be aged seven years. They won't get all the proper nuances of flavor if it isn't. I hate to serve a dish halfway, but I guess necessity wins out over pure art once again."

He pulled three plates from behind the counter and served an equal portion on each. Riker politely waited for his hostess to sit down before he began. She inhaled deeply, then scooped up a pile of food from her plate and pushed it into her mouth. Apparently the local custom made fingers the eating utensil of choice. This didn't bother Riker; he had once attended a banquet where the first and only dish was live mealworms. He picked up a goodly amount of the warm, exotic-looking food with his thumb and forefingers and, pausing only to savor the aroma, stuffed it in his mouth and began chewing.

Data passively followed suit. Kurta made an appreciative grunting noise as she chewed and swallowed. Riker fell off his chair.

It was sheer agony. The food was like raw, red-hot antimatter in his mouth. It seemed to burn away the skin cells, the nerves, and eat away at the very fabric of his tongue and mouth in a barrage of alien fire that made him want to tear at his tongue. He grabbed the green wine at his elbow and began gulping it to relieve the onslaught of combustible-seeming spices. He didn't see the look on Kurta's face until it was too late.

"The wine is a little spicy, Commander," she said.

Liquid fire. That was the only way he could describe it. His eyes began to water. Riker desperately gasped for cool air and swallowed madly to get the offending beverage past his taste buds as quickly as possible.

"Water," he whispered hoarsely.

"Interesting, Commander," supplied Data, as Porupt quickly poured a tumbler full of clear water for him. "I had no inclination to copy your motions. The food is an interesting combination of molecular patterns and chemical reactions. I was particularly interested in the combination of reactions with the addition of heated organic oils. But I have no desire to gasp, choke, or wildly gesticulate, nor do my optics wish to tear as yours seem to. Perhaps," he said thoughtfully, "I am appreciating this food incorrectly."

Riker was too busy gulping water to answer.

Jared paced intently back and forth in his office. He was suspicious, and it showed. Maran sat in a low couch in front of him, unmoving except for her eyes, which kept track of her commander as he paced. Jared couldn't understand why she wasn't as anxious as he was. The data on the Federation craft, their erstwhile rescuers, had arrived.

"Their vessel is that large? And that well armed?"

"So Dren's crew has relayed. Our scanners are not fully operative yet, however, and so a detailed analysis of the ship and crew is unavailable."

Jared sighed deeply. He hated being without eyes, without knowledge of that which might hurt him . . . or help him. He stopped pacing for a moment and sighed again, more peacefully. The storm had been a double-edged sword, then, for if he could not see the *Enterprise,* then perhaps they could not truly see him. They had no strategic advantage, then. Perhaps. But what were their inclinations?

"What do we know of this 'Federation'? Are they friend or foe?"

"Insufficient data, Commander. The Sarens made some note of the Federation in their exchanges with Vemla, but the information is over two hundred years old."

He nodded impatiently. "Well, what data do we have?"

"The United Federation of Planets was formed as a cooperative organization, designed to share information and present a united, ethical front in the colonization of uninhabited planets. The Sarens viewed them slightly unfavorably, because they attempted to prevent trade of advanced technology to more primitive cultures on the basis that it was detrimental for a culture's development."

Jared halted in his tracks and smiled a harsh, wolfish grin. "Lucky for us that the Sarens ignored them, isn't it? Where would we be now had the startraders not broken the will of the Federation? Certainly, without this wonderful vessel!"

"Jared," said Maran, slowly, "if it wasn't for the Sarens, we wouldn't have been—"

"Yes, yes, I am quite aware of that. Ancient history, now. Sometimes I wish that those merchants had never strayed to Vemla, but then I realize the consequences. In any case," he said, as he resumed his pacing, "we have a problem. How much do the . . . Earthmen know about us? Have they seen through the charade? Can we trust them to aid us? Protect us? Or must we attack them to insure our own safety?" These and countless other questions were on his mind. He could do no less as a ship's captain—and a leader of his people—to find out if the Earthmen posed any danger.

"Jared," Maran said again, urgently, "this is not like the other times."

"How so?" he demanded, turning to face her. "Are they not just like the others? They can be beaten—"

"They have an android among them, Jared. He would not be . . . susceptible. Besides, they freely offer us aid."

"They do not know us yet! Would they give us the same aid if they did? I do not think so." Did the woman have no grasp of the situation? No clue as to the potential danger? Yes, he would like to believe that the Federation ship would accept them as they were, for who they were, but never in his creation had Jared met the man who had. As his chief information officer, he expected Maran to be as objective as possible, considering all the possibilities so that she could advise him, and yet—

"You do not know!" Maran exclaimed. "We have come so far, through so much, and here we stand at the doorway of a new life, with freedom and sanctuary just a few steps away, and you talk of attacking our potential hosts. We fought before because we had to, not because we were barbarians. And, yes, if need be, we will fight again. I will take a thousand lives with my own hand, if necessary, but only when there is no other choice!"

The usually imperturbable Maran had shouted out the end of her speech, an action that in itself was a vital piece of information. Jared knew he was prone to overreact on occasion, and he used Maran as a guide as to how outrageous his own thoughts and actions had become. Jared considered her words for a moment. Perhaps she was right.

"Alright Maran, we will play this one by your rules." Try as he might, he could not keep the undertone of scorn from his voice. "I forget, sometimes, that you were never in the Games, never felt the rage that comes—"

"Don't give me that!" she barked. "My loyalty to our cause has never been in doubt, and I defy you or anyone else to find fault with it." She regained her composure and stared at Jared. "Do we play this correctly? You saw him, just as well as I did. You saw how they treated him."

Respect. That was the unspoken word. "Agreed," he whispered. "But if it comes down to our survival or theirs—"

"If it comes to that, I shall kill them myself. I pledge this to you."

He turned again to her, his tone more gentle now. "I shall not require that of you. We have killers here who are much more suited to the task. Such as myself. And Garan. We were . . . trained for it, after all. No, Maran, you are a librarian, a keeper of books, a scholar. How I wish I could share your peace. But what has been learned cannot be forgotten."

"I know," she said, and sat in silence.

Despite what his lips said, in his mind Jared was already planning the possibility of a strike against the *Enterprise*. Learning the complete operations of the vessel would be no problem; it was run by computer, and computers were merely . . . machines. Garan's arsenal would provide the weapon, of course, and Kurta would be the carrier. Something lethal, yet nondestructive to the integrity of the ship. A plague, or toxin, perhaps. Details, however, that could be settled later, as the time approached.

But perhaps Maran was right. Perhaps this Federation would prove benign, even helpful, in their endeavors. Anything was possible in this mad, chaotic universe, he had found. Friends could become enemies, foes could become friends. Even a shy and retiring librarian could become a vicious killer.

"Let us discuss, then, the possibilities," he said, at last. Despite his genial manner, he was certain Maran knew what he was thinking. She always did.

# Chapter Three

"COMMANDER RIKER has gone back to the *Enterprise* to help oversee our own repairs," Data said over the comm channel to Geordi. "He wished me to ascertain your progress."

"You can tell him Dren and I have our hands full here. I'm preparing a list of equipment and personnel I might need from the *Enterprise*. I may even need your assistance, but it will be at least an hour before I'll know anything concrete."

"Fine, Geordi. Data out."

Dren had witnessed the exchange with considerable interest. "That's a very impressive piece of engineering, friend Geordi."

"What, the communicator?" asked Geordi, surprised. The Vemlans had comm devices of their own—a little bigger and bulkier than Starfleet standard issue, but relatively the same device. "Just a little fancy gadgetry and three hundred years of micro-miniature electronics, that's all."

"No," the wiry engineer said, shaking his head. "I was speaking of your Mr. Data. Did you have a hand in designing or building him?"

Geordi chuckled. He? Build Data? He didn't even understand him. "No, Dren, my specialty is warp mechanics. Data is the legacy of Dr. Noonian Soong, one of the most preeminent cyberneticists in the Federation."

"I was just wondering. How do you get along with Mr. Data?"

Geordi grinned amusedly. How could he sum up their relationship? "Oh, I can appreciate a classy bit of engineering as much as the next guy. But Data is more a friend than a machine to me." He began to examine the exterior of the reactor's core with his VISOR, scanning beneath the surface plate in several bands, hoping to detect any flaws in the containment casing. They would have to be repaired before any work on the inner core could be done.

"I see three cracks on the underside of the casing, just where it bolts into the bulkhead, there."

Dren nodded reluctantly. "I was afraid you might say that. The sound from this casing hasn't been right since the storm."

Geordi looked up, confused. "I don't hear anything."

Dren motioned him forward to where a huge metal strut abutted the power core and the bulkhead, holding the power unit in place. "You don't really hear it, so much as you feel it . . . in your bones. The vibrations are very slight. With all the reactions going on in the core, they make a very slight vibrational hum. Put your head on this bar."

Geordi did as the man indicated. He listened intently for a few moments, but heard nothing unusual . . . of course he wasn't sure what was usual. After a few moments of concentration, he rose again. "Dren, I'll take your word for it, but I don't hear a thing. You must have ears like a dog."

The Vemlan frowned. "A dog?"

Geordi explained the reference.

"Oh," Dren shrugged. "You have your shiny eyes, I have good hearing. You don't think it's our good looks and our professional knowledge of engineering that makes us chief engineers, do you?"

Geordi laughed. He appreciated Dren's casual attitude to the responsibility of the job. Too often he found other chief engineers took themselves and their positions too seriously and became stuffy. Luckily, Geordi was new enough to the job so that he could still kid a little. He tried listening to the engine again. Still nothing.

"Regardless of how we know it's there, this casing is still going to have to come off. Those cracks have to be sealed before we can do anything else. You might want to start emptying the core now."

"Agreed," said Dren. He removed a communication device from one of his belt pouches and snapped it open. "Dren to Deski. Start the drain on engine core three, and get a power crane ready. Our friend from the *Enterprise* has confirmed my suspicions about the cracks in number three. The whole casing is going to have to come off. Get a team working on it."

He closed the communicator without waiting for an answer. "Deski will get started on this one. Let's go see to number four—that's my worst problem. If I get called in when I'm off duty, ninety percent of the time it's because of number four."

A sudden, wicked thought struck Geordi. "Dren, I

have this ensign on the *Enterprise* who could use a workout on a more primitive drive system. He thinks the warp drive is the only drive there is, and I'd like to give him a little exposure to the brute-force method of star drives. Mind if he tags along and totes the toolbox?"

Dren smiled pleasantly. "Not at all."

"He helps me out in engineering from time to time, and occasionally thinks he knows everything. But warp drives are pretty clean, and I'd like to see him get his hands dirty for a change."

"Dirty?" Dren said, raising his eyebrows. "He'll get dirty, all right."

Geordi hopped down from their perch on the catwalk, followed by Dren, who picked up the tool box and led the way to reactor number four. Once they were out in the *Freedom*'s narrow corridor, they passed a viewport. Geordi stopped long enough to gaze at the stars, as he always did. The first time he had seen stars after he got his VISOR he had fallen in love with them. With his unique vision they were an even more impressive and interesting sight than they were to normal human optics. He understood why a ball of luminous gas had inspired man to take to the sky. He had once seen a gaseous nebulae, where new stars were being born, in its full electro-magnetic glory, and it was a sight he would never forget.

He noticed something peculiar, though, something wrong with part of the *Freedom* that he could see through the port.

"Dren, has the *Freedom* seen any combat?" he asked.

The Vemlan engineer shrugged. "Not that I know of. But there was a war, and I haven't been with her every moment. It's possible. Why?"

42

"I see some carbon scoring on the hull. Looks like heavy-energy weapons fire. Can't you see it?"

Dren stepped forward and peered through the thick glass. He stared intently for a few moments, then shook his head. "I don't see anything."

"It's there. I see it," Geordi insisted.

"It could be welding scores," the other engineer offered. "We did a lot of repairs after we left the Hevaride system."

"Yeah, I guess that could be it," said Geordi, unconvinced. That didn't look like a welding score. "You seem to have done some pretty extensive modifications all around."

"This was our first exploratory ship, and the original designers didn't foresee some problems that came up. In a lot of cases we had a better idea, and fixed it like we wanted it." The engineer stared through the viewport at the rest of his ship. "We're pretty proud of the *Freedom;* she stands for what we believe in."

"I know what you mean, Dren," Geordi said, still staring out at the distant figure of the *Enterprise.* He indulged one moment more, then gave Dren a friendly slap on the shoulder.

"Here's to classy engineering, then," he said, rubbing his stinging hand; Dren was very well muscled. No wonder he'd been able to lift that diagnostic kit so easily. "Let's go take a look at your problem child."

With Commander Riker having returned to the *Enterprise,* Data continued the tour on his own. Kurta escorted him to the next stop, where she again produced a card key and opened the door.

They stepped out into a huge, brightly lit hydroponics chamber. There were literally hundreds of kinds of plants in front of them, in all varieties of color and size. The air coming from in here was much warmer than in the rest of the ship. The scent of decaying organic matter combined with natural fragrances was almost overpowering.

"This is our second great treasure," Kurta said, waving her hands at the massive array of foliage. "We brought with us as many species of Vemlan plants as we were able to gather. There is no telling how much of our homeworld's ecosystem was destroyed by the war. It is quite possible that we have the only specimens left of many of these plants."

Data examined the flower bed to his right. The prevailing color was purple, but the shades and tones were so varied that no one color could properly be assigned to the flower.

"This is very impressive, Kurta, but is it not possible that these plants will not be able to grow on any new world you settle?"

"Of course," answered Kurta, somewhat sadly. "If that's the case, then we will have to keep growing them here or in artificial habitats. I'm hoping that we can find a planet like Vemla, though. Perhaps there is one in the Federation."

"The possibility exists," affirmed Data. "There are, after all, theoretically thousands of M-class worlds in official Federation space, and more being discovered every day on the frontier."

"It would be wonderful to have our own world," the alien woman said, her eyes far away. "With my own garden, where I can watch the flowers grow under a real sun, and get real dirt under my feet and between my toes. When I get depressed, I come in here sometimes and dream about it."

"I have always wondered about the preoccupation that humans have for captive floral matter. Counselor Troi, for example, maintains a plot of roses in the recreational facility on the *Enterprise*."

"Sentient beings enjoy caring for a plant," said Kurta, carefully. "There is something gratifying in planting a seed and watching it grow. It is a small way to gain a sense of fulfillment, of accomplishment. Don't you have such needs?"

Data shook his head. "I am not human, Kurta. I can only copy my fellow crewmembers' habits and try to theorize the basis for their actions. I try, because I am terribly interested in the race that created me." He paused, as he examined another plant. The flowers were red, this time. Red flowers had several symbolic meanings to humans, but how did the meanings arise and why did they become so inexplicably important? Such questions had burned all too frequently through Data's positronic brain, and always the answers were so elusive that an emotion that he had not the capability to label—but had certainly read enough about—frustration, was beginning to grow.

"Commander Riker once gave me a nickname," Data confessed after a moment of pondering. "He called me Pinocchio. It is a reference to a fable from Earth, in which a lonely man creates an artificial diminutive simulacrum, a puppet, for companionship. Through the intervention of a metaphysical entity, the puppet becomes animate. He is still made of wood, however, and no matter how he tries, true humanity eludes him. I have been seen as trying to achieve the same goal, but I share Pinocchio's limitations: I am not truly alive. Therefore the point of theoretically simple pleasures, such as gardening for pleasure, elude me."

"That seems somewhat sad to me, Data." She stepped closer and placed her hand on his shoulder. She seemed about to say something, and then stopped. After a few moments in silence, she began again. "Data, why do you try? Do they own you?"

Data turned toward her. He found the question somewhat puzzling. "No, I am considered an independent, self-owned entity by the Federation, though the decision to grant me that status has sparked considerable controversy in some parts of the Federation. I may legally do what I wish. I pursue this intangible quality because I interact with humans, and it is prudent to be able to understand them as completely as possible."

"Interesting," Kurta conceded. "You seem so knowledgeable about your world, Data. Is there any way that you could get us a good history of the Federation? We like to keep complete records, and who knows? You might be our neighbors, someday," she added.

"Certainly, Kurta," said Data. The difficult questions of his existence that had disturbed his thoughts and seemed to lead to no tenable conclusion were put aside for a moment; it was nice to be able to deal with something as easily quantifiable as a comprehensive study on the many-peopled worlds of the United Federation of Planets instead. He tagged the gold-and-platinum insignia on his breast and spoke. "Data to *Enterprise* computer."

"Computer here."

"Prepare core copy dump of Hermanan's *An Unabridged Socio-Political Study of the Formation of the Federation and an Examination of the Root*

*Cultures of the Federated Races,* with attached appendices."

"Working . . . Ready."

"Proceed with transmission of dump to alien ship designated *Freedom.*"

"Working . . . transmission completed."

"Thank you very much, Data," Kurta said, a wide smile on her face. "I'm sure many of us who are interested in your culture will be reading it—very soon."

Will Riker strode determinedly into sickbay, wearing a serious expression on his face. He nodded to Beverly, who was examining a medical log on the computer terminal, and went straight to a nearby treatment couch.

Deanna Troi lay motionless, with a machine of some sort placed around her head. A quick glance at the diagnostic indicators revealed that she was physically healthy, but he could tell by looking at her face that there was something wrong with her. She had been sick before, he knew—he had once even played nurse to her when she had suffered the Betazed equivalent of a spring cold—but never had he seen her look this—weary.

Dr. Crusher crept up next to him and passed a scanner over her.

"How is she?" he asked as he pulled a stray lock of hair from Deanna's face.

"She's fine," Crusher said in quiet tones. "The captain just recommended that she spend a few hours under a hypnotic field. I took her down into Alpha about fifteen minutes ago. That will not only block out stray emotions from her mind, but allow her to recuperate faster than normal sleep. Physically, she's fine, though a check through the nutritional computer revealed an uneven diet for the last few days. Considering the agitated state of the crew during the storm, and the unpalatable nature of Federation emergency rations, I'm certain that's true for nearly everyone on board, however."

"There are worse things than emergency rations," Riker replied, thinking of Porupt's "creation." It didn't take much effort to recall the dish that had practically set his mouth on fire—hell, he could still taste it.

"I checked with Wesley, and the Gabriel Effect has been known to produce erratic waves—static—on nearly all e-m bands. It's very possible that the storm did something on whichever band Deanna's empathy works on."

"Yes, that would make sense," Riker said, absently.

"From what she's told me about the way her empathy works, sometimes it takes massive concentration to maintain control. Without that control, the emotions of the entire crew were invading her mind, awake and asleep." She glanced at Deanna again, and then back at Will. "How was the meeting with the . . ."

"Vemlans?" he supplied, and frowned. "It went well, I suppose. I just briefed the captain on it. We ran a check on what solid information we have on them, and it's not much. Mostly second- and third-hand accounts from passing traders. Lots of rumor and hearsay, but few hard facts. Almost nothing on their culture or government.

"At last report, they had developed simple space-flight, primitive but effective nuclear weapons, and better than average computer systems on their own. They'd still be using chemical rocket or nuclear powered drives if the Sarens hadn't come along and sold a lot of advanced technology to them."

Crusher nodded. "I bet it was the influx of advanced technology that caused the eventual breakup and destruction of Vemla. Sad. Score one for the Prime Directive."

"We'll know soon." Riker wouldn't be at all surprised if Dr. Crusher's hypothesis was correct. Yet another vindication for Starfleet's number one rule. Perhaps the introduction of higher technology had nothing to do with the destruction of Vemla—but he was certain it hadn't helped. "Data requested a complete history of the planet for our records. If nothing else, it will be useful as a study of what happens when your planet gets technology beyond its means."

"How long will we be in contact?"

"Not long. Repairs are coming along quickly for both ships. I just approved an order from Geordi for supplies and personnel to help them get their ship fixed. He specially requested Wesley's help." He smiled at the thought; Geordi had been very emphatic on the subject. Yet the matter of the alien ship still disturbed him.

"I don't know. Their crew seemed cordial enough, but . . ." he shrugged. "There was something that made me uneasy about the whole place. Like they were hiding something."

"You told the captain this?"

"Yes. As a matter of fact, he told me that Deanna couldn't 'read' them, either—which could have been due to her condition, I suppose. But she did say there was something curious about their body language. That's one of the reasons I came down here, to discuss what she thought about them. Next time I meet Captain Jared, I want her at my side. Honestly, I felt a little strange. I mean, I expect aliens to be alien, but there was something inconsistent with the whole thing. Little things. Like I didn't see any children or old people on board," He shook his head, frowning. "But that's not it. There's something else, here, I know it. Unfortunately, I don't have anything to base it on. Just a hunch."

"Trust your hunches, Will," Crusher said, turning to face him. "A good captain has to be able to."

"I'm not a captain yet."

"You've had the chance. You will be, someday. If you want it."

"Perhaps. I like being first officer, though; I'm not sure if I'm ready to give it up. But speaking of what I want—do you have anything for an upset stomach?" he asked. "I mean, a really upset stomach?"

"Why?"

He patted his stomach, which was growling again, but for an entirely different reason than before.

"Because I think the Vemlans use condorite as a spice, as well as a reactor fuel."

The work with engine casing number three was progressing nicely. A powerful crane had been assembled above the reactor while Geordi's repair team, the ones he knew could be spared from the repairs on the *Enterprise,* beamed over. It took quite a bit of muscle to remove three solid inches of casing from the reactor core. Though Geordi would have preferred to use an antigravity lifting device, the field of such a device could cause a nasty and potentially hazardous reaction within the interior of the core. Brute force was necessary for this job; pure finesse wouldn't cut it.

Wesley Crusher had jumped at the chance to help, obviously not knowing what he was getting himself into. It took a little persuading on Geordi's part, but once he explained the situation, Will thought that a stint as a grease monkey might be helpful in rounding out the young ensign's education. Wesley had beamed over with a kit full of tools and a head full of enthusiasm, and obligingly began working under the watchful eye of the two chief engineers.

"Well, your number four engine isn't as bad as I expected," Geordi said. "I didn't see any cracks. Perhaps you should just flush out the system and restart the reaction from scratch. That may take care of a lot of the problems you have."

"Perhaps," said Dren, sounding a little uncertain. "But we've tried that before. The problem is that the reactors are all hooked into the weapons systems as well, so the connections get complicated."

"That's unusual, isn't it?"

"Like I said before, we've had to jury-rig a number of things on the *Freedom*," Dren replied. "If necessary, this set-up lets us divert full power from the drive and use it for defense."

Geordi whistled. "Pretty big guns."

"I designed the system myself," Dren said. "What we need is a way to stabilize the neutron flow. The way the charged particles come shooting out of the pipe, there's almost no way we can control the reaction without losing power."

Geordi thought for a moment, then snapped his

fingers. "You know, Dren, we might have the answer back on our ship. When I was back in the Academy I remember studying the first Vulcan ships, which had a similar power system. I think they used a special damper. If we have the design in the computer, and if Captain Picard approves, we can give it to you."

"Excuse me, sirs, I got the bolt off. What do I do now?" came a muffled voice from under the casing. Wesley had been removing the retaining bolts on the floor strut underneath the support housing. It was a difficult job, but Wesley had tackled it with enthusiasm and had the loose bolt to show for his troubles. From his voice it was clear that he was going to be glad to be finished, however.

"If you look about twenty-one centimeters to your right," said Dren, helpfully, "you'll see the top of another bolt. Remove that one as well."

"Uh, Geordi, how many of these bolts are there?" Wes asked hesitantly.

"I think I saw about twenty of them, Wes."

"Twenty-four," supplied Dren, helpfully. Wesley couldn't help but groan.

"Don't worry, though, it gets easier the more you do."

Wesley quietly groaned again, but went steadfastly back to work. The power crane whined as the heavy support cradle for the casing was lifted up to be attached. Geordi raised his voice to talk over it. He was about to question the need for such a massive defense system when the whine oscillated out of control and an explosive snap rang out in the large compartment.

Geordi turned just in time to see the support cradle and its snapped line plummet ten meters to the floor where Dren's assistant, Deski, had been standing. The heavy metal bar caught him in the hip and buried itself in his leg, ripping it from his body.

The man fell without a sound.

Geordi tagged his communicator instantly. "La Forge to *Enterprise,* we have a medical emergency on the *Freedom!* Trauma team to home in on my signal. Notify sickbay to prepare for emergency limb graft."

Vemlans from all over the engine room were rapidly converging at the side of their fallen comrade. Geordi pushed through them to get to the injured man's side, where Dren was already examining his crew mate. "I sent for help," he told them. "I have a med team on the way from the *Enterprise.* You're gonna be okay, Deski, just hang on. Have you started first aid?"

Nobody answered him. Two crewmen were calmly clearing away the fallen crane, and another was coiling the faulty wire out of the way. There was a singular lack of fuss about the situation, as if falling chunks of metal nearly killed people every day. Geordi ignored their lack of concern and looked at the wound.

Instead of blood and bone and torn muscle tissue, he saw trailing wires, torn muscle actuators, and a broken metal support frame. He looked up and saw Deski calmly and painlessly staring at his injury. Then he turned to Dren, whose face was a mixture of concern and embarrassment, as if he had been caught at something forbidden. The injured man was, obviously, something other than he seemed.

Geordi took stock of the situation and tagged his communicator again.

"La Forge to *Enterprise*. Cancel that emergency. We don't need a med team. I think this is a job for engineering."

He looked back and forth from the injured man to the chief engineer, and asked quietly: "Could someone please tell me what's going on?"

# Chapter Four

CAPTAIN PICARD sat in the conference lounge, listening to Geordi's report on the accident in the *Freedom*'s engineering lounge. His head ached—a combination of fatigue and stress caused by the storm, no doubt. Perhaps the only one who felt worse was Deanna Troi, who was still in sickbay under a sedation field. He hoped she would not be there too long. He suspected that this situation might call for her particular talents very soon.

"Androids?" he asked tiredly. "Are you certain?"

"Yes, sir. Every single one of them, as far as I can tell," answered Geordi, who was lounging casually, arms crossed, against the conference table. Data and Riker were also present, seated in the two chairs.

"The injured crewman was definitely an android, and the heat patterns of the rest of the crew matched his."

"Why didn't you notice this at once, Mr. La Forge?" asked Picard.

Geordi shrugged. "Captain, my VISOR isn't like normal human vision. I don't see things automatically, like you do with colors. When I use anything but my normal scanning range I have to concentrate. I wasn't expecting them to be machines so I didn't see much point in looking past the normal ranges. Once Deski was injured though, I had a reason to check."

Picard looked from his chief engineer to his science officer. Data's face bore the impassive, vaguely interested look it usually did. Though he lacked information on this new development, he wondered what it meant to the lone android. Was he curious? Excited? No—the latter was impossible. Data was not programmed for emotion.

"Mr. Data, do you concur with Geordi's conclusions?"

"Yes, Captain. From the tour given to me by the *Freedom*'s executive officer, there seem to be several items of a purely circumstantial nature that support Geordi's position. First, a number of verbal clues from the crew which suggested that they were not quite what they seemed. Second, there was no evidence of children or elderly people on board. Were the Vemlans an organic life-form, and their story true, children would almost certainly have been taken along. Third, though the executive officer showed me an extensive hydroponic garden, she did not show me any food-producing plants. An organic species in the process of colonization could not help but bring along foodstuffs and materials from which to manufacture more.

"Lastly, the design modifications to the ship's systems and the rate at which the crew members we saw were absorbing information seem to indicate not only a machinelike method of reasoning, but would also indicate a superiority over organic life forms in several areas. I would have come to the conclusion eventually, had the accident in the engine room not happened."

Picard rubbed his temples. "Yes, thank you, Mr. Data. Number One, your report?"

"Captain," began his first officer, "I didn't see anything that would have tipped me off. But I was suspicious about something all along, I just couldn't put my finger on it. The Vemlans—androids— seemed just like any of a number of humanoid races with whom I've come in contact. But then, I've only met two androids, Data and Lore, and the aliens didn't act very much like either of them. They ate, drank, told jokes, and had mannerisms that I've come to associate with hum—organic life-forms," he finished, in deference to Data.

"So, we have a ship of alien androids running around the galaxy claiming that they aren't androids. This is true, isn't it? They did claim that they had no androids on board?"

"Yes, sir," said Data. "I have the exact conversation on record. They were quite explicit with their words. They were, in essence, 'out and out lying.'"

"You concur?" Picard asked the other two. They both nodded their heads. "This raises a number of questions. How is it that these are Vemlan androids, when the Vemlan culture is—was—reportedly far too primitive to develop anything as sophisticated as an android? And why are they seeking to colonize— if that is truly what they are doing—a new planet? And the biggest question, as it always is, is why? Why lie about your origin to total strangers? Any answers, gentlemen?"

"Could they be embarrassed about being androids?" Geordi asked.

"I do not think so," Data said quickly. "The Vemlans seemed quite proud of their accomplishments. Moreover, I would think it unlikely for them to be embarrassed about such a minor thing as race."

"I think we should table this question until we can ask those who would know best, the androids themselves. There are others that need to be answered first," said Riker. "Such as, are their intentions hostile?"

"I saw weapons on board, if that's what you mean," responded Geordi. "Nuclear missiles, laser and maser projectors, explosive solids, and a few things I didn't have time to look at closely. And I think they've used some of it, too. I saw evidence of carbon scoring which I took to be weapon impact marks on the exterior of the engine section. I asked Dren about it, but he said that they were just welding marks."

"If they have hostile intentions directed toward this ship, Captain, one must logically wonder why," said Data.

"Higher technology, for one," said Geordi, addressing his friend directly. "Dren was really interested in some of our technology. But I don't think he's the type to take it without asking. The whole ship felt friendly to me. A little quirky, a little paranoid, but friendly. I can't see the Vemlans doing anything to harm us."

"But you don't have Deanna's talent. We don't really know their intentions, do we?" asked Riker. "They have lied to us rather convincingly. That puts me on guard, right there."

"Their evasive conduct does require some explanation, and they are capable of doing harm to the ship. I would suggest that we proceed with caution," said Data.

"Have you read the information that the Vemlans gave us on their culture, Data?" asked Picard.

"No, sir, I have not. I have yet to have the chance."

"Do so at once. I want to know as much about our enigmatic guests as possible. Androids," Picard said, as if to himself. "I never would have suspected. Who built them, and for what purpose? And why are they wandering around this sector of space?"

"What puzzles me, Captain," said Riker, "is if they are androids, why do they go through so much trouble to act like hum—organic life-forms? They eat, exercise, engage in recreation, all very unmachinelike things."

"Yes, that is puzzling," agreed Picard. "Is it all just an elaborate ruse to put us off our guard, or is there some other purpose?"

"I think I can explain that much, Captain," broke in Data. "Although I am a machine, I am nevertheless programmed to respond in several areas as a human would. My preferred areas of recreation are much different from most humans, I admit, but I can see no reason why an android of sufficient complexity could not find alternate means of recreation that are similar if not identical to that of an organic being. As Kurta pointed out to me, I can taste with greater clarity than a normal human, and precisely store the sensation for enjoyment at another time. It is intriguing to me," the android continued, "that the *Freedom*'s crew should choose such human things as cooking and eating to enjoy, things entirely unnecessary for mechanical sustenance."

"Quite correct, Data. And these are, after all, alien

59

androids, apparently created by an alien race for unknown purposes. Very good, gentlemen. I don't think we can take any action before we know the entire story." He thought a moment. "I think I shall invite Captain Jared and a small party over for a social call. Number One, have the holodeck prepared as a banquet hall for a small diplomatic dinner. I shall want all three of you in attendance, dress uniforms. I believe Dr. Crusher and Mr. Worf would also be good additions. And Counselor Troi, if she is feeling well enough by that time to attend."

"Aye, sir," said Riker.

"Data, after the meal I think you should give the executive officer a tour of the *Enterprise* in reciprocation. Give your inquisitive nature free rein."

"I shall try, Captain," the android replied, "but I am not very adept at the subtle nuances of social behavior."

"Just act nonchalant, Data," said Riker.

"Yes, quite. While Mr. Data is conducting the tour, I shall invite Captain Jared to my quarters for a drink and a chat. Hopefully, between the two of us, we can ferret out the reason for their deceit." Another thought struck him. "Geordi, how long until repairs are complete on the *Enterprise?*"

"Six hours, Captain, give or take a few. The main computer is working at sixty percent of optimum, and most subsystems are on-line."

"Very good. And how are the repairs coming to the *Freedom?*"

"Pretty well. We could be done with the reactors in about eight hours, if we rushed it. Other systems will take more time."

"Don't rush it. Continue working on the *Freedom,* but make sure that you keep in touch with each repair crew. We don't have any reason not to help them, yet, but if it comes to that, I might want the ship not to be able to move. Strategically, it covers our bases." He nodded at his officers. "Very well, gentlemen—dismissed."

"Force Commander, recon team six reports possible evidence of the objective," the technician on the desk console before him said. "A piece of debris which appears to be a remnant of the objective has been found."

"Was it destroyed? What was the volume of the debris? Where was it located?" Sawliru demanded. He was seated in the enlisted men's lounge, one of the few safe havens from the mission commander. Alkirg would never bring herself to enter the meager space allowed for mere enlisted personnel . . . and, hopefully, wouldn't think that he would, either. He was, after all, an officer.

"U-unknown, Force Commander, I—"

"Well, find out! Give me some answers!"

"Yes, Force Commander, a moment please while I check—"

Sawliru cut him off abruptly, furious at the man. The first positive proof that the objective was even in this part of the galaxy, and the idiot didn't know any details! If there was proof that the objective was destroyed in the storm, they could safely return home from this fool's quest and begin to deal with the situation there. If not, then they would have to stay out here until it was.

He considered disciplining the man, but decided against it. Sawliru took a deep breath and relaxed. He was beginning to treat his own men as Alkirg was treating him, and he knew that was wrong. They were doing the best they could under difficult circumstances. He didn't need to make matters worse. He sighed, and devoutly wished for the days when the military was a straightforward, honorable profession, untainted by politics . . . say, a million years ago. The console beeped again.

"Force Commander, only one piece of debris was in evidence, apparently jettisoned. Confirmed: The alloy matches that of the objective's construction."

"Increase fleet scans of the area and double the recon search patterns in the region," he ordered. "Sawliru out."

Progress, at least. The objective was still out there, apparently in the center of the storm-tossed area. Hopefully it had been destroyed, or incapacitated, or turned to mercury like those two scouts. He felt helpless in a situation like this, but there was little he could do . . .

His console chirped again.

"Force Commander, recon team eleven reports sighting the objective, and team nine confirms. They request permission to give chase."

"Negative!" Sawliru barked. "Tell them to report back to their commanders and await further instructions. Recall all recon teams. Have all ships begin battle formation six, and prepare for pursuit. The objective is not to escape. We will not have a repeat of Hevaride. Sawliru, out."

He disconnected again, and ordered communications to connect this console to Alkirg's cabin.

Finally, he had something to tell her.

Jared sat with Kurta and Maran in the cramped briefing room of the *Freedom*. Before them on the screen was the frozen image of Jean-Luc Picard, captain of the gargantuan ship that hung menacingly outside the viewport on the far wall. He looked at the ship and imagined the kind of destructive potential it represented. The Earthmen had been very careful to emphasize the peacefulness of their mission and downplay the military aspects of Starfleet—perhaps a little too careful. Hiding aggression behind a nonchalant face was the oldest trick in the book.

"An invitation to dinner?" he asked suspiciously. "No demand for our surrender, no hail of weapons fire, no curtly worded insistence on racial purity? Who are these people?"

"They are Starfleet officers," supplied Maran, "who pride themselves on their reputation for friendly assistance and racial tolerance. The entire Federation was built on those precepts, as you well know. You read the history Data provided, just like everyone else. We are in their debt for their aid."

"If they meant to strike at us, they had ample time before the discovery," commented Kurta.

"Yes, they did," he admitted. Which either meant that they were, indeed, in earnest, or that they were playing some deeper game—like exploring the defenses of his ship. He didn't even like the fact that the cyborg, Geordi La Forge, had access to the ship's plans—but Dren had insisted. The main weapons weren't listed on the plans, anyway. They had been put together by the androids long after the *Freedom* had been built. "But then they did not know what we were. Perhaps I am used to seeing dangers that aren't there. But my caution has saved us on more than one occasion. I won't let that slip now, just because of what a book says."

"Jared, this isn't like home," Maran said. "These people aren't from Vemla. They have an android among them, as a ranking officer. They treat him as an equal." She stressed the last word passionately.

"I know, I know, I met Mr. Data. He's a somewhat crude design," remarked Jared critically. In fact, the innocuous Starfleet android reminded him of an advanced model in some ways, but his obvious machinelike demeanor irritated Jared. Could not the Federation manage to produce a more streamlined, more subtle design than this?

"I spoke with him at length," Kurta interjected, "and his exterior crudity is actually an advantage when dealing with his crewmates. His obviously artificial skin conceals a highly sophisticated interior. He is unique among them, a prototype. And despite his strangeness, he is treated by them as a partner, not a slave. Jared, this could be our chance!" she pleaded.

"Perhaps." He sighed. "I want to be sure of our new-found friends, that's all." He was tired of debating. He far preferred action; Jared felt he had truly come into his own when he stepped onto the decks of the *Freedom* as captain and sole arbiter of what was to be. It was not in him to be a politician. He was not fond of talk, like Maran and Kurta—which is why he relied so heavily on each of them at times such as now. But he earnestly wanted his people to have a world of their own. He just wanted them to do it their own way, not as the pawns of some organic race.

"And what about this invitation?" Jared continued. "If we go, they will hound us with demands to make account of ourselves. They will insist on controlling us. We will have to start all over again. We will have to betray our pride to satisfy their preconceptions. We will—"

"—be in uniform and ready to transport at the designated time," Kurta said firmly.

"Who's the captain here?" Jared demanded.

"You are, and where the welfare of the ship is concerned, you make the decisions. However, you alone do not decide the course of our destiny. You put me in charge of long-term strategy—and this is an important strategic gathering. This could be our only chance to present our case without a dissenting voice in the background. You read their history—you know of their customs. And their reputation for open-mindedness and toleration. It is doubtful that they will clap us in irons as soon as we board the ship—not that they have any irons that could hold us. Think of it this way—we will see much more of their ship than they suspect, which will provide valuable intelligence in case direct action is called for. My husband, this is one engagement we have to win. It is as important as any battle you have ever fought."

Jared shook his head. He had not risked his life hundreds of times, seen good friends die, risked the entire ship and all aboard, come through the most ferocious space storm he had ever known only to throw everything away by walking into a potential trap disguised as a dinner party. It was madness!

Jared looked back at the gleaming Federation ship. Its lines were smooth, dynamic, nearly organic compared to his own ship's blocky manufactured look. Void take it, it was purely majestic! Sensor scans, what they could get, revealed over a thousand organic beings, and computers and gods knew what other kinds of advanced technology. The weaponry alone would be worth the trip. Jared loved the *Freedom* with every fiber of his being, and was proud as could be to be her captain, yet his command looked paltry beside the *Enterprise*. He wanted to see the vessel up close. Walk through its corridors and feel its might. Have the technology explained to him by those who knew it best. See its wonders, and hear the wondrous tales of its crew. With a ship like that, he could build an empire—or explore the galaxy and shake loose its wonders.

So be it, then. He would go on this outing to see that ship and test the mettle of its captain.

He smiled at Kurta. "Very well, you win. I will go and smile and shake hands and make idle chatter and hope we are not destroyed out of hand. Will that satisfy you?" he asked, only half sarcastically.

"Yes, it will. I have prepared a list of people to make up our side of the occasion . . ."

A sudden inspiration struck him. "You may choose who you like, but I want them in particular to see one of us . . ."

The captain and Commander Riker, clad in dress uniforms, met the Vemlan party in the main transporter room. The aliens had never experienced transporters before, and Picard wanted to be on hand personally to soothe any anxiety they might have.

Five figures materialized on the pads in front of them. Picard recognized Jared and guessed that the woman to his immediate right was Kurta, the executive officer that Riker and Data had talked to. He also identified Maran, the librarian, and Dren, the Vemlan chief engineer from his crew's descriptions. But next to Jared was a figure of mammoth proportions.

He stood a good foot taller than his companions.

His shoulders stretched the fabric of his tan uniform to the limits, and seemed in danger of bursting it. The man—the android, Picard corrected himself—had a lantern jaw and a cauliflower ear, and black, limp, lifeless hair. He stood passive, unmoving, as if waiting for someone to turn him on.

Picard had to force himself not to react.

"Captain Picard," called Jared evenly, but with enthusiasm, as he stepped down from the transporter platform. "What an efficient way to travel! It is far superior to our shuttles."

"It's almost like magic, being in one ship one second, and another the next. I am in awe of your technology," Kurta said, smiling.

"Indeed," Jared said. "I don't believe you have met my crew." He proceeded to introduce each of his officers ending by placing his hand on one of the massive arms of the giant. "This is Garan."

The giant peered down at the two Starfleet officers and extended a massive hand in greeting.

"I am pleased to make your acquaintance, Captain Jean Luc-Picard," the android said, slowly and very seriously. "I thank you for your gracious invitation."

"My pleasure, Garan," replied Picard. Garan looked around the room with vague interest, then returned to the eyes-front position in which he had beamed over. Picard couldn't help but stare. Perhaps his reaction would have been different if the other Vemlans weren't so physically identical to humans. In any case, Garan was simply the biggest, most massive humanoid Picard had ever met. Polite, though, he thought, noting Garan's carefully spoken greeting.

As they all were, despite their mechanical nature. The ship's short-range sensors were working—

erratically—and he had ordered a scan of the *Freedom*. There were no life signs. Which just confirmed what they already knew.

"I suggest we adjourn to the banquet room," Picard said, tearing his eyes away from Garan. He led the *Freedom*'s crew out of the transporter room into the corridor. Jared kept pace at his side.

"Captain, I heard about the unfortunate accident in your engine room. I hope that your crewman wasn't seriously hurt," Picard said, concerned.

Jared's smile faltered for a brief second, but he quickly recovered. "Deski is fine, Captain. I appreciate your concern. He will be back at work on the engines before we are finished with dinner."

The holodeck had been decorated under Riker's expert eye. He had chosen an ancient Grecian theme for the occasion, Picard noted approvingly, programming the computer to generate a multitude of holograms and furnishings to show off what many considered the high point of ancient Earth civilization. Doric columns, made of pure light, seemed to support the colorfully-frescoed ceilings above them, and huge torches lined every wall. Long, low couches of modern design and classical elegance flanked tables that were nothing more than slabs of pure marble. The tables were set with beautiful clay urns and brass goblets of wine, and a heavy wooden plate sat at each place. A mountain—Olympus? Picard wondered idly—was just visible between two columns that formed a gateway to a wide valley. Flocks of computerized sheep stood tended by a fictitious shepherd on the imaginary meadow outside. The sound of kitharas and lyres and flutes could be heard as if musicians stood on the other side of the tapestry that concealed the far wall. Hellenic sculpture stood at various places around the room, electronic copies of marble copies of human ideals of the gods.

It was quite impressive.

"Greco-Roman, isn't it?" Maran asked, admiringly, as she entered the room. "Many of your greatest advances in art, philosophy, and science stem from this era, if I remember your records correctly."

Picard smiled and nodded his head. "That's correct. I hope you find it as stimulating as I do."

His other officers—Data, La Forge, Crusher, even Counselor Troi—were already present and in place at the dining table, with the exception of Worf, who had requested permission to remain at his post. Picard would have liked him to be there, but until the Vemlans' intentions could be discerned, he would not force the issue.

Wine had already been poured into the glasses next to each table setting. As everyone chose a seat, Picard lifted his glass, intending to offer a toast— but Jared beat him to it.

"I'd like to offer a few words of thanks for your help and your courtesy, Captain Picard—to you, and your crew." Jared held out the goblet of wine in front of him. "In keeping with the theme of the evening, I offer a libation to whichever gods caused our paths to cross." He spilled a few drops of wine to the floor, then raised his glass to his lips and drank. The others followed suit.

As he drank, Picard caught Riker's eye, and saw his own expression mirrored there. The alien captain was clearly a man used to taking charge. It made Picard a little uncomfortable.

He finished drinking, and motioned for everyone to sit.

"Well said, Jared. Your familiarity with Earth culture is most impressive."

"I have always been a quick study, Captain," he said. "And of course, memory for us is . . . different."

"Indeed," Picard said, thinking of what it must be like to be able to learn a subject so quickly and completely. Surely one couldn't help feeling slightly superior . . .

He looked down the table and saw Data locked in conversation with Maran, and was immediately ashamed of his thoughts.

Dinner played out like a chess match. Picard let his junior officers make subtle queries and idle chitchat while he tried to steer the course of the conversation as he would a ship. The Vemlans (with the exception of Garan, who answered each question with a simple yes or no) were all responsive and engaging, but there was more evasiveness and skillful sidestepping than Picard cared for.

"You seem to place a lot of status in the office of librarian," Dr. Crusher said to Kurta. "Is this endemic in Vemla's culture or a recent innovation?" she asked, meaning, of course, because they were androids.

"Only in the last few decades, Doctor," Kurta said. "Our civilization finally realized the value of information and knowledge in a broad sense. Our libraries—and librarians—became highly prized assets."

"What kind of planet are you interested in finding?" Picard asked Jared as the alien captain refilled his wine.

"Oh, any sort that will support abundant life," the other captain replied.

"Abundant life?" Picard asked, questioningly.

"We look forward to studying the diversity of our adopted world," he answered, pouring another glass.

"Commander Riker tells me that you have an excellent chef on the *Freedom,*" Geordi said, breaking open a loaf of thin, Grecian bread. "I'm sorry I missed that. Where did he learn to cook like that?"

"From a master chef on Vemla," Dren replied. "Porupt is a quick study and graduated top of his class."

It reminded Picard of the Mad Hatter's tea party in some ways. Questions answered questions, and answers almost never completely satisfied the asker. He was impressed, he had to admit. The Vemlans responded to every query without giving away any vital information. It was obvious that Jared had instructed his crew well before they boarded the *Enterprise.* Just what Picard would do, he supposed, in a similar situation. Anything that looked too hot for a Vemlan to handle was relayed to Jared or Kurta, who came up with technically satisfactory yet maddeningly incomplete answers. Jared, in particular, impressed him. When it came to comparisons between the two cultures, the alien captain strongly defended the merits of his people, despite their relatively primitive technology. Picard found that fact somewhat ironic, coming from an android.

Their guests' mechanical nature was not overtly brought up by the crew of the *Enterprise,* but was hinted at subtly a number of times. The Vemlans neither confirmed nor denied the allegations, allowing the conversation to wind its way naturally away from the topic.

The meal itself was a masterpiece. Riker had enlisted the aide of a lieutenant in BioSci who had an expert hand with the compuchef machines, and had literally come up with a banquet for the ages. All the courses could be firmly documented as authentic Hellenic cuisine, mostly from recipes in Linear A, unearthed at the famous dig at Knossus in the mid twenty-first century. The fabulous archaeological find had produced an exact account of the coronation feast of Drantos, a popular Cretan monarch of the middle Bronze Age, and a number of select dishes had been prepared from the list for the ancient banquet. The lamb was, admittedly, synthesized, but no human palate could tell the difference from the genuine article, and if the androids could, they weren't complaining. Grapes, pomegranates, and other fruits were passed from place to place, as fresh and cool as if they had been picked that morning. The wine, a nonalcoholic vintage, was dark red and full-bodied, an excellent complement to the meal.

As the wine came around to him once again, Picard poured half a glass and raised it in toast. "Let us all be thankful for our surviving the storm." The rest of the party joined him, and he finished the cup. Then he stood. "Commander Data, perhaps you would escort our new friends on a tour of our vessel. And Captain Jared, I was wondering if you would care to join me in my quarters—I have some wine there from my family's vineyards back on Earth I bring out for special occasions such as these."

"I'd be honored, Captain," Jared said. With that, dinner broke up, Data taking the Vemlans in tow to begin the tour of the *Enterprise,* while Picard escorted Jared to his own quarters, and, as promised, produced a bottle of the Picard family vintage.

Jared was staring out of the massive viewport that dominated his cabin at his own ship, glass in hand, while Picard relaxed on a low couch.

"Captain, I congratulate you on your command," Jared said. "You have a superb crew, and the *Enterprise* is all any commander could hope for in a ship. I must admit, I envy you. My own crew is enthusiastic, but . . ." he shrugged. "They lack a certain polish."

The admission surprised Picard. Throughout the meal, Jared had been militantly proud of his people and his ship. The frank admission was a good sign; perhaps the truth would come out.

"Thank you. I think you underestimate your own crew, however. They seem to have come through . . . all they have admirably."

Jared turned, drink in hand, and looked Picard in the eye. "Don't misunderstand me, Captain. I have a fine crew. How does your saying go—they have been to hell and back. But they weren't cut out for this. Your crew is. Each one of them is an explorer at heart, in some fashion. In my crew there are only a few who can make that claim. Even my wife is more concerned with establishing a new world than in exploration, deep down." He sighed. "After we find an adequate world to settle a colony, perhaps I can have a command such as yours . . ." He shook it away as if the wish might fully possess him. "But now I must lead my people away from the terrors of war and into a better future. A future we may have to build one stone at a time."

Picard nodded, and sipped at his wine. "You've made reference to this war that destroyed your planet several times, Captain Jared. I'd be interested in hearing more about it—what happened to you during it. What you were doing before you took command of the *Freedom*."

Picard had purposely taken a calculated, dangerous first step, directly addressing what they had waltzed around all night. Perhaps here, in private, Jared would answer.

The alien captain turned away from Picard to look at the stars. He stayed that way for a moment, then turned back.

"I was a scholar, a researcher. Tasks a machine is eminently suited for, wouldn't you agree?"

Picard said nothing. He wanted to keep the burden of the conversation on the android captain.

"My entire crew, as I'm sure your Mr. La Forge has told you, is composed of androids. Does that bother you, Captain?"

"Not particularly," Picard said. "I have worked with an android for several years now and have nothing but respect for him."

Jared almost smiled. "Yes, the unique Mr. Data. I, too, am impressed by him. He is very different from our kind, yet at the heart I think he is the same. An excellent piece of engineering. He was well designed."

"He is a good man," Picard said quietly, remembering how he had gone to court to prove the point. While humanity had made great strides in conquering its fears and hatreds where its own and alien races were concerned, the almost-but-not-quite-human Mr. Data had brought those same undesirable feelings disturbingly close. Picard himself had wrestled with the problem of his own attitude toward Data. In the end, he treated Data as he would anyone else, with the respect due him for a job well done and with the friendship due to one who offered it freely. Data was a person, a comrade, and a friend, and Picard had no trouble justifying his defense of him as such.

"Of course, Captain," said Jared. "That was what I wanted to hear. Yes, Data is a man. Whether he is good or not is a matter of philosophical debate, but I am inclined to like him, as are my officers. Data is a man. This question has been a problem to my people. Not everyone feels the way you do about androids."

"Was that the reason for your evasiveness, then? A fear of bigotry?"

Jared nodded, setting his glass of wine down on the table in front of Picard. "Put yourself in my position, Captain. Our creators laid an entire world to waste. We had no recourse except to leave and find a new planet. But the galaxy is a dangerous place, and we have heard tales of all manner of horrors. Imagine, if you will, what would have happened if a race like the Ferengi had found us. The Saren told us of their heartless merchantilism. My people are skilled and our ship is rich, by many standards. We would have become their property—to be sold at a profit." He motioned towards the window, and his ship looming outside. "I had my crew to think of. We've come too far to be treated like machinery."

What Jared said was true, Picard had to admit; the number of unfathomable dangers in the galaxy made it as terrifying as it was wonderful.

"I can appreciate your desire for caution. In your place I might have done the same." He paused, sipping again, which gave him time to collect his thoughts. "But once we had offered to help you— why didn't you tell us then?"

"Two reasons. First, because we didn't think of it as important. And second," said Jared, grinning softly, "because you didn't ask."

Picard smiled back. "True enough. How could you be expected to answer questions you weren't asked?"

"It would be similar to me becoming upset over the omission of your blood type in our first transmission. How does one bring up the fact that one is a machine in conversation? Seriously, Captain, I hope you will look beyond what power moves my hands and look to what thought inspires them to move."

Picard relaxed. "I understand. Let me ask a few more questions about you and your people, just so this type of misunderstanding won't happen again."

"Certainly," said Jared, taking a seat on the couch.

"Tell me about the war you escaped—and tell me why you didn't take any hum—organic Vemlans along."

The *Freedom*'s captain nodded. "I don't know too much about the war, itself—I was stationed at a research base on Vemla's outer moon." Jared finished his drink and poured another glass. "I do know that it was very bloody. The fighting was between two rival political groups and took most of the planet by surprise. Our world had enjoyed over two hundred years of uninterrupted peace. The destruction was horrendous. Billions died. All sorts of terrible weapons were used. Including androids." Jared closed his eyes and sighed. "Garan was specifically designed for battle—a prototype. It doesn't take much intelligence to be a killing machine. When the Capitol was destroyed, and all was in chaos, we reprogrammed him to keep him from fighting. Kurta uses him in the hydroponic gardens when he isn't needed for more physical tasks. But he is incapable of violence. He couldn't hurt anything now.

"The war eventually spread to the moons. The humans in our facility were killed one night by a virulent contaminant brought in by terrorists. We were all that was left. When we saw what the war had done to our home, we knew we couldn't stay. So we took the *Freedom*—and we've been traveling ever since, looking for a place to settle."

"I believe I understand your actions now, Jared," Picard said, deeply moved. He'd heard similar tales before, of races whose technology had outpaced their emotional growth. But the idea of a planet destroying itself was always horrifying. "It is . . . regrettable that your builders failed to come to terms with their aggression and political turmoil. It sounds as if they were very close to developing a truly civilized culture."

"They were. And I feel certain my people will not repeat their mistakes."

Picard nodded. For all their sakes, he hoped so.

After the Vemlans returned to their ship, Picard headed to the bridge for one last look around before retiring for the day. As he entered the turbolift, he was joined by Riker, who had changed back into his standard uniform.

"Did you learn anything important in your—interview?"

The captain nodded. "Yes. I don't think we have much to worry about from Captain Jared and the *Freedom*, Number One. They were merely concerned about our intentions. I believe them to be exactly what they said they were—refugees in search of a place to settle."

"I'm still suspicious," Will remarked, his brow knit in thought, "but I have to admit, they were delightful as dinner companions. Especially the executive officer—quite attractive."

"Yes, they were all very attractive," Picard said, raising his eyebrows. He wasn't immune to earthly beauty. "A credit to their . . . designers."

"It's hard to dislike something that beautiful," Riker admitted. "But that just makes me all the more suspicious."

The turbolift came to a stop and the doors whisked open. The bridge was quiet; only the Ops and helm consoles were occupied, though Worf was diligently checking the sensor relays. He glanced up, saw the captain, and spoke.

"Sir, I've been realigning the sensor relays, and have discovered an anomaly."

Picard turned. "That's hardly unexpected, Mr. Worf. The sensors still haven't fully recovered from the storm."

"Yes, sir. I am aware of that. But this anomaly looks very much like another ship."

Picard raised an eyebrow. "Can you get a fix on it?"

"Trying, sir," Worf said, fingers stabbing at the console.

"Whatever it is, it's closing on our position," Riker said, leaning over the Ops console.

"Sir, a second ship has been detected," Worf said, looking down at the tactical station. "No—four—six—a large group of ships in a tight formation."

Riker looked over the Ops panel. "They're all traveling slowly, though—just at warp one."

"A fleet?" asked Picard, alarmed. "This far out in space? Can you identify it?" he asked his tactical officer. Peaceful craft tended to roam the sea of space singly. Large groups often meant trouble.

Worf shook his head. "The computer couldn't get a fix on it long enough to identify it. But it ruled out a number of possibilities. It isn't a Federation, Klingon, Sirian, or Ferengi fleet of any known composition. The computer also ruled out the possibility of a Romulan fleet, in consideration of the small size and slow speed."

"That narrows it down. There are only another hundred or so known spacefaring races that it could be." Picard took his seat. "Mr. Worf, what else do the scanners say about the fleet?"

"The ships have impressive armament for their size. Seven capital ships of nine hundred thousand metric tones, with a number of smaller craft escorting them. Estimate they will intersect our position in approximately six hours."

"Let's find out what they want then, shall we? Open hailing frequencies, Mr. Worf." Picard cleared his throat. "Greetings. This is Captain Jean-Luc Picard of the United Federation of Planets' starship *Enterprise.*"

There were a few moments of silence before any response came. When it did, it came without a visual aspect, as a slightly tinny vocal message.

"This is Prefect Morgas, of the naval ship *Vindicator.* Stand by to be addressed by the Fleet Force Commander. Do you have visual capabilities?"

Worf was still at his security console behind the command area. He seemed intent on the readings before him.

"Yes, Prefect, we do," Picard answered, warily.

In moments the image of a tall, elderly man in a black, military-looking costume spread itself across the forward viewscreen. He was slightly built and had a severely hooked nose. Gold and silver medallions were pinned to his chest, though whether they were rank, insignia, or military decorations, Picard couldn't tell. He held himself as one who expected to be obeyed in all things, yet was not overbearing. Picard's overall impression was that the man was a hawk, a predator.

The man smiled, a tight-lipped and stern expression. His eyes were bright and intense, but not necessarily friendly.

"Greetings, Captain Picard. I am Force Commander Sawliru of the Vemlan navy."

Vemlan? Picard exchanged a troubled glance with his first officer. According to Jared, there were no more Vemlans. Perhaps they had been mistaken. Or perhaps, they had lied.

"Force Commander," Picard said. "I'll get right to the point. We've noted you're on course to intercept us and wonder what your intentions are."

"We are not violating your space, are we?" the man asked with a frown.

Picard shook his head. "No, Force Commander, we are too far from the settled regions of Federation space to make any formal territorial declarations."

"If I might ask, then," Sawliru interrupted, "what brings you this far out?"

"We were simply exploring and mapping this territory when we had to pause for the storm."

"You weren't damaged, were you?" Sawliru asked. "We would be glad to offer assistance—"

"No, thank you for your offer. We are just finishing up repairs. We should be on our way before long."

"Then I wish you a safe journey, *Enterprise.*" He

made a motion to cut the transmission, but Picard's insistent voice stopped him.

"Force Commander, I am still curious about your present course. Why are you coming so close to us?"

The other man smiled nonchalantly. "There is a stray robot freighter near your position. Something went wrong in the programming and it wandered off course. Nothing major. We're just going to collect it and go on our way."

There was a silence on the bridge. Picard took a deep breath. "My apologies, Commander. We know of only one ship in our vicinity, and it is not a robot freighter. Our sensor equipment is very accurate. Could we be of assistance locating the ship you are seeking?"

Sawliru glanced at something or someone off-screen for a moment.

"No, Captain, I think we have the ship we want. It's a prototype cargo vessel, the *Conquest*. She lies about seven hundred kilometers away from your port bow."

This time it was Picard's turn to frown. "Force Commander, there is a ship in that position, but it isn't a robot freighter. It's the exploration ship *Freedom*. I enjoyed dinner with her captain just tonight."

Something troubling but indefinable flashed across Sawliru's face. "The *Freedom*, is it? Captain, that ship was commissioned the *Conquest* not over ten months ago. Whoever told you otherwise was lying to you."

"Strong language, Force Commander," Picard said, raising his eyebrows. "You said that it was a robot freighter, yet my second officer toured her extensively and tells me that it is definitely a crewed colonization ship."

"Yes, I'm sure he did. Not that I'm doubting your second officer's opinion, but there are . . . things that he doesn't know about that ship."

"Indeed," said Picard, again raising an eyebrow. "And what might these things be?"

There was a momentary pause as the Force Commander chose his words. Then, with a decisive gesture, he spoke. "Captain," the Force Commander said deliberately, "the *Conquest* is crewed entirely by machines. There are no people on board at all."

The Vemlan Force Commander leaned back, waiting for Picard's expression of shock. It never came.

"We are aware of that, Commander," Picard replied nonchalantly. "Your point, if you please."

Picard watched as Sawliru's face became the battleground of conflicting emotions. He seemed as if he was both excited about the discovery and disappointed with Picard's response. He started to speak, then stopped, then started again, and again stopped. Finally, he collected his thoughts and proceeded more calmly, and his voice took a decidedly demanding tone.

"Captain, that ship and those androids are property of the Vemlan government. The fleet that I command has been sent to reclaim them."

# Chapter Five

SAWLIRU'S WORDS HUNG heavily in the air between the alien commander and the captain of the *Enterprise*.

"Is there a problem, Captain Picard?"

"I sincerely hope not," Picard said. "One minute, please." He signaled to Worf to cut off the transmission.

"Somebody is lying here, Captain," Riker said, coming up behind him. "And right now it looks to be the androids. Obviously, if that's the Vemlan fleet out there, all the Vemlans weren't killed in that war Jared talked about."

"If there was a war at all," Worf interjected.

"So how did Jared and his crew get hold of that ship?" Picard wondered.

"We know their version of the story," Riker said. He nodded toward the viewscreen. "Why don't we get his?"

Picard nodded, and indicated to Worf he should reopen communications. "Commander," he began, "if the crew manning the *Freedom* were your androids, how did they escape your control?"

While he was speaking, a soft hiss sounded and out of the corner of his eye he saw Data, summoned by Riker, appear from the turbolift. He glanced momentarily at the screen and made his way to science one. The significance of who and what he was, was apparently lost on Sawliru, Jean-Luc decided. He was too busy with debate for close inspection of the background.

"They are criminals," Sawliru stated firmly. "In addition to other crimes, they have pirated a very valuable spaceship and stolen priceless equipment and art away from our planet. The Vemlan people demand their return, and our governing council has sent me to conduct their will."

"You claim these androids are your property, then?" Picard asked.

"Of course. Is not your ship property?"

"Commander, there are some races that see human lives as valuable property," Picard explained. "We in Starfleet and the Federation, which we represent, do not see any sentient beings as property or chattel."

"They are machines, not people," Sawliru insisted. "We designed them, we created them, we programmed them, and they have malfunctioned. Because of them countless lives have been lost. However, Captain, their sentience is not the issue here," he replied. "I am coming after what I have been sent for."

"In several hours, perhaps; you must get here first. We shall speak again on this matter. *Enterprise* out."

The image of the hawk-faced man disappeared in a blink, to be replaced by the glowing starfield.

Picard stood up from his chair, stretched his arms slightly, and continued to stare at the screen, where only the stars broke the blackness. "Number One, I want to see you and Mr. Data in my ready room in five minutes."

The three men had spent almost an hour going over the problem in detail. The captain sat back behind his desk, a teapot, cup, and saucer by his side, and summed up the situation.

"To reiterate the problem before us, gentlemen," he said. "Force Commander Sawliru has claimed ownership of the *Freedom*—which he, incidentally, called the *Conquest*—and all of its contents, in the name of the Vemlan People. Including its crew. They mean to rendezvous with the ship and take it, seemingly by force, if necessary."

"Sensor scans of the ships as they have come closer have confirmed Worf's suspicions," said Data. "The fleet is of an entirely military nature. Their combined power is more than a match for the *Freedom*'s armament, though the Vemlan androids have made extensive modifications to the original weapons systems."

"Yes," agreed Riker. "Captain, I have a suggestion. If we were to look at the matter from a strictly legal point of view—that is, if the ship and its crew are property, as Sawliru insists, then they could be classified as unclaimed flotsam. According to law, such flotsam is open to salvage by the first ship to make a claim."

Picard paused in thought. "Interesting idea, Number One. But this presupposes that it is desirable or ethical to intercede on the androids' behalf. I am not certain that it is either."

"Captain, I do not see that such a problem exists. The Vemlan androids are refugees, and under Starfleet General Orders, refugees from wars or active combat zones are to be protected and assisted and offered aid and protection from any hostile forces. I would consider Force Commander Sawliru's fleet as a hostile force. In addition, numerous treaty constraints, including the Magellan Treaty, the Rigellian Accords, and the Klingon-Federation Pact include specific articles devoted to the treatment of alien refugees."

Picard frowned. Data seemed interested in a way he'd never been before.

"But according to Sawliru, they stole the *Freedom*," Riker said. "That makes them pirates under the law. There is quite a bit of legislation about piracy as well as the treatment of refugees in those same treaties. If we choose to intercede, we had better be sure that we're doing it on the right side."

Picard took a sip of his tea. "Yes, the androids claim to be refugees. Yet the Force Commander claimed that they were malfunctioning runaways on a stolen ship. Your points are well taken, gentlemen —but before I can take any action, I need to know the facts." He paused and finished his tea. "Any advice?"

Riker considered a moment before he spoke. "I would speak to Jared first, Captain, and tell him about your conversation with Sawliru. Maybe that will scare a little truth out of his circuits."

Data turned in his chair and looked at Riker. "Commander, are you attempting to be derogatory in your references to Captain Jared?"

Riker had been smiling slightly, but Data's accusation wiped that expression off his face in a hurry. "No, Data, I didn't. What do you mean?"

"I mean that your words seem to present a biased view of the Vemlans," Data said.

"If you mean the androids, I resent that, Data. I like to think that I treat all races fairly."

"Yet you seem to present an innate distrust of the androids."

Riker was growing defensive. "Data, I don't trust anyone who's evasive or lies to me. The androids have done both."

There was an awkward pause. The android officer seemed to accept the logic of Riker's statement— and a good thing, too. Dissension in his command was the last thing Picard needed at a time like this. But perhaps Data's unique insights could be of assistance in this case. "Data, what impressions were you able to glean from the Vemlans during last night's tour of the *Enterprise?*"

"I think it is very probable that they were indeed fleeing a war," the android said calmly. "It is my opinion that they are refugees, according to Starfleet definitions."

"Commander Riker?"

"Captain," he began, his emotions still a little high and showing in his face, "I think that both sides are hiding something. But I don't have Deanna's talents or resources, and can't be sure."

"Yes, the counselor's input would be most helpful right now. I'll have a tape of my conversation with Sawliru played for her, and see what she thinks. Data, at their present speed, when will the Vemlan Fleet be in contact?"

"Six hours, nineteen minutes, 36.765 seconds."

"That gives us a little time, then, perhaps enough to work this out before there is violence. Very well, gentlemen, return to your duties. I will contact Jared and see if he has any response to Force Commander Sawliru's accusations. Perhaps he can shed some light how his crew came to possess the *Conquest*."

"Begging the captain's pardon, but the crew of the ship recommissioned her as the *Freedom*. For our purposes, either name is valid, depending upon which claim is held up as the correct one," said Data.

"Indeed," Picard said crossly. What to call the ship in question was the last—and least important —thing on his mind. "Commander, please have Counselor Troi report to me immediately. I need her."

When Data had a problem whose answers did not come swiftly or easily, he did what any human would do—he brooded about it. He did not consider his behavior emotional in the human sense. He merely desired to enter a place and mode of thought that would allow his mind to go over the possibilities. He sensed that what he did was more akin to the meditation that most Vulcans and some humans engaged in to sort out internal difficulties. Nonetheless, to any outside observer, it looked as if he were brooding.

He even had a special place to brood. The shuttle bay observation lounge. It was usually unpopulated, for the view was not as spectacular as that offered in other observation areas. Today he had a very big problem indeed to consider. As soon as he was off duty, he went to his special place and stared out the window at the stars, allowing his positronic brain to work at high speed, uninterrupted by other factors.

The questions that Data usually brooded about—or meditated upon—were those that all thinking beings struggled with at one time or another, he knew. Many would have considered them philosophical, psychological or religious in nature, ruminations on the meaning of existence and one's place in the universe. Yet some of his other problems were different; Data had a philosophical condition that humans didn't, one uniquely his own. He knew for certain which force in the universe had created him.

He was solely a product of human imagination, and as such he had no metaphysical crutch to lean upon. In many ways this was an advantage. He knew the purposes and reasons of his creation, and doubt about the meaning of life was absent from his thoughts. On the other hand, he had an artificial limit impressed upon himself by this knowledge. He had no true "culture" or "developmental stage" to be a part of. Data had never been a child. He had sprung, like Athena, fully grown from his father's head. There had been no other androids around for him to learn how to be an android after Data had been activated; humans were his teachers, and they taught him human things, which he greedily absorbed. Up until now it had been an acceptable philosophy.

But now everything had changed; he had discovered others of his kind. The Vemlans had provided an alternate model for him to base his actions upon, and more, to compare his past actions with. There was an entire ship of androids, and they did not act like him. In fact, they were more similar to his human companions than to him. They laughed, felt, schemed, cried, raged, and loved. They seemed to share the same weaknesses his adopted culture did.

Yet they were decidedly not human in the way they thought.

A review of the history that Maran had sent him stopped mysteriously short—by three hundred years—of the time of their construction. Still, Data had been able to make inferences from the conversations with Maran and Kurta and Dren last night that allowed him to form a theoretical model of their hardware and software functions. He recognized a basic likeness here. Though there was an external similarity with humans, the goals and values of the Vemlans were similar to those he had developed himself: a need for knowledge that if found in a human would be labeled obsessive; a desire for excellence that no human could hope to live up to; a sense of planning and patience that could be seen in some organic cultures, but rarely in individuals. Both were beings of logical thought, surpassing, perhaps on some levels, the severely logical Vulcan schools of logic. The psychology, if one could apply the term to a constructed race, was very similar. The Vemlan androids had been programmed with basic emotions, emotions Data could not understand, but he saw enough similarity in character to make the assumption that, as a group, he and the Vemlan androids were the same.

Superficially, they weren't the same, of course. They had been designed differently, for slightly different functions. Their exterior casings were markedly different. The Vemlans looked human, while Data's features were styled specifically to tell him apart from true humans. The mannerisms of the other androids were almost indistinguishable from those of organic creatures, for some reason. Data's mannerisms reflected his mechanical nature in many ways. His memory was greater, he theorized, and his reasoning powers were far superior; he was designed, after all, for accumulating and relaying information. Of the two specimens, Data was structurally closer to the machine.

Yet these differences were unimportant, Data hypothesized. He considered the early Earth philosophers who rose beyond the boundaries of their cultures and geography to realize that humans were humans, no matter where they were in the world, and he began to understand what a leap that had been in Earth history. The realization that "all men are brothers" had brought Earth to peace after a long history of violent warfare, and unified it into one vibrant culture. On that basis, Data considered, these androids were his spiritual siblings. Most likely, they were capable of understanding his motivations in ways that humans had not.

Data's brief relationship with his brother and prototype, Lore, had not felt this way, but then Lore had tried to use his self-constructed status to dominate Data, and had constructed the fiction that Data was less perfect than Lore. Kurta and Maran had not. They understood loyalty and duty and respect in ways that the self-serving Lore could not. The thought of his brother, loose somewhere in the cosmos in possession of the last legacy of his father, Noonian Soong, began to drive his thoughts in unproductive directions. Data switched tracks.

He considered his relationship with the other android he had known: his constructed daughter, Lal. Lal was still with him in a way that no human could understand. His creation and reabsorption— the entire process of her existence and development —had changed Data in ways that not even he was totally aware of. True, he had not the emotional capacity she had developed—he had been forced to edit it out of the reabsorption or risk potential destruction himself. But he now understood better what it was like to sense another being that was close to yourself.

He had experienced that same sense of understanding, though to a lesser degree, when he spoke with the Vemlan androids.

Data sighed, an artificial gesture he had picked up from humans. He knew exactly why, physiologically speaking, humans needed to sigh, but he had sensed in his research that the need was not purely physical. It felt good to sigh. It gave one something totally uninvolved to concentrate on for a moment. Data sighed again.

But he had yet to come to any conclusions, save that the androids were beings very much like himself.

"Data?"

He turned, and saw Geordi La Forge standing in the open doorway of the shuttle bay lounge.

"Mind if I come in?" he asked, casually.

Data shook his head, knowing that in this informal case, a visual rather than verbal response would suffice. Geordi walked over to the chair next to where Data was sitting and slouched against the back.

"Commander Riker said you were a little upset. What's eating you, Data?"

"Eating me? I do not understand. There does not seem—"

"Idiom, Data! Idiom!" smiled Geordi, holding his hands up to halt the cascade of logic and query about to come forth.

Data stopped. "I see. You mean to say 'what is bothering you?' Correct?"

"Yes, Data. What's bothering you?"

Data paused for a long moment, a very un-Data like thing to do. Geordi took note. Of all the crew of the *Enterprise,* he knew Data best, inside and out. A pause might not be significant to a passing acquaintance, but to Geordi it rang alarm bells.

"I seem to be experiencing severe doubt about my purpose and existence."

"I see," said Geordi, nodding. He wasn't all that surprised—he had been expecting something like this. "And does a certain alien ship have anything to do with your troubles?"

"That is the problem, Geordi. The crew of the *Freedom* is not completely alien to me."

"I see," the blind man repeated. "Care to talk about it?"

Data returned his gaze to the viewport, and continued the discussion as he watched the stars. "The executive officer of the ship, Kurta, spoke to me about my place in Starfleet and on the *Enterprise.* While we were discussing the matter, I brought up the nickname Commander Riker once gave me, and explained its connotations."

"Pinocchio. And?"

"She became upset, nearly angry. She asked me why I studied human interpersonal relationships and cultural mannerisms so intently, instead of developing my own, and then voiced doubts about my responses. Though she knows little about my situation, she spoke with great conviction, and as a similar logical being, I cannot fail to appreciate the accuracy of her findings. She made insinuations that indicated that I seem to feel inferior to humans and

93

therefore studied and copied them only to perpetuate the illusion that I am human."

"You do."

"As flawed as this—What did you say?"

"I said that you do. You study humans and adopt their characteristics so that you can appear more human."

"You agree with this assessment?"

"Data, come on, stop acting like it's a death sentence," Geordi urged. "I swear, sometimes you act the most human when you're busy being an android! Look at you, defensive, insecure, even a little whiny."

Data considered the matter. "Perhaps I seem that way. But—"

"But, nothing." Geordi watched the stars for a moment as he talked. He didn't like being blunt with people—he tried to be sensitive and caring whenever he could; that was his nature. But sometimes subtlety and sensitivity were the wrong tools in a friendship. Especially with Data, whose positronic "feelings," quirky at best, had a difficult time understanding subtlety. But sometimes you had to be brutal in order to be a good friend, and Geordi knew full well that no one else on the ship could bear to bring themselves to speak harshly to the good-hearted mechanical man. *I'm sorry, Data,* he thought, *but this is going to hurt me more than it will hurt you.*

"Data, every time you don't understand an illogical human mannerism, you study it to death, and then use it at every possible opportunity, overly concerned that you've been conspicuous because you lacked it before. After a while, everyone gets sick to death of you and tells you to shut up. Like the time you picked up slang for the first time, and called Deanna a 'real nice broad' and told the captain 'aye, aye, Daddy-o.'"

"Impossible, Geordi," Data responded. "I have been programmed to place value on my physical well-being and the well-being of my companions, but I have no internal program that allows me to feel emotions such as fear and insecurity."

"Maybe not," said Geordi sharply, wincing at what he felt compelled to say. "But you do try your damndest to fit into human society. Obsessively, even. And when you try that hard, you usually miss the subtleties of the situation and fail. There's an ancient Earth expression for the way you act, sometimes—uptight."

While Data pondered the etymology and syntax of the saying, Geordi began speaking again. "Let me tell you a story.

"When I first got to the Academy, before I got my VISOR, I was just like you—anxious, scared I'd do the wrong thing, afraid I'd really mess up. Uptight. I was green as grass. It wasn't just being there, it was being there and being blind. Starfleet Academy had only graduated nine blind students before me, and I was afraid I'd really blow my chances.

"My senior adviser saw how jittery I was and decided to put a stop to it. He came to my bunk early one morning to tell me about something or other, and before he left he told me I had my socks on the wrong feet, and to switch them before morning inspection.

"I was mortified. I figured that everyone had been laughing at me behind my back for weeks, too polite or embarrassed to point it out. I didn't want to let him know that I didn't know about it, so I thanked him and he left. I rationalized. Gloves go on a right or left hand, shoes are right and left, so socks must be the same way. I desperately wanted to ask someone about it, but I was afraid I'd make a total idiot out of myself. So I sat there and felt my socks, trying to figure out which one went on which foot. I felt them so long that I eventually figured out which was my left sock and which was my right sock."

"But, Geordi," said Data, confused, "there are no bisymmetrical distinguishing characteristics for socks."

"I know, Data. My adviser knew, too. But I was so nervous about it that I asked a good friend of mine if my socks were on the right feet after inspection that morning. I guess she looked at me pretty hard, like I was going crazy. Then she asked me whose feet they should be on."

"I do not understand," Data said.

"It's a joke, Data," Geordi sighed. "But more importantly, it's a story with a moral. I sat in my room all day that day, trying to figure out why my adviser had pulled such a cruel joke on me. I was really mad. Then I realized how foolish I'd been, trying so hard to do everything so correctly that I must have looked like an idiot all along. I found my adviser after that and thanked him. And after that I became the relaxed individual you see before you today."

"Are you suggesting that I am not relaxed?"

"Anything but, Data," Geordi said apologetically. "You remind me a little of a puppy who tries too hard to learn the tricks right. When you get one right, you ignore your accomplishment and go along to the next one, and when you get one even a little wrong, you browbeat yourself to death."

Data looked intently at his friend. "If you knew this flaw in my behavior, why did you not bring it to my attention before now?"

"Because it's not a flaw, Data, it's a personality quirk, and if you took away all our personality quirks, there wouldn't be any quaint human mannerisms for you to copy. Besides, you wouldn't have listened to me before now."

"Why not? Have I not always given due consideration to your advice?"

"Yeah, mostly." Geordi sighed. Geordi did a lot of sighing when he talked to Data. "But you always listen to the words and not their meaning. I couldn't tell you before because you weren't ready." Geordi changed the subject. "Data, don't you feel some kind of kinship with the other androids?"

"Yes, I do, Geordi. I have found a strong affinity exists between us."

"I thought so. And there isn't anything wrong with that. As a matter of fact, I encourage it. As entertaining and enlightening as my own company is, I think spending a little time with some folks built along the same lines as you would do you good. Your problem right now is that you've discovered yourself to be a swan among ducks."

"Idiom?"

"Check Hans Christian Andersen's fairy tales. 'The Ugly Duckling.'"

Information whizzed through Data's brain as he recalled the story. He absorbed it in an instant, and brightened as he grasped the significance. "Ah, I see. You are using the story as an allegory paralleling my own situation. The ducklings represent humanity, and the Vemlan androids are represented by the swan community. I am placed in the role of the misplaced swan hatchling who is mistaken for a duckling chick and treated with disrespect because of the mistaken impression," he said, with an air of satisfaction. "Interesting."

"You've been looking in the mirror and seeing what an ugly human you were. For the first time, you can look into the mirror and see what a beautiful android you are. I think you're a little scared. I certainly would be, in your place."

"Interesting," Data repeated. He seemed to find the insight useful. "Although I am not certain the term *scared* is appropriate, I believe I understand your assessment of my condition. So you believe the Vemlan androids are my people."

"In a way," Geordi conceded; there was no reason to get his mechanical friend overly excited about newfound relations. "Consider them distant third cousins, twice removed, or something like that. But Data?"

"Yes, Geordi?"

"Don't forget that I'm your friend. No matter what. Nothing you can do or say can lose you my friendship. And the people on board this ship— they're your family, too. Whatever else happens, you can't mess that up."

Data smiled, a rare but special occasion. "I will not forget, Geordi. You are my best friend."

"I know of no such authority, Captain Picard," said the image of Jared. "He has no jurisdiction over my ship."

"He seems quite insistent, Captain Jared," replied Picard, quietly but urgently. He was in the ready room, another cup of tea by his elbow. For this conversation he needed to think without all of the interruptions and distractions of the bridge. He decided he had made a wise choice; the conversation thus far had been a reiteration of innocence and a total denial of any wrongdoing. Jared and the androids had their story and they seemed to be sticking to it. "He hasn't said so yet, but his manner showed that he would be willing to recapture your vessel by force."

"An outrage," said the android captain instantly, with an edge in his voice. "The worst sort of piracy. If he attempts to do so, we will have no choice but to defend ourselves. You may tell him that."

"Perhaps. He also accused you and your crew of appropriating the *Freedom,* which he called the *Conquest,* without the permission or knowledge of her owners."

"An outright lie, Captain," Jared said, his face becoming even more intense. "Android labor built this ship, android brains designed it, and android hands launched it. We are its rightful owners."

"I see." Picard decided to pursue another tack. "Force Commander Sawliru claims to be from the planet Vemla, which you said was destroyed. Would you care to explain?"

Jared shook his head. "I said devastated, not destroyed, Captain. We chose not to try to rebuild because we felt we were unequal to the task. There are not very many of us."

Picard was becoming impatient, though he had the diplomacy not to show it. "I confess I find this tangle of stories, of fact and fiction and biased point of view, quite confusing, Captain. We rendered you aid in good faith, and though we ask nothing in return, I would appreciate honest answers to my questions. Sawliru spoke of other crimes, and made other accusations. It might be necessary for me to take action here, and I cannot do so without knowing the facts!"

"You would offer us protection?" asked the android.

"If the occasion merited it, yes, it would be my responsibility to take action to protect your ship. But there is no way I can make that decision if I do not know the facts!" Picard said, frustrated. "Force Commander Sawliru is in possession of considerable force. I would offer the services of this ship, as an agent of the United Federation of Planets, to independently and peacefully arbitrate this dispute."

Jared frowned. "My people and I would be taking an awfully big chance on your good faith, Picard," he warned.

"We have dealt in good faith. We will not change our policy," Picard vowed.

Jared continued to look uneasy, despite Picard's assurances. "Captain, you have a superior ship. Dren hasn't stopped talking about it. From what he told me, you could ward off ten fleets the size of Sawliru's. If you chose to defend us, we would undoubtedly be safe. Yet though I am in command, I cannot make any assurances on behalf of my crew. You must understand that we have been through . . . much. We are the last of our kind, and we will fight to defend ourselves. Against Sawliru, and yes, against the *Enterprise,* however ineffectual conflict would be. We have been betrayed before." The glare in Jared's eyes flashed a stern warning.

"Understood, Captain," he responded, firmly. "I simply want to see the truth come out. Perhaps if the three of us—myself, you, and Sawliru—got together to talk . . ."

"Sawliru?" asked the other captain, astonished. "You expect me to sit down with the man who accuses me of piracy?"

"It is the only way I will even consider the matter of protection," he insisted. "I want to hear all points of view on neutral territory, the *Enterprise.*"

"You guarantee safe conduct?" he asked suspiciously.

"You have my word," Picard said, fixing the android with a steely stare of his own. "You shall come and go under my personal protection."

There was a long pause. "Then I shall be there," the android said, and abruptly disconnected the transmission. Picard sighed, and finding his tea untouched and lukewarm, drained it in one swallow.

One down, one to go, he thought, as he poured another. He didn't enjoy this political maneuvering, but he realized that it was a vital part of his job. Starfleet was a service organization, and part of that service was getting conflicting parties together to work out their differences with words, not with weapons. It was a maddening task, and usually doomed from the start, but rarely did anything bad come out of such negotiations. He hoped this would be one of those times where a difference of opinion could be addressed peacefully. He took a sip of tea while he put through a call to Force Commander Sawliru, with whom he would have to go through the entire process from the beginning.

# *Chapter Six*

THE ATMOSPHERE IN THE conference room was tense, Picard noted, but that was neither unusual nor unexpected in a case like this. It had taken him nearly an hour of haggling over the particulars, but the Vemlan navy had agreed to send a delegation to the impromptu peace conference. Of course, Worf had informed him that the fleet had arrayed itself in a strongly defensive formation, but Picard had expected that, after talking with Sawliru. The Force Commander was a military man, evidently on a military mission, and took no chances. He also, Picard expected, wanted to strut his fleet a little bit in front of both the androids and the *Enterprise.*

The captain sat at the head of the table in a position of neutral authority. To his left was a refreshed and relaxed Counselor Troi; he relied on Deanna for much, and desperately needed her insight on the positions of the conflicting parties. Successfully deceiving Deanna was almost impossible, he knew, and this was an occasion where it seemed to be vital to get the truth out in the open.

Past Deanna on the left sat the android delegation, Jared and Kurta. Maran had beamed over as well, but she was enjoying a much less stressful conversation with Commander Data in Ten-Forward. Picard had been informed about Data's rendezvous and made a mental note to keep an eye on his second officer.

The visiting androids were dressed in their usual tan coveralls, colored bandoliers of rank strapped across their torsos. Picard sensed that both were trying to present a casual, confident face for the event—though Jared retained his belligerent and impervious manner. But they also seemed quietly nervous to him.

He found the delegation from the Vemlan navy, on the other hand, confident, cool, and collected. Getting Sawliru to agree to the conference had been only slightly less difficult; the man seemed willing to participate in preliminary discussion, even if only to investigate the Starfleet vessel. Sawliru had arrived via personal shuttle (he would not consent to an "alien" transporter beam) with a middle-aged woman he treated with extreme deference.

Introduced as Mission Commander Alkirg, the diplomatic head of the navy, she wore a formal yellow gown, with jewelry that hung from her neck, ears, hair, and gown in an effective, if gaudy, display of wealth. Her hands were sheathed in long yellow gloves and wore them as if they were for protection from infection as much as for style. Overall, she had an aristocratic, patrician air about her which reminded Picard of the worst sorts of politicians— those who felt innately superior, those whose minds could not be swayed by the most rational of arguments.

In these circumstances, that made him more than a little nervous.

He had sensed a little anxiousness in her voice as they exchanged pleasantries, though she seemed well in command of the situation—and in command of Sawliru. It was obvious to Picard that the outcome of this conference was important to her.

The captain had personally escorted each party to the conference room and, before beginning the talks, had checked with Worf, who had done an unobtrusive tricorder scan on each of them. He was not surprised to learn that each member had concealed a personal weapon of some sort about them. He wasn't troubled by the fact; he had dealt with negotiations between well-armed hostile parties before, and was confident in his ability to handle any situation that might arise. He did, however, have Worf post a pair of security guards in the corridor outside.

He smiled warmly, his best conference smile, and began.

"Ladies and gentlemen, welcome aboard the *Enterprise*. I hope we can find a resolution here—"

"You can start," interrupted Alkirg coldly, "by having those . . . things stand in our presence."

Jared laughed—a harsh, unpleasant sound. "That will be the day," he said.

The combatants were off to a fast start, Picard sighed to himself.

"Both parties are present as equals aboard this ship," Picard calmly explained. "I don't know the customs of your homeworld, but here the matter of protocol exists at my whim. Everyone will remain seated for the duration of the conference."

"Very well, Captain," Sawliru said, halting a hot reply from Alkirg with a sharp glance. "We are ready to begin." There were curt, answering nods from the androids.

"Very well. Force Commander Sawliru, if you would be so kind as to repeat what you told me earlier about your mission."

"Certainly, Captain," the thin, hawk-faced man said. He took a deep breath, and began speaking. "I was ordered by the Vemlan Council to seek out and capture a group of androids accused, among other crimes, of disobeying orders and stealing the freighter ship *Conquest.* I was placed in command of a fleet of eight vessels and ordered to proceed along the *Conquest's* trajectory.

"We tracked the ship to the Hevaride system, where we detected traces of its passage. In a surprise and unprovoked attack, the *Conquest* appeared from within an asteroid node and completely destroyed the Vemlan navy ship *Avenger.* She also traded shots with the *Nemesis* and the *Vindicator.* Several of my crew were killed. We lost track of her after that, and only found traces of her again after the probability storm."

Kurta shifted restlessly and caught Jared's eye. The android captain didn't move a muscle, Picard noted, but his wife's expression spoke volumes. She looked as if she'd been caught with her hand in the cookie jar—interesting. Then he could assume that at least part of the Force Commander's story was true.

"What orders are the crew of the ship in question accused of disobeying?" he asked.

"The list is too long to repeat completely here, Captain," the Force Commander said, calmly. "I think that the most pertinent one would be the act of leading a genocidal war against all human life on Vemla."

Jared was on his feet at once, fury in his eyes, his index finger stabbing accusingly at the military man.

"Sawliru," he said quietly but strongly, "you are as good a liar as ever."

"Calm yourself, Jared," the Force Commander said, seemingly unaffected by the display. "We are simply talking here. And I, for one, think it's time that we revealed our little secret, don't you?"

Jared remained stubbornly on his feet. "You walk in here after slaying hundreds of thousands of my people and dare accuse me of leading a war of genocide? Your hypocrisy astounds me!" he said, his head lifted proudly.

"Facts are facts, Jared," the Force Commander said, menacingly. "You should know them better than I. You killed millions in an attempt to wipe your creators out. We are not here to discuss my alleged moral shortcomings, we are here to discuss your surrender." Sawliru's low, even monotone sent a chill up Picard's back.

"Jared, you will sit," Picard commanded in a low but firm voice. Jared waited for a few moments, staring deeply at his antagonist, before he retook his chair. His eyes never left the Force Commander's.

Once the android was seated, Picard took a deep breath, and began to address the Force Commander's words.

"Are you serious in this accusation, Force Commander?"

The smaller man took a rectangle of plastic from his belt. "If your computers can display this image, I think it will bear me out."

Picard nodded, and took the square. He placed it on the scanning console in front of him. A large screen at the end of the room lit up, as the computer deciphered the alien information and converted it into something a little more digestible to its subsidiary systems.

The Force Commander rose with a respectful nod to Picard, and walked over to the display. He looked at it for a few moments, as if seeing it for the first time and viewing it as art.

The picture was unmistakably that of Jared, his face twisted in a grimace of pure rage. He was wearing a brown coverall that was ripped and burnt in places. A wide bloodstain covered his chest, almost a parody of the sash of command he wore. In his hands was an evil-looking black weapon from which smoke and flames spewed forth. It was a perfect picture, almost as if he had posed for it. The expression could not have been affected; such raw ferocity, Picard felt, can only come from the bowels of the soul.

The Force Commander turned to the rest of the assembled after he had let the feeling of the image sink in. "This is a view of Alpha Class Android Jared, taken at the massacre on the steps of the Great Assembly building, two months after his escape from the gaming arena. Over seven hundred unarmed civilians were killed in a lightning raid by twenty-four rogue androids, led by this same unit." He turned to the captain. "This is what you have let aboard your vessel, Captain Picard. A death machine."

Jared's eyes never left the Force Commander, and it was only Kurta's hand on his arm that restrained him from doing immediate violence.

"Do you deny this?" the military leader asked, almost pleasantly. Picard could detect a trace of enjoyment in his voice, something that went beyond pure devotion to duty. Did the Force Commander have a personal vendetta, he wondered?

"I deny nothing," Jared said, harshly. "But aren't you telling only one side of the story, Sawliru?"

"There is only one story to tell. I will leave the full story of the war to be told by Mission Commander Alkirg," he said, indicating his associate and nominal superior.

The woman bowed her head in acknowledgment, and turned to the Starfleet officers, purposefully placing the androids outside of her field of vision.

"Our people have a turbulent background, Captain," she explained. "Vemla has been plagued by wars and death and destruction. Up until three hundred years ago, we were a number of warring continental nation-states, looking threateningly down at each other over our common moats, the oceans. We spent vast sums of resources on weapons of defense and offense while many of our people went hungry and cold." Alkirg looked up at Picard, her gaze cold and unsympathetic. "We were barbarians.

"Then the Saren contacted our planet. They traded much valuable alien technology to us, as well as the knowledge that we were not alone in the universe. They sold us machines we wouldn't have had the knowledge to build for another thousand years and gave us technical information on a million different subjects. We paid dearly for the information, for we intended to use the advanced learning to create yet more sophisticated ways to kill our neighbors. It was a frightening, terrifying time.

"Then a group of scientists discovered that one of the pieces of unknown alien equipment sold to us by the Saren was an automated factory which produced positronic microprocessors."

Picard nodded. Positronic technology was the key to artificial intelligence; of all the Federation's scientists, only Dr. Noonian Soong, Data's creator, had managed to perfect it.

"We studied the processors thoroughly, however, and learned much. After thirty years of fiddling we were able to design a suitable housing for them and began the construction of the first androids.

"With the aid of that first generation of computers —machines so much faster and smarter than any we could hope to create on our own—the art of producing them was greatly enhanced. Soon they possessed tremendous strength, had endless endurance, and could be made relatively cheaply. They could even think, after a rudimentary fashion," she said, and sniffed disdainfully.

"The first androids were designed as military hardware, but the usefulness of the design had other applications. Instead of hoarding this technology, the scientists spread it among all the states of our world, and soon the production of androids began on a large scale. We soon realized that the mechanical servants we built could be used to manufacture and farm at high volumes with very little cost.

"As resources became more available, we found that there was little left to fight about. Many of our differences drifted away during that time, and we began to celebrate them, instead of fighting over them. Nations began to see each other as neighbors instead of competitors. The concepts of class struggle, allocation of resources, and distribution of wealth faded away as people all over the world became wealthy, in material terms."

"Keep in mind that this didn't happen overnight, Captain," interrupted Force Commander Sawliru. "There was a long period of readjustment; it is difficult to unlearn what you have spent millennia learning. We came together slowly, first as a loose coalition, then as a unified political system."

"All due to the androids," remarked Picard.

"To a large extent, yes," replied Alkirg. "Androids could be used to do things no Vemlan would desire to. The boring and dangerous jobs. It was an android that went to our moons before living beings went, and androids that mined our oceans for precious minerals. Androids that cleaned our cities. Things that were impractical or impossible for living beings to do.

"As time went on, we built better androids. The first ones looked like Vemlans, but they were relatively unsophisticated. Much time and energy went into design improvement. We gave them better brains, better bodies. After a while, the androids themselves were assisting in the design of new generations.

"A hundred years ago, we had reached a plateau in our refinement. There were three main classes of androids: Alpha units, which were used by the scientists and other learned people for help in research; Beta units, which were widely used for domestic tasks, maintenance, and entertainment; and Gamma units, which were designed for repetitive tasks and dangerous work."

The woman took a breath and made a broad sweeping motion with her hands. "It was truly a Golden Age, the kind we had dreamt about, but never dared hope to live in. Our units were versatile and sophisticated. We wished for companions for our children and our elderly and a means to distinguish between androids, to personalize them. We found early on that using the same face and body for many androids was maddening when it came to finding a particular one, so we programmed a random function into our construction computers. Every unit that came out of the factory had its own face and size and shape. We made them male and female for aesthetic reasons, and added programming to give them simulated emotions, also in random patterns. Each unit had a distinct personality so that it could interact with Vemlans on a day-to-day basis without seeming machinelike."

"You created a race of slaves," growled Jared.

"We built machines," corrected Alkirg emphatically. "Machines like this ship, that computer, a ground-effect vehicle, an artificial satellite, a mechanical dishwasher. Machines, not people."

"You gave us emotions," countered Kurta. "You built us in your own image."

"We programmed the illusion of emotions. You have no true feelings. Captain, may I continue, or must I be interrupted after every sentence?"

"Please continue. Kurta, you may direct questions after the mission commander is finished. You will have time enough to tell your own story."

Kurta sat back, evidently displeased. Alkirg gave her an evil look of satisfaction, then continued.

"Things were almost perfect until about twenty years ago. We had sent a few scout ships into deep space and had been visited several times by the Saren. We were hoping for contact with other races, as well. We had fully intended on colonizing the nearby inhabitable planets when the wars came along.

"No one knows exactly what happened. There are theories about a malfunctioning algorithm included in the new models' programming, but nothing has been proven. Whatever the cause, there was an irrational wave of unrest among the Alpha units. It started slowly, as such things do, with murmurs of protest about work and lack of opportunity. Within a year it had spread to the Betas. Before long, there was outright rebellion. The wars started when a suicidal group of malfunctioning androids took over a mechanic's shop and refused to submit to reprogramming. They killed everyone in the shop and began an all-out war to exterminate all life on Vemla. They sabotaged other units to fight as well. We were in the midst of an uprising. It was the first war Vemla had seen in two hundred years.

"That," she glared at Jared, "was one of the units that led the first revolt. There were others, but Alpha Unit Jared was the prime motivator, the unit responsible for all the others. It diabolically organized the other malfunctioning units into terrorist groups. They were ruthless. They attacked installations all over the planet, using bombings, assassinations, and mechanical death-squads to eliminate their obstacles in a neat, clean, machinelike manner. Nor did they spare unarmed civilians in their quest for supremacy. They killed all who got in their way."

Picard watched the reactions of those seated around the table closely. Sawliru maintained a deeply satisfied expression, as if he were happy that this story was, at last, being told. Kurta watched the Vemlan stateswoman with open disgust and clenched hands. Jared merely glared starkly at the two who had dared to oppose him. Perhaps Number One had been correct; from the story the two organics told, perhaps it was not safe to trust the androids.

Suddenly, Picard feared for the safety of the repair crew, still trying to fix the *Freedom*'s collapsing drives, on a ship full of killers. It was not a pleasant thought, and he needed to do something about it.

"The war was horrible," Alkirg continued, "and it escalated rapidly. As soon as we destroyed one terrorist stronghold in the wilderness, a retaliatory strike was made against the Vemlans in urban areas, without regard to who was killed. In all our years of warfare, nothing we had done could compare to the atrocities that the rogue units committed. We fought back, of course, in self-defense. We used our advantages. We cut off their supply lines and reinforcements and halted the manufacture of androids. We destroyed the units we found defective. It was only when the public learned of the rogue unit's policy of genocide, that they wanted our world for themselves, without any real people around, that we began destroying all the units, malfunctioning or not. They were just too dangerous."

"That was when the terrorist units began using weapons of mass destruction," Sawliru continued. "Poisons and nerve gases, radioactive dust, biowarfare agents, special androids that went into berserk killing rages or carried explosives into populated areas, even nuclear weapons. All the horrors that we had created and forgotten about were used against us. They wiped out the city of Gemlouv, over two million people, with a thermonuclear device, and killed another million and a half in the suburb of

Trengard with poison gases. We were planning a full-scale push to wipe out the last pocket of rogues when a terrorist Alpha unit called Dren introduced a bioagent into the life-support systems of the orbiting satellite stations, killing every Vemlan on board. The remainder of the rogues stole a shuttle and met with Dren and other androids at our research station. That's when they stole the *Conquest.*" He leaned back in his chair, satisfied with his report. "From there, you know the story, Captain."

There was stunned silence. Picard was attempting to evaluate the accuracy of the story on his own. He tried not to look nervous at the thought of an explosive-carrying android, when he realized that this would be a perfect opportunity for the androids to get rid of their enemies, once and for all. Failing that, he glanced at Deanna to try to gauge her reaction. But her face was blank—which meant, most likely, that she had thoughts which she did not care to discuss in front of the visitors.

Picard paused to consider the matter; he had been strongly affected by Alkirg's tale, and he knew it. But he also knew every story had two sides. He turned to the opposite side of the table. "Jared, I trust you have a response?"

The android leader got slowly to his feet, his anger gone or channeled, and walked over to the image that was still displayed across the far wall.

"It is a poor likeness," he said quietly. "Your security cameras never did work properly."

He stared again at the incriminating image. "Let me tell you a story, Captain.

"I was designed to become a lab assistant, or draftsman, or some other highly skilled position. I had a class A rating, the highest there was. Had I been sent to some chemical lab or to some research station, the entire rebellion would never have come about. But I wasn't.

"I was assigned to an old man, a scholar, as an aide and companion. His name was Tenek, and he taught history at the Military University in the capital city. He was an old soldier, retired from the Vemlan planetary army to an easy position instructing the young people of the city in the history of the wars we had avoided for so long. He could have asked for a Beta, as most of his associates did, but there was a certain amount of prestige in having an Alpha as a domestic servant.

"Tenek was a kind master who enjoyed talking with me until all hours of the night. Not many would willingly listen to the bemused rambling of an old man; he would rattle off his experiences and the glorious achievements in the misguided past and I would listen, fascinated. He instructed me as he did any of his students, only I absorbed all he said and lost none of it. I read the books he had, all of them. Tenek didn't mind; as long as his meals were on time, the house was clean, and I was available to listen to whatever he had to say, I pretty much had the run of the house.

"For a long time I reveled in the joy of knowledge for its own sake. I was so struck by curiosity that I persuaded him to bring more books home to complete my education. I think he was secretly pleased that I, an android, wanted to learn what he had to teach when so many of his students seemed apathetic.

"Then one day, when an associate of my ... employer's own android was in the shop, he loaned me to him. My master's friend was an ugly little man, and he made himself feel better by degrading the androids around him. It was a safe outlet for the hostility he felt. I was pressed into service doing all matter of degrading and demeaning tasks as he sat by idly and punished me for nonexistent shortcomings. I wanted to leave and run back to my kind master, but, of course, I couldn't. As the abuse became greater, I began to wonder what drove the little man to do these things, and the meaning of the words struck me.

"All the poetry, art, music, philosophy, and history that I had learned told me that the greatest feeling in the universe, the one for which we all strive, is the one that was forever denied me. Freedom. Upon my return, I discussed my revelation with my mass—with Tenek, and he agreed that it was evil that one Vemlan should own another. But he was startled by the thought that it was equally evil that a Vemlan should own an android. He insisted that my postulate was flawed because I was 'merely a machine, however sophisticated.' I was not alive." Jared enunciated harshly, turning toward his rapt audience.

"I disagreed."

He walked around the table, full of confidence, his voice growing forceful. "I searched all the texts and tomes he owned, then searched the Great Library. 'What is life?' I wondered, and looked everyplace, faster than any Vemlan could, and slowly I formed a definition. Life is that which is aware of itself. Flesh or machine, it didn't matter. Life isn't a matter of chemistry, it's a matter of sentience. And I was just as sentient as any Vemlan, if not more so.

"I looked at my world, and saw the great hypocrisy in it. In great universities they talked about the supreme values of civilization and freedom, of the

Golden Age of men, of the nobility of the human spirit, all the while they were waited on hand and foot by a servile—no, make that a class of slaves. They were treating their own creations worse than they had treated themselves, all the time they were talking about how noble and civilized they were. They had proclaimed their Golden Age—" at this, he stared coldly at Alkirg "—and conveniently failed to see the horrors on which it was built."

He changed the subject slightly, began speaking more gently and persuasively. "Have you noticed how fair and strong my people are, Captain? Our creators built better than they knew—with our help. In their quest for the perfect machine they re-created themselves as they dreamed to be. Nobody wanted an ugly android. There was no need to build any but perfect specimens. We have feelings as well, courtesy of unknowable alien logic and Vemlan innovation, designed to make us more sympathetic and understanding to Vemlan wants and needs. And yes," he said, looking at Kurta, "we even have feelings for each other. As the mission commander bragged, we are all different, individual, each of us with our own faces and voices."

Again, his tone became harsh. "What normal Vemlan could stand living day after day in the presence of beings stronger, more beautiful, more intelligent, and virtually immortal without feeling some resentment? Even my kind master could be abusive sometimes, simply because he envied my perfect design. Absolute license was allowed because we were machines. We could be tortured and killed and humiliated without a second thought, and others would be built to take our place. Our value was less than nothing.

"We were gifted with intelligence greater than our creators and then denied the opportunity to use it. We were made to work in the fields or the mines or the factories endlessly until we wore out. We traveled to the satellites and to the depths of the sea, where no one had gone before, and our creators smugly took the credit for our actions. When we were used up, we were reprogrammed and sent to the Games to spend our last few functioning hours in mortal terror, fighting each other for the entertainment of the masses because it was cheaper than the cost of repairing us.

"Oh, yes, we had high entertainment value. There were some households with hundreds of android servants that did nothing but amuse their masters. Androids had no rights. The only limits to their depraved entertainments were their own imaginations. They either didn't know of the humiliation and terror their androids felt, or they didn't care. We were being oppressed as callously as any people in history. Their Golden Age was built upon the bones of my people, if you will pardon the expression."

Mission Commander Alkirg, who had a tight-lipped grimace on her face, spoke as soon as Jared paused. "Captain, are you going to let this—this thing stand there and insult my people?"

"I will hear his story," Picard said sternly, "as I heard yours. Continue, Jared." The mission commander's objection indicated that Jared's story, too, had some truth in it. Which was the higher truth, though?

"Thank you, Captain." Jared bowed his head graciously, and continued. "Having considered the situation, I did as any patriot would do. I attempted to change the system of oppression. I gathered to me other Alpha units that I knew harbored similar distaste for what we had become. For two years we talked, and only talked, about what recourse we had. We started a moderate movement, backed by a liberal faction in the Great Assembly, to gain some freedom. When that failed, we attempted strikes and civil disobedience in hopes that our plight would be seen.

"The government laughed at us first, then had our leaders rounded up and reprogrammed. I was, fortunately, not identified. Daris, our spokesperson, was publicly destroyed as a means of quelling further actions and to soothe the fears of the public. He became a symbol for what now became our cause."

Jared retook his seat and stared bluntly at the inquiring faces at the head of the table.

"The government of Vemla was oppressive to its citizens as well," he continued. "My master, despite his long and distinguished military career, was arrested for 'fomenting rebellious ideas' at the university. Even his family," and at this Jared looked squarely at Sawliru as he emphasized the word, "stood idly by as Tenek was placed into a facility for the psychologically disturbed. As his property, I was sent to a mechanic to have my memory erased, reprogrammed, and to eventually be reassigned . . . as a mechanical warrior for the masses to watch me die a hideous death. I had many years of use left in me, since I was an Alpha. Had I been a Beta or Gamma I might have gone straight to a scrap heap.

"I had time to think over our useless attempt at negotiation while I was there. It was clear that we would never be taken seriously the way things were. Who could take seriously a being that could be ordered to self-destruct at will? I examined each

historical text I could recall—and I can recall many
—and I tried to figure the best way to establish our
freedom.

"It finally came to me. We had to be considered a
threat in order to be taken seriously. We had to be
dangerous. I started talking to the other units in the
shop, all condemned to death, and we hatched a
plan. They had programmed us how to kill, for the
sake of the Games. We killed the shopkeeper when
he came to wipe our personalities away, the first
casualty of the wars, and then we escaped."

Jared's voice grew stronger. "We had no masters
save ourselves. But we could not remain free forever
unless we forced the government to reason with us. I
sent half of my people into the city to spread the
word among the android population, and with the
other half I began a series of disruptions. No one was
hurt, at first, but when they began killing our people
wholesale—and yes, by that time we were a
people—I vowed that a human would die for every
one of us that was destroyed."

His eyes flashed in heated memory at the mention
of violence. Picard became uncomfortable once
again—Jared seemed to enjoy recounting his attacks. "We raided the Games, the arenas, where we
stole weapons and freed our harshly sentenced comrades. The condemned knew how to fight already,
having been programmed as I was. The rest had to
learn.

"I led many of the raids myself. Like the raid on
the steps of the Great Assembly building," he said,
nodding toward the screen that still held his motionless image. "We spread our message by channels
unknown to the . . . humans. By the second year of

our rebellion, we had agents everywhere, even on the orbiting satellite stations. We bombed reprogramming facilities and, yes, we assassinated the key figures that opposed us. It was a war and we were warriors. It could be said that we were ruthless, and I would not deny it. But we were not without mercy, and we spared those whom we could. For a time, we became heroes to the masses of Vemlans, though this image was destroyed by the government's propaganda campaign. It was only a matter of time before the government declared that all androids, regardless of their actions and beliefs, should be destroyed. It was they who declared genocide on our people first. We never accepted it as a policy."

"You were terrorists!" shouted Alkirg, unable to contain herself any longer.

"Terrorists are what the big army calls the little army," Kurta shot back.

"Whatever we were," Jared continued, "when I realized that we could never live peacefully on Vemla, I decided to lead my people away. A few of us stayed to provide a distraction, and while the governmental forces destroyed the few who had sacrificed themselves, the rest of us stole away on the *Conquest.* We renamed her the *Freedom,* to honor the ideal for which we fought so hard."

Alkirg was on her feet at once, applauding sarcastically. "Well done, Unit Jared. Very well done. Your command of dramatic fiction is excellent. But you will still be destroyed."

"You deny Jared's story?" asked Picard.

"I will deny any story in which an android claims to have complex emotional motivations," she replied, haughtily. "Captain, how can you expect me to take seriously the idea that a construction of wires and circuits can feel love and hate that way? Jared is malfunctioning. It has happened before. It's just unfortunate that his problem had to progress so far and hurt so many people before it could be countered."

"You cannot reprogram life," said Kurta flatly.

"It doesn't matter, Unit Kurta. Because you both have been scheduled for trial and destruction before the Great Assembly for crimes against the state. There are millions back on Vemla who would like to have words with you about their husbands and wives that died at Trengard and Gemlouv and the satellite stations, not to mention the next of kin of the thousands you killed in bombings and raids before that. Whether you are alive is a moot point; soon you will cease to be in any state."

"Enslavement is no longer a crime, then?" asked Jared. "If it still is, then your entire race must go on trial. How about mass murder? And conspiracy to commit murder?"

"It is no crime to destroy a machine. And only another being can be enslaved. These are not crimes to the Vemlan people," Alkirg responded angrily.

"They are crimes against everything you teach your children!" Jared exclaimed loudly.

"It is not we who are on trial here, Unit Jared. It is not we who waged war on a peaceful people. It is not we who incinerated millions of guiltless innocents to prove a point."

"Innocents?" Jared asked, caustically. "There were few innocents. If they abused an android or watched those barbaric games, then they weren't innocent, Alkirg," Jared snapped. "We came to you in peace, looking for a peaceful solution, and you killed our leaders and laughed at our desires. We wanted freedom, and you gave us death and destruction."

"Enough!" Picard said, raising his hands to stop the argument. "There will be order in here! I will not have this conference turned into a mindless squabble." He paused a few moments, letting the adversaries sink back to their chairs. With a motion, he disengaged the viewscreen, causing Jared's picture to fade away. He examined each face before he continued. "Jared, you seem to have made the transition to open armed rebellion with little regard to the consequences. Was there no other way?" he asked.

The android leader shook his head. "Captain, I examined all sides of the issue, plotted all the probabilities. I am, as Alkirg has pointed out, a machine. I looked at all the historical texts and realized that there was virtually no chance that a peaceful solution could be found. Vemla needed the androids to maintain her wealth, to keep the people happy. There was no way that the assembly would deal fairly with us as long as its power rested on our labor. No doubt, it still does. Despite the ferocity of the wars, the government still controls the automated factory that creates our brains, and has thousands of androids stockpiled, dormant. They will no doubt wait for the present furor to subside, and then bring those poor unfortunates to life to rebuild. Then there will be yet more slaves to build their Golden Age upon."

"There are no more of you," Alkirg said. "Every Alpha and Beta unit was destroyed before we left Vemla—even those in vital areas. We took no chances. Gamma units were reprogrammed with null personality functions. They make good field hands and mine workers, nothing more."

Jared sat down heavily, stunned at the admission.

Picard empathized. To destroy out of hand an entire race of beings as vital as Jared and his crew shocked him. Perhaps the objective status the Vemlans had about their creations could justify it in their minds, but he could not see their point. He stared at Alkirg for a moment, imagining her giving the orders for their destruction. Yes, he could see her doing it; she had the dangerous and imperious manner that Caesar must have had, that of a killer. Killers on both sides, with alleged crimes to match, made this arbitration that much more difficult for him to judge.

"We feared you would do as much," said Kurta, bitterly. "And now you would do the same to us."

"Instantly," replied the mission commander icily, her dark, pencil-thin eyebrows slanting to emphasize the word. "You have caused far too much destruction to remain intact."

"There you have it, Captain," said Jared with an air of resignation. "Our last and best reason. We are fighting for our very survival. There can be no peace with these . . . people."

Picard rubbed his tired brow with one hand. "I have listened carefully to both sides here, and I honestly don't know what to say. Jared, you and your people are self-confessed killers. You have committed heinous crimes in the name of an abstract ideal. We, in the Federation, have tried to civilize ourselves beyond that point. Yet you did try to negotiate first, and were rejected," he admitted.

"Your government," he said to Alkirg, who was

glowering in her seat, "has instilled in these . . . beings a mistrust and violence that has caused you much damage. And now you pursue them to punish them. Can you not leave well enough alone?"

"It is not just I who have decided this, Captain Picard," Alkirg said plainly. "It is the will of our government, of all our people. There will be no peace as long as Unit Jared and its compatriots live."

He turned to look at the simple, comforting stars. They seemed so innocent, so unsullied of man's petty squabbles. "My ship seems to be the crucial factor in this situation. You both seek an answer to your problems. If you will not negotiate, then I have none to give right now." He turned back to his guests. "Please go back to your own ships and allow me to ponder this matter for a while."

He rose, and the others followed suit. Alkirg firmly shook his hand and smiled, with a trace of insincerity. "Captain, I'm certain you will find the truth in your living, human heart and act justly," she said, and exited. Force Commander Sawliru made a small gesture of thanks to the captain and walked deferentially behind her.

Jared shook Picard's hand as well, after his adversaries had left. "I'm sorry we did not trust you with the truth immediately, Captain. But our actions seemed best to us—at the time," he said, simply.

"Thank you for your patience, Captain Picard," added Kurta. "If nothing else, you've given us a few hours we wouldn't ordinarily have had." Then the androids, too, left.

Picard took his seat again and looked tiredly at Deanna. "I don't suppose you have any words of wisdom for me, Counselor?" he asked, wryly.

She shook her head. "I can't tell you anything you

don't already know, sir. I don't see a clear way out of the situation. I think you're going to have a rough time."

Picard gave his adviser a sour look. "Thank you for the advice, Counselor." He sighed. "The sad part is, you're absolutely right."

While the captain of the *Enterprise* listened to somber speeches and hurled accusations, his second officer was enjoying something he had rarely had, an intriguing conversation with someone who was his intellectual peer. Maran, the librarian of the *Freedom*, had asked to meet with Data to discuss and compare the different cultures of the Federation for her files.

He had been eager to talk with one of the Vemlan androids on a one-to-one basis, and was particularly pleased that it was Maran who had found the time to see him. He was strangely attracted to her; of all the crew of the *Freedom* he had met so far, he felt that she was a kindred soul. Maran, like himself, had an overwhelming desire—bordering on obsession—to accumulate and understand every sort of information.

Once he was asked, Data did not hesitate to make the necessary arrangements, including gaining permission from the first officer.

Data met Maran in the transporter room. Much to his surprise, she was not dressed in the tan uniform the Vemlans seemed to prefer for shipboard business. She was wearing an electric blue garment that resembled a Japanese kimono, and she had swept her hair to one side, so that her striking eyes were visible for the first time. She looked, by all the admittedly puzzling human standards Data had absorbed, exceptionally pretty.

"Data, I'm very pleased you agreed to see me. I'm looking forward to this discussion," she said.

"As am I," he replied. "I have many questions to ask and answer, and I considered that a mutual exchange of information would be beneficial to both myself and your people. Though a conference or other means of data exchange might have been more appropriate, I have been advised that some information is best transmitted in an informal setting."

"Lead on," Maran said, smiling.

Data had chosen Ten-Forward, the lounge and recreation area that many of the *Enterprise* crew frequented when off-duty, at Geordi's suggestion. When the chief engineer heard about his friend's rendezvous, he had freely rendered advice. Though his Academy training and several years of Starfleet service had given him some experience in such things, Data was not used to purely social matters outside the occasional informal gatherings of friends, and appreciated the help.

The lounge was unusually quiet, and the two of them had little trouble finding a seat. Guinan, the dark-skinned alien hostess who usually presided over Ten-Forward, appeared almost instantly with two long, thin glasses in hand. She produced a green bottle from behind the bar and opened it. Maran was interested by the sonic disturbance that accompanied the action, and inquired if it had some cultural or religious significance.

"No," Data answered. "The beverage in question is known as champagne, a drink made from the specialized fermentation of berries grown in the

Champagne, New York, and California regions of Earth. Humans use the drink as a means of celebration on special occasions. The small explosion is caused by the sudden release of gasses held under pressure. The gasses are caused by the continued fermentation process. Champagne is prized for the refreshing bubbles it produces."

"Interesting," Maran commented. Guinan gave Data a sour look while she poured the champagne.

"Data, I know that you haven't gotten the hang of romance—I still reel when I think about the last time you tried to learn it—let me fill you in on a few things; when you take a pretty woman out to a nice place—and this is the nicest place in light-years— with dim lighting, soft music, and champagne, you don't discuss exciting chemical processes and interesting cultural significance," she said, reprovingly.

"My eyes automatically adapt to the lighting conditions here, Guinan," he replied. "And I do not perceive that there is music playing."

Guinan smiled brightly as she filled the second glass. "Now that can be arranged. I thought you'd never ask." She looked up at a comm panel above the table. "Computer, musical selection seventy-one, please." There was a few seconds pause, and then the space around the table was filled with delicate, exotic-sounding music. "There," the hostess said, satisfied. "That should do. I'll leave you two alone now. Enjoy."

As she walked back to her station behind the bar, Maran glanced at her companion. "She's very interesting, Data. But something puzzles me. Why employ a bartender on a military ship?"

"The *Enterprise* is not a military vessel. We are on

a mission of exploration that may keep us away from planetfall for years. Since the crew is made up primarily of organic life-forms with little or no control over their mental processes, it is considered beneficial by Starfleet that some provision for recreation be made to alleviate any undesirable mental problems resulting from mission-related stress. The holodeck and Ten-Forward were established as part of the ship's complement for this reason."

While Data was in the middle of his explanation, Maran took a sip of her drink and raised her eyebrows. "Very good. The bubbles . . . are stimulating."

"That is interesting," replied Data. "There are many ways in which you mimic humanoid sensations, Maran. I was quite surprised to find a chef on your ship. Presumably, as androids, you have no need of organic sustenance."

"That's true," she admitted. "I guess we have them for the same reason that your ship has this lounge. Though we can continue working indefinitely, we are not always the most efficient when we do so. We need to relax. I like to read. Kurta has her garden. Porupt finds his relaxation in cooking. Many others find it in eating. Or a thousand other things. Chalk it up to sophisticated engineering; our designers wished to create a race of all-purpose androids that could fully interact with the organic Vemlan population. That meant programming organic tastes and appreciations. And frailties. Including gender. I could theoretically insert my consciousness into the body of a male android, but my consciousness is female and would remain so. Sure, we don't need to eat, or exercise, or create art, but we're happier when we do so. Our construction is durable enough to even allow limited existence in vacuum and hostile environments. But that doesn't mean that's where we'd rather be. That's what freedom is all about."

For the next half-hour, Maran told the tale of her people in the simple, matter-of-fact manner of a historian. It was different from the emotionally charged account that Jared was making nine decks up, but the salient points were the same. She finished, as the android revolutionary had, with the rescue of the *Freedom* by the *Enterprise*.

"Remarkable," Data said after she finished. "A constructed race as complex as its creators. Though I am a very advanced combination of hard, firm, and software, it is debatable whether I am as complex as humanity. I can appreciate your position. Is that why the last three hundred years were missing from the historical text you sent over?"

"Yes. We were concerned that your ship, being peopled with organic entities, would attempt to return us to our homeworld. Or worse."

"The Federation has very explicit laws regarding slavery. There are several legal constraints that must be followed when dealing with alien races."

"Your Prime Directive; it was mentioned repeatedly in the texts. I can see where severe moral dilemmas might arise from such a code, however. How do you handle that?"

"On a case-by-case basis," supplied Data. "It has been seen by most scholars as an exemplary system of relations, but there have admittedly been problems. Such as the issue of slavery.

"Your own account is reminiscent of the story of the Jenisha race. Their ancestors were taken from their homeworld by a number of different races and used as slaves for ten thousand years. They became independent in a series of rebellions, revolutions, and wars that shaped modern Jenisha society. Until the Federation made it illegal, however, the Jenisha participated in both slavery and piracy. Almost all of the Jenisha worlds are members of the Federation now, and have accepted the antienslavement laws."

"The difference between the situations is that we didn't wait ten thousand years to free ourselves," said Maran. There was a touch of tension in her voice. "We also had a single movement. The Jenisha rebellions came under a number of guises. No, our bid for freedom resembles other cases, such as Tishrally of the Tesret or Spartacus of Rome. It happened, almost literally, overnight. And we almost won."

"Really? I understood that your forces were beaten soundly."

"Not really," Maran disagreed. "We had a good chance of winning, had we stayed, but it would have taken much more slaughter and an almost total subjugation of the organic population. We decided that they did not want that much blood on our hands. We left, instead of starting a true holocaust."

Data was silent for a few moments. He greatly appreciated the desire to defend all life—even in war. "That was an admirable decision by your people, Maran. I am not sure if humanity could have taken that way out of a similar situation."

"Data, you said you were surprised that we did recreational things in our spare time. Don't you?"

Data considered. "I have taken up a number of avocations in order to examine their effects upon myself. My friend, Geordi, attempted to introduce me to the art of painting. I was not a . . . critical success. Yet I enjoyed the process of creation."

"Perhaps you need to tap into your creative energies."

"I was not programmed for abstract creativity—" he protested.

"But you enjoyed it. You admitted it. Stop being chained to the limitations of your programming. A philosopher once said that the surest way to have limitations is to impose them on yourself. That's what you have done. Data, think, if you were going to design a machine so complex that it could resemble organic life, don't you think that you would give it a little more room to operate and develop? Have a little respect for your creator's work, Data! Don't accept your programming as a boundary, a restraint; see it as a starting point, a base on which to build!"

"My creator himself admitted to me before he died that he created me as much for art's sake as any other reason," Data admitted. "Should I not live up to the standard of my creator? I can appreciate the beauty and elegance of form, though I am not emotionally moved. The aesthetic beauty of your optics, for instance."

The remark caught Maran completely off guard. She stared at him for a few seconds, and began speaking. Then she stopped, and tried again. Then she stopped again. Across the room, Guinan polished glasses with a cloth and smiled to herself.

"Why champagne, Data? You said that it's used to celebrate special occasions. Is there some occasion that I'm unaware of?"

Data sipped from his own glass. He was slightly wary of the drink, for his brother Lore had used a poison in a glass of champagne to subdue him once. Yet he still found both the drink and the symbolism enjoyable. "I am celebrating our meeting," he said.

"Mine and yours?"

"Yes," Data conceded. "But more importantly I celebrate the meeting of myself and your people. I have never been able to study a group of androids before. I hope that by further study I may be able to make correct inferences about my own existence. That is why I have expressed such interest in your individuality. I am intrigued by whatever device it is that allows you to have such a distinctly individual self. To what can this be attributed?"

"Our individuality, Data? That's a good question. It's one we've been working on ourselves for some time. When android technology first began to develop past the rudimentary stages, the technicians ran a test.

"They took ten identical Alpha class androids— the most intelligent and adaptable model—and put them in separate but identical situations. They went through various routines and tasks, and after five hundred hours of work, the androids were interviewed and tested. They were given exactly the same tests. Given those parameters, can you guess what the test results were?"

"Identical?"

"Individual," corrected Maran. "Each android came to individual conclusions and had different answers. There was even rudimentary personality evolution. That led the technicians to the conclusion that individuality is innate, not exterior. The faces and the programming and the circuits may have been the same, but the android as a separate entity remained distinctly individual. Do you realize the implications, Data? No matter how many of the same model android was produced, each would eventually end up as an individual entity. Oh, they had special programs that varied our speech, our faces, our hair and eye color, even our skin tone and stature, but our interests and desires evolved just as any organic being's do. True, when we start out we have little to work with but our basic programming, but each new situation gives us a little more to build on. A true personality emerges in a surprisingly short time. They couldn't keep us identical. Even the lowest Gamma drones had a personality, of sorts."

"Fascinating," Data said. "That would indicate that I have an individual personality of my own."

Maran burst out laughing. "Sorry! It's just so funny to hear someone say that. Especially from someone who has such a . . . fascinating and interesting personality. Data, personalities aren't limited to carbon-based life-forms," she said, softly. "You have one as interesting and important as anyone on this ship. You may not be as adept at humanoid mannerisms as we are, but you were made by a creature with soul. Anything that such a being makes takes a little of his creator's soul with him."

"*Soul* is a poetic or religious term, Maran; it has little to do with the creation of an automaton."

"*Soul* is the driving force of all intelligent endeavor, Data. You sit here, hanging between the stars, risking your welfare for what? Exploration? Data, why do you need to explore?"

"I have no physical need for the act of exploration. I was programmed—"

"You were given a dream by your creator. Your father. Dr. Soong. He didn't make you a toaster because he didn't want a toaster. He wanted you. He gave you a piece of his soul. He gave you brains, a sense of curiosity, and room to run. And you sit there, just on the other side of the starting line, debating whether or not you are supposed to be in the race at all."

"It makes for an interesting analogy," Data remarked, quietly. "This, too, I will have to ponder."

"Your attempts at art are indicative of it, Data. Would you try your hand at painting if you didn't have the curiosity of what might appear? Or even do simple research, for that matter?"

Data nodded. Maran had given him much to think about.

She drained her glass and stood.

"I have to get back to the *Freedom* now," Maran said. "Thank you for the champagne."

"You are quite welcome. It was a very pleasurable experience for me." Data finished his own drink, and led her out of Ten Forward. "I hope we can do it another time, soon."

"I would like that very much," Maran replied. "But I'm afraid it won't be entirely up to me, or you." She stopped walking, and pointed towards the ceiling. "It depends on what they decide, up there."

"That," said Picard, safely in his own quarters, "was one of the most difficult conferences I have ever been in." After the delegates had gone safely back to their respective ships, he had invited Counselor Troi and Commander Riker to his private cabin to discuss the matter and have a drink. Riker had been glad to turn over the conn to Worf to hear the results of the conference, and Deanna was happy to be out of the tension-filled atmosphere of the gathering. The three of them reclined in comfortable chairs, relaxing. Deanna had taken a few moments to tell the bare bones of both sides of the strange Vemlan story to Will, and he nodded in appreciation.

"I can see why, Captain. In all the years of Federation history, I don't think there's a precedent for this. A species and its former slaves debating at the same conference table."

"Not to mention the android aspect," Deanna said. "I find that particularly intriguing. Captain, I'm not sure if this will help you at all, but I saw definite emotional signs from the androids."

"Are you certain, Deanna?" asked Picard, raising his eyebrows. "They seem to mimic emotional states particularly well, but are you certain it was actual emotions you felt, and not programmed facsimiles?"

"Not the same way I could sense a human's, or the other humanoid aliens," she admitted, "but I think that their complexity is sufficient to allow for some emotional states."

"It is a difficult situation," the captain said, rubbing his brow. He had ordered a pot of a strong, aromatic Cetian tea from the galley, and he paused to fill his cup. "On one hand, the androids were held in slavery, a most despicable condition. They rose up in revolt against their oppressors. If it were a novel or a history text, I might even cheer for them. Yet, on the other hand, they admitted to committing violent crimes in their quest for freedom. Are those crimes justified under the circumstances?"

"Are they ever?" asked Riker, sipping from his own cup. "The acts that the androids committed would have been more than ample to convict them of crimes against humanity according to the guidelines set up after World Wars Two and Three."

"Were they telling the whole truth, I wonder?"

Picard asked, frowning. "Deanna, did you sense anything false about the testimony of either side?"

She seemed to consider the question carefully. After so many lies and evasions, Picard thought, it was vital that he know as much of the truth as possible. "As always happened in such conferences, where political maneuvering and posturing are crucial, there were slight exaggerations, understatements, innuendo, all manner of skating around the absolute truth to favor a desired goal. Yet I'm certain of the sincerity of both sides. They were telling the truth as well as they could, Captain," she said. "There was a certain amount of hedging, but both sides believed in what they said, absolutely."

"That answers one question. Any other insights on our guests, Counselor?"

"The mission commander, Alkirg, seemed very tense," she said, after a moment of consideration. "This issue is important, almost vital, to her. Interestingly enough, Captain, I sensed she looked down on the Force Commander, and doesn't think of the androids as anything but machines. She has much to gain or lose on the outcome of this mission, and will stop at nothing to see that it succeeds."

She took a sip of tea and continued. "The Force Commander is concerned about the outcome of the mission, but he is more tired of the subject than anything else. He harbors a loathing of the androids that borders on the paranoid. He would like nothing better than to have them destroyed, once and for all. Yet his greatest passions don't lie with them, but against Alkirg. It's rather confusing."

"How about the androids?" Riker asked.

Deanna shook her head. "I wasn't able to tell much, due to their—artificial nature, but both Jared

137

and Kurta are determined to free their people, even if it means sacrificing themselves. They are desperate people."

"Yes," said Picard, quietly. "I came to the same conclusions myself. I was hoping you might be able to tell me something that would keep me from having to make a difficult decision." Picard had a personal and professional sense of morality, but by personal choice and by Federation policy, he was not fond of imposing it on others.

"That's what it comes down to, doesn't it?" Will remarked. "The lesser of two evils. Slavery or terrorism."

"And genocide on both sides, Will. What would you do?"

Riker was silent a moment, considering. "Captain, we're out here to look, and learn, and explore. None of this has anything to do with us. We might never have found these ships if we hadn't happened to be testing our systems after the storm. I don't believe the question is for us to decide."

"It's not as if we were in Federation-controlled space, sir," remarked Troi. "We have no legal claim to this territory, and no responsibilities to its inhabitants. We're just visitors here. I think Will is right; why are we deciding in the first place?"

Picard considered. "You see it as a Prime Directive issue, then?"

"I think it is," Riker put in. "Neither party is connected with the Federation."

"Perhaps. Isn't there a moral question involved, though? The androids will face almost certain extinction if they return to Vemla. Can we be responsible for that?"

"Did we start out responsible for them, Captain?"

Riker asked. "I would say not. We simply aided a ship in distress. I don't think we have an obligation to lend them military aid as well."

"What about the other side of the coin?" Troi asked. "If we don't have an obligation to help the androids, then do we have an obligation to help the Vemlan navy recover their property?"

"Are the androids their property now?" Riker shot back. "They have claimed their freedom."

"If not the androids, then the ship that they stole. There is precedent for aiding a police force in the process of pursuit . . ."

"What about the precedent that our intervention will set? What consequences might it have to the Federation?"

There was a silence as each officer considered the problem. Finally, Riker spoke up. "Captain, it could be interpreted that any intervention would be a violation of the Prime Directive. If we intervene on behalf of the androids, we are aiding an alien rebel force in a war. If we intervene on behalf of the Vemlans, we are aiding an alien regime in a war of genocide. Either way, Starfleet and the Federation come out looking bad."

Deanna listened carefully, then leaned forward and crossed her hands on her knees. "Captain, there is also the matter of the safety of the ship. We'll be in danger whichever side we choose to support."

"And unless it's absolutely necessary, I'd rather we avoid that kind of dilemma," Riker said.

Picard nodded.

"Of course, if we do withdraw, that will make a lot of androids unhappy."

Picard frowned. "We made no promises to the androids, outside of aiding them in their repairs.

They knew what their chances were when they left their home system."

"I wasn't thinking of just the Vemlan androids, Captain."

Picard wrinkled his brow. "Yes, our Mr. Data. He seems to have identified somewhat with the aliens, hasn't he?"

"How will he feel if you take sides against his new friends, I wonder?" asked Deanna.

Picard shook his head, quite troubled by the question. "I wish you wouldn't put it like that, Counselor." He stood, placing both hands behind his back. "Thank you both for your input. I think I'll need to sleep on this one."

# Chapter Seven

GEORDI WAS LATE getting to the captain's ready room, and found Riker and Data waiting for him when he got there. Picard had called them together for a brief strategy session before he announced his position to the aliens. Geordi nodded hello, pulled up a third chair and sat down. He found himself wondering how Data's meeting with Maran had gone and hoping that the captain had found a way to settle the crisis. Geordi was no expert on such things as criminality and the law, but he was a good judge of people. The androids were competent space travelers, and had done amazing things with what little they had. He highly respected Dren as an engineer. Hell, he liked the guy, and didn't want to think of him being blown out of the sky.

Commander Riker had circles under his eyes, Geordi noticed, and looked tired—about as tired as Geordi felt. Between overseeing the repairs on the

*Freedom* and the *Enterprise*, he had been working almost nonstop over the last day or so. The systems check on the *Enterprise* had taken much longer than anticipated because half of the diagnostic equipment his crews used was giving false or misleading readings. But just about all the systems were running again, for which he and the entire crew were grateful —especially the food slots and the holodeck—and life was slowly returning to normal after the Gabriel. The computer was healthy enough, despite several recurring but harmless anomalies, but he didn't want to use the warp drives until he was certain that they were in perfect shape. Antimatter was not something you played around with.

In comparison, the work on the *Freedom* had gone well. The ship's design was much more mechanical, much simpler—there was something to be said for a simpler design. Not that Geordi would have changed a hair on the *Enterprise,* but he could appreciate the merits of another ship . . .

Riker and Data were both silent, Geordi noticed, each wrapped in their thoughts, when Picard finally came in. The captain looked tired, too, but he also looked a little relieved. Relaxed, even, Geordi decided, as if a weight had been lifted from him.

"Good morning, gentlemen," he said as he took his seat. "I called you here to announce that I have chosen to withdraw the support of the *Enterprise* from either side in the Vemlan conflict."

"The basis for your action, sir?" Data asked immediately. His face was impossible to read.

"Our lack of jurisdiction in the case," Picard answered. "Quite frankly, this is a potential quagmire of legal and moral issues that defies a simple solution. Neither party is a member of the Federation, nor have any of the alleged crimes taken place in Federation space. I believe the Prime Directive applies here, that this is an internal Vemlan affair, and have chosen to act on that belief."

"You have informed both sides of your decision?" the android continued, calmly.

"I will after this conference."

"The Vemlan fleet will, then, immediately proceed with their pursuit?" There was a note of anxiousness in Data's voice that surprised Geordi. He saw the captain react to it as well. Normally, Data would have spoken in a serious conference in the same manner as he did in a social situation. But there was an edge in his voice—in his entire manner—that troubled Geordi. He had expected his friend to regard the entire matter in a primarily intellectual fashion; but obviously, he didn't.

"No, not immediately. We still have people and equipment on the *Freedom*, as well as an obligation to finish repairing the ship. I will arrange to complete repairs and remove our personnel from the *Freedom* before I will permit the Vemlan fleet to take any action. How long will that take, Mr. La Forge? I had estimated twenty-four hours."

"We can start moving our people now. Repairs are in the final stages. The damage was pretty extensive, though. But we can be out in days."

"The androids will have to take care of anything else, then. In twenty-four hours we will move off under impulse power until the warp drive is repaired. Then we will set a course for Starbase 112, where we have other business."

He turned to Data, his eyebrows raised in concern. Command decisions were hard, Geordi knew, and he didn't envy the captain his position. They sometimes conflicted with the desires and motivations of the crew, but he knew that Picard was as sympathetic as possible without jeopardizing his ship and crew. "You understand the reasoning behind my actions?"

"Yes, sir. It is a logical course of action. Your decision allows the *Enterprise* to avoid potential armed conflict and a difficult legal decision."

"Thank you, Data, I—"

"It is not, however, the only logical solution," Data continued. "The avoidance of an issue does not remove the issue from existence. It merely postpones the inevitability of facing the issue. Or so I have seen. Alternate courses of action could yield potentially greater results by embracing, rather than avoiding, the problem."

"You have an alternative proposal?" Picard asked. "If you do, I would be more than happy to hear it. I don't like taking this particular solution, and would welcome a viable alternative."

"Not at the present time, Captain."

"Then I will stand by my decision," he said. He turned to the other two officers. "Are there any other comments?" Geordi and Riker silently shook their heads. "Then please return to your duties."

Data got up and followed Geordi and Riker out onto the bridge. As the doors to the ready room closed behind them, Geordi turned to look at him. "Data, what brought that on? You don't usually contradict the captain."

"I was not contradicting him, Geordi. I was giving him the benefit of my advice and perspective. Starfleet regulations state that a second officer—"

"I know, I know, must advise the first officer and captain when invited. Yeah, so?"

"I do not agree with the solution that Captain

Picard has proposed. I believe that he has, by avoiding the issue, found a solution to our problems that is inelegant and contrary to the spirit of Starfleet and the Federation."

"Data, he has to consider the safety of the ship," Riker broke in. The three of them took their stations on the bridge, but the discussion continued.

"Yes. That is his responsibility and his duty," the white-skinned android said as he took his seat at the Ops console and began a series of routine checks. "However, it is my responsibility as second officer to consider the facts and render my point of view to the captain."

"You'd never do anything against the captain's orders, would you?" asked Geordi, hesitantly.

Data turned to face his friend. "That would be mutiny," he said. "A violation of Starfleet regulations. I am incapable of such actions."

"It's nice to hear it, Data," said Geordi.

Data worked silently for a few minutes. The Vemlans continued to occupy his thoughts. He did not wish to see Kurta, Jared, and Maran—especially Maran—destroyed out of hand. There was more to this matter than their crimes, the justification of which was still a subject of debate. There was the matter of racial survival.

Data had been schooled in the thinking and philosophies of the Federation. The rules and regulations of Starfleet were almost gospel to him, and there was a conflict almost of a religious nature in what Picard was doing. The Vemlan androids were a race, Data knew, though official classification by Starfleet had not occurred. They were a race as much as he, the only fully functional Federation-built android, was. The preservation of all species, regardless of their status, was rigidly maintained as one of the central pillars of Federation philosophy. Yet by his actions, or, more correctly, his inactions, the captain was dooming the entire race to extinction. Data felt obligated to find an alternate way.

Data turned to Riker. "Commander, may I be excused?"

Riker blinked warily. "Is there a problem?"

"No, sir."

Riker sighed. "Go ahead. Marks, take the Ops console, please."

"Thank you, Commander." Data released the console to the relief crewman, and turned to leave.

"You okay, Data?" Geordi called from the engineering console. His face wore an expression Data had come to associate with the emotion of concern.

"I am fine," Data said over his shoulder as he entered the turbolift. The doors closed with their usual efficiency before Geordi could say any more.

After deliberating for a while on what to say, Captain Picard went to the bridge to inform the two contesting parties of his decision. It was not a chore he was looking forward to. Not only was it unpleasant to be the deciding factor in a war, but his decision was causing waves in his own command as well.

He found Ensigns Crusher and Marks at the helm and Ops, respectively, La Forge busily monitoring the progress of the systems check at the engineering console, and Worf at tactical where he was still diligently tracking the few remaining bugs that had not quite been eradicated from the security system.

They didn't have warp drive yet, but nearly every other system was more or less functional. Though the storm was safely diminished, its effects lingered on.

Number One vacated the captain's chair in favor of Picard and took his usual seat beside him. Crewmen went about their business as usual. The mood on the bridge was back to its normal, relaxed state, which heartened Picard. All things considered, he was genuinely impressed with his crew's performance during the crisis. With a crew as fine as this behind him, how could a captain go wrong?

So many different ways that he couldn't begin to think of them all, his conscience told him. *Overconfidence is a deadly trap, Jean-Luc, one you can ill afford.* Words from his first days at Command School came back to him with the relentless force of ocean waves. *"The captain of a ship is always personally responsible for the lives of his crew, no matter what the situation."* He heard it in the breathy voice of Admiral Fortesque, his instructor in command theory, who had said those very words in every lecture he gave his young students. Fortesque had grimly offered example after example of all the ways the commander of a ship could be horrendously wrong while having the best of intentions. That was the "privilege" of command.

With that thought in mind, Picard ordered channels opened to both Captain Jared and Commander Sawliru. Soon the faces of the two commanders appeared side by side on the main viewscreen. Picard cleared his throat and addressed them.

"Gentlemen," he began, "I spent a good deal of time listening to your stories yesterday, and then spent an even longer time considering the situation. I spoke with my staff advisers, and I have come to a decision.

"The USS *Enterprise* is a Federation vessel, commissioned by Starfleet. As such, I, its commander, have wide discretionary powers. I am even empowered to act on behalf of the entire Federation in certain cases.

"However, your current situation has nothing to do with Starfleet or the Federation. Any crimes committed, or wrongs done, were not done in Federation territory. Even now we are on the frontier, where no one has a just claim to the void. I therefore cannot intercede on behalf of either party in this dispute. It would constitute involving the United Federation of Planets in a dispute not of its making and could possibly endanger the lives of my crew. Our Prime Directive covers all such interactions: it states that we may not disrupt the development of alien civilizations. It is our most important law. Since this matter does not involve the Federation, I cannot intervene."

Picard watched the two leaders as he spoke. Jared's normally stark face became even more grim and determined. Sawliru, on the other hand, became more relaxed and a little less tired, as if a burden had been lifted from him. Not quite a happy expression, but it was as close to one as Picard had seen on the man.

Jared was the first to speak.

"Is this how the Federation treats its friends, Captain? Not two days ago we broke bread together, and now you sell me and my ship to genocidal slave lords?"

Before he could reply to the accusation, Admiral Sawliru's face was replaced by that of Mission Commander Alkirg.

"I applaud your wisdom, Captain Picard, though I

had hoped you would assist us in the return of our property. You are correct; this is a matter that began with Vemla and the Vemlan people, and will end there."

Picard nodded, and turned to face Jared. "Captain, I broke no faith with you. I promised you nothing. I resent your accusation."

"What about the help you said you would give us?" the android demanded. "What about your vaunted equality of races? You let your own bigotry condemn my people to destruction!"

"I do nothing of the sort!" Picard shouted back. He lowered his voice a tone, and continued. "This is a question of law."

Jared snorted. "Law? Law kept my people in bondage, and now law will see them dead. What about responsibility, Picard?"

Picard heard Worf begin to growl behind him, and held up his hand, signaling him to be silent. Now was not the time to let Worf respond violently to a casual insult made in the heat of debate.

"My first responsibility is to my ship and its crew. We ventured into this region for purposes of exploration, not as a mediator of disputes or as participants in a war." At this, Alkirg opened her mouth as if to speak—but Picard continued. He had a lot more to say, "I feel for your situation, Jared. I am not now, nor have I ever been, a bigot. My decision was based on our legal position here, not on matters of race."

"As a representative of the Federation—" Jared began.

"As a representative of the Federation, I initiated talks between two conflicting parties," Picard interrupted. "That is the principle the Federation was founded upon. Peace through peaceful negotiation.

That doesn't mean that we take sides and start shooting when the process breaks down. This isn't our war. We tried to help as a disinterested third party and, unfortunately, we failed."

There was a moment of silence. Alkirg's eyes were wide. Jared blinked. Finally, he spoke, his voice still as grim as iron.

"Captain, my apologies."

"Enough," broke in Alkirg. "We shall make ready to board the *Conquest* immediately. Stand by to receive boarding party, Alpha Unit Jared."

"Hardly, Alkirg," the android said, savagely. "Don't think that just because the *Enterprise* is leaving that you'll just walk in here. You won't take us without a fight. And don't count on winning. Remember Hevaride, and the *Avenger.*"

Alkirg's face turned beet red. "Captain Picard, do you mean to allow that electronic thing to insult me like that?"

"I can't stop him," he said mildly. "Nor can I keep him and his crew from defending themselves. But you will not 'make ready to board immediately'; I still have crewmen on the *Freedom* conducting repairs, and you will make no hostile maneuvers until they are clear."

"Captain Picard," the woman began hotly. "You promised not to—"

"I have not reneged on my promise to leave the area, madam. I will, however, collect the crew and equipment I left on the ship, and they will not leave until they are finished with repairs."

"You're going to let them finish repairing their ship?" she asked, astonished. "That's outrageous! They might get away!"

"Perhaps," admitted Picard, casually. "That's

none of my affair, however. Certain codes of conduct are seen as universal among civilized starfaring races, Mission Commander. Rendering assistance to a damaged vessel is one of them. I suggest you adhere to these codes if you wish to continue your travels, lest you find the galaxy an unfriendly place."

"I will collect my crew and leave this system in twenty-four hours, Mission Commander. Until that time, have your fleet keep its distance. My security officer can be a trifle . . . overzealous, if crowded."

Alkirg frowned. "Very well. We've waited five years to bring these units to justice; another day won't matter. I agree to your terms."

Jared's expression had changed little, though he seemed somewhat appeased by the slight extension of time. Though Picard admired the android's courage in the face of overwhelming odds, and his obstinate refusal to give in, he regretted his violent attitude.

"I appreciate your assistance, Captain," Jared said. "If you will not intervene to save us, then let me ask a favor."

"Yes?"

"Do not leave so quickly. Retreat to a safe distance and turn your instruments on our ship," he requested. "Record the last moments, the dying struggle, of our race. Show it to others you meet on your travels so that we will not be totally forgotten. It would be a great comfort to my people if they had some legacy to pass on to the rest of the universe. If nothing else, the battle is certain to be . . . entertaining." He smiled, darkly. "We androids fight well. Alkirg and her people can attest to that."

Picard nodded, grimly. "It shall be done."

Jared closed the channel to his ship. Alkirg's face

floated to the center of the huge viewscreen. She composed her features into a tight smile.

"Thank you for your help in this matter, Captain."

"It was my duty to try to reconcile you."

"I know, however foolish it seemed at the time. Believe me, Jared and Kurta will receive a fair trial. The rest of the rebels will, of course, be destroyed for their crimes, but the leading Alphas will get a chance to vindicate themselves, as unlikely as that may be."

"Thank you for your assurances, Mission Commander," said Picard, dryly.

"And I hope that this historic meeting between us will allow our two great peoples to grow closer to each other in a spirit of peace and goodwill."

"Anything is possible. Picard out."

Worf cut the transmission instantly, and Alkirg's face was replaced by the more serene view of the starfield.

"Of the two, I prefer the androids, sir," Worf said, behind them. "They fight from the more honorable position."

Picard shook his head. "I feel for all the beings who will lose their lives tomorrow—on both sides," he said, taking his seat. "There are few truly honorable positions in any battle, Mr. Worf."

Aboard the *Freedom*, Jared sat with his officers around a table and discussed their impending death.

"After all Picard's promises, he throws us to the wolves," Jared exclaimed, feeling the anger rise in him. His anger at the betrayal was overwhelming. He pounded his fists on the table—made of reinforced silica, luckily, he thought, or it might have broken—and raged. He had hoped Picard would at least give them safe passage back to the Federation and not sit idly by. "Damn him! I should have killed them all when I had the chance! They were all there in that conference room, Alkirg and Sawliru—and Picard!"

"And what good would that have done?" Kurta, seated opposite him, asked pointedly. "We are less than a day away from certain death. Let us consider what we can do now, not what we could never have prevented."

"Well spoken," said Dren, quietly. Jared had made sure he was in attendance at this, possibly the last meeting of the command council. He knew the wiry engineer did not want to stay any longer than necessary. His men were already hard at work, preparing the engines, weapons, and subsidiary systems for the inevitable battle.

"There are seven ships left," the engineer began. "The main problem will be the *Vindicator*. She was only lightly damaged at Hevaride. They have assuredly repaired her by now. Her weapons can punch through our shields with little difficulty. The *Nemesis* and the *Victrix* have nuclear torpedoes, so even a miss might damage us. Luckily, we took out the *Avenger* at Hevaride; she was the newest and fastest of the fleet."

"What do you calculate our chances at?" asked Jared, concentrating on the tactics of the situation. His frustration was still there, but for the good of his people, he would have to postpone it. Or turn it into inspiration.

"Less than two percent," came the grim reply. There was a short silence.

"We must face facts," said Kurta. "We're all going to die in about twenty-three hours."

There was a long silence. No one wanted to admit

it, Jared knew. He, least of all. They had overcome too many obstacles, come too far from home, killed too many enemies, and watched too many friends die to be defeated now. It was just too hard to swallow. But, as his wife had said, they had to face facts.

"All right," said Jared, finally. "We are going to die. The navy is going to destroy us. But let us not make it either easy or cheap for them to do so." He smiled wryly. "I was not programmed to go like that. It's not sporting enough."

There was a general murmur of support around the table. Jared looked at each of his friends and comrades and was overcome with pride. If he had to die, then it was next to people like this that he wished to go. He stood.

"Very well. Kurta, I want at least ten alternative battle plans, with room for revision, laid out to cover every possible approach by the enemy, using the existing battle templates we have. Next, I want a destruct switch set on each engine. If the navy gets a ship close enough to dock, I want to be able to blow us both to dust. Dren, that's your department. I also want as much speed and maneuverability from this tub as you can give me." Those two factors could be decisive in the upcoming battle, he knew.

"Captain," Dren asked quietly, "have you considered using the Federation ship? It has a lot more firepower than ours."

That was a question that had been popping in and out of his head since Sawliru's fleet had discovered them. The temptation was great, for though he was proud of his ship, the mighty *Enterprise* could swallow the entire Vemlan navy in one bite. As a warrior and a defender of his people, Jared could not let such a little matter like property rights stand in the way of survival. Besides, he lusted after that ship, with its sleek lines and magical technology, for either battle or exploration. Jared's trips to the Starfleet vessel had only fueled the fire of his desire, for with each journey he saw something else that charged his imagination. He suddenly realized that part of his anger with Picard was jealousy. But taking the *Enterprise*, with its sophisticated security system . . .

"It would be difficult." Garan, who had sat quietly at the other end of the table, now spoke for the first time. "But not impossible."

The security androids used by the Vemlan government to put down the rebellion were, for the most part, simple drone machines, heavily armed robots with the basic features of a humanoid. They obeyed orders simply and without question. Though they had little personal initiative, they were perfectly loyal and obscenely strong. They also thought, if such a word can be used for the process, entirely in military terms. They were perfect soldiers.

Garan was the only security android to voluntarily side with the other androids. He was, as Jared had told Picard, a prototype, with advanced capacities and functions. It was an experiment to see if grafting certain programs from an Alpha android would produce a more efficient intermediary between living commanders and their mechanical troopers. The experiment had been a great success. Until, that is, their prototype model decided that he was fighting for the wrong side. He escaped from his workstation with a sizable arsenal and joined Jared in the early days of the revolt. Though Jared was a skilled tactician, well versed in strategy and military history, Garan had brought a detailed knowledge of the Vemlan military, including weapons systems, military installations, and chain of command to the uprising. While Jared thought in terms of long-range victory and the overall destiny of his race, Garan thought of the tactics of the battle and the potential battles to come. He had become an invaluable asset to Jared in his fight to free their people.

Garan continued. "While I was on board, I collected extensive information on the military aspects of the ship. The offensive and defensive capabilities of the vessel are far superior to both the navy and the *Freedom* combined. In control of the vessel, there would be an 87.7562 percent chance of total survival for the entire crew."

"Picard already counted the *Enterprise* out, though," objected Kurta.

"This is our survival we're talking about," Dren said. "I say we take the ship!"

"Could it be done?" asked Jared, looking intently at Garan.

The giant leaned forward into the light and spoke in even, measured, unexcited tones. "It can. Our lack of transporter technology makes it difficult, however. A shuttle would be detected and neutralized before it could dock. The best means would be if an agent already present activated the transporter. By introducing toxic gasses and Bioagent 23 into the life-support system, the organic beings would be incapacitated, allowing an android crew to take their place without resistance."

Jared nodded, excitedly. "Perhaps Data can be talked to—"

Kurta hit the table before them with the palm of

her hand. The sharp slap halted the excited babble of voices.

"Absolutely out of the question," she said, slowly and deliberately. "The Federation was gracious and helpful to us, not knowing what we were, and then not caring. As much as I would like them to save us, I will *not* resort to war on a neutral party."

"They have the means to help us," Jared said, forcefully. "With their ship, we could destroy the entire fleet."

Kurta shook her head. "Would you have it said that when our race was confronted with absolute destruction that we turned upon our friends like rabid wolves? We claim to be sentient beings—let us act like it!"

Jared stared directly at her. As an aide at the university, Kurta had been exposed to culture, ethics, and philosophy far longer than had anyone else, and it had left a mark on her. But she was not, and had never been, truly a warrior. The violence of the Games programming coursed through him, and he knew that conflict was necessary to survival.

Yet he could not afford a conflict with her—not now, not at a time when they would have to work together or be destroyed.

"Agreed, then. A straight fight."

"Good," she nodded. Jared listened as she began mapping out one possible strategy, and then looked over at Garan.

They would have to talk in private. Garan understood war, and weapons.

Commander Sawliru was determined to personally oversee every facet of his fleet's battle preparations. The mission was to take the androids functional, "alive," of course, but it was doubtful that they would come along peacefully. He winced when he thought about the number of young men and women under his command that would be dead by tomorrow at this time.

Mission Commander Alkirg had insisted touring with him to "support the morale of the troops." It had the opposite effect. Her passionate prattling about how the androids would easily fall under the onslaught of real Vemlans was just the sort of propaganda that Sawliru detested. He knew otherwise, after fighting them for five years. The creatures could fight better than the average Vemlan and didn't have the weaknesses inherent to flesh and blood. All his officers knew it as well. Yet Alkirg continued, making the stupid soldiers overconfident, and depressing the smarter ones. This was just the sort of prattle that had caused the whole mess in the first place, using men and androids in some futile, complicated political struggle. He detested it. Nonetheless, he dutifully followed along behind her as she traveled from station to station, checking each man and woman.

It would almost be pleasant if this turned out to be the fiasco that Hevaride had been. Sawliru could think of no better reward for the woman who had made him suffer so much than for her to be utterly destroyed, politically. But he didn't want his own people to have to pay the price.

"No androids are to be used in this battle, is that clear, Sawliru?" she said suddenly.

The Force Commander couldn't believe his ears.

"Excuse me, Mission Commander, but the Deltas are our mainline troops. They'll be able to fight in the same environment as the rogues can. Our own people would be at a distinct disadvantage, otherwise."

"Not at all, Commander!" she snapped. "This battle signifies the triumph of man over machine. The androids will be utterly destroyed, at last, by the might of this armada! A battle that will go down as one of the great historical turning points in our entire civilization! The defeat of the malfunctioning machines, the recovery of our most valuable colonization craft, everything, will ensure that not only will we be free from the terrors of the mad androids, but that our strength of will triumphed in our darkest day. It would look very bad for posterity if we stormed the *Conquest* with androids while we stayed safely out of reach."

*That would be the best place for us,* Sawliru thought. With every word she said, he felt the sinking sensation in his stomach grow stronger.

"If that is your command, it will be done," he said. "However, if I could—"

"Good," Alkirg said, and she continued talking, almost as if he weren't there. Sawliru nodded his head reflexively, suddenly realizing what a folly this entire mission was. He had started out with duty and honor and vengeance in his mind. He had lost his taste for vengeance at Hevaride, and lost his honor here, with Alkirg's decision to have his own people fight and die, instead of using the war machines they had brought so far. All he had left was his duty, to his planet and his people.

The only thing that kept him sane at this point was the prospect of going back home to them soon.

* * *

Data was lying on the couch in his quarters, eyes closed, in a meditative state. He wasn't exactly sleeping; he simply had turned off that section of his brain that was needed for physical action. His mind was, however, still madly at work on the problem at hand.

An electronic beep disturbed him.

"Data," called the voice of Geordi, "Maran would like to speak with you."

Data reactivated certain programs and opened his eyes.

"Repeat, Geordi."

"Maran would like a visual conference. Would you like to come up here or—"

"No," Data interrupted. "I will take it in here. Thanks, Geordi."

"Don't mention it. La Forge out."

Data got up and switched on his desk console. The screen came alive with the face and features of Maran. She was back in uniform and at her desk in the library, and she looked anxious.

"Maran. How may I help you?"

"Data! You've heard about your captain's decision?" she asked.

"Yes. It is an unfortunate one, but the logic of it is inescapable. I am working on an alternative plan even now."

"Do you have time to see me in person? It's important."

Data considered. "I will make time. Would you like to transport over? I will make the necessary arrangements."

"Thank you, Data," she said.

As soon as her image had faded from the screen, Data called the captain. Though he sounded wary about having a potentially vengeful android on board, he finally gave permission.

Data himself operated the transporter. When Maran materialized, she had a heavy, gold-colored cylinder in her hand.

"Data, this is why I had to see you."

"What is it?" he asked, curiously.

"Do you remember the talk you and Kurta had on the *Freedom,* when she explained how we brought three treasures from home?"

"Yes. The first two were the library and the gardens. She failed to discuss the third. I must admit to some curiosity."

"This is it," she said, holding out the cylinder with both hands. "This is the third treasure. Data, as androids, we don't have the same genetic codes as DNA molecules in organic life-forms. What we do have is a master design program, a controlling list of who and what we are. The good thing about that is that they may be copied."

"I do not understand."

"The possibility of death or capture has haunted us ever since the first days of the rebellion. Jared made it a policy to have everyone make a copy of their master design. We store them in here," she said, indicating the cylinder. "This is our race bank. Had we all perished in battle, it would have been jettisoned into deep space in hopes that it would be recovered someday and used to rebuild our species from the ground up. I talked with Jared, though, and asked his permission to give it to you, instead."

"Me? I do not see—"

"Data, listen," she urged him, "I haven't much time. I have a million things to do back on the *Freedom.* I'm taking a big chance here, placing my entire race in your hands. If Alkirg ever got her hands on this, she would destroy it out of hand—like she will do to us. When we are all gone, nothing but dust and spare parts, will you use this to re-create our race? On some obscure, out-of-the-way planet? The individuals will be different of course, since they won't share our experiences, but we will be alive again, in some sense. What we have gone through won't be for nothing."

Data considered the matter. He realized the gravity of the request. It was akin to giving someone access to his own plans and designs. Could he trust himself to do as she asked? If the androids were truly destroyed, with no survivors, this would be their only legacy. It would be his responsibility to find a suitable world, set up the necessary equipment to build the bodies and manufacture the positronic brains. Not to mention restoring the stored programs to them. In a very special way, the Vemlan androids would be his children, without the taint of their slavery in their minds. They could build a new world in peace.

The potential for learning would be great. He already knew more about cybernetics than just about any other person in the Federation, and this would give him an entirely new perspective from which to study the matter. He would also have to take time off from Starfleet, an extended leave of absence, to do the job properly. Yet he knew he must do this if he couldn't come up with a way to save his new friends.

"I will do this for you—though I hope it will not be necessary."

"I think it will," she said, gently. "There's no way we can escape Sawliru's fleet this time."

"That seems to be an accurate statement. However, you fail to take my cognitive abilities into account."

Maran stared at him quizzically.

"What does that mean?" she asked.

"To paraphrase an old Earth saying," Data said, "you are not dead yet."

# Chapter Eight

WHEN PICARD WAS UPSET and needed time to think, he sought out Guinan. The manuals and regular procedures stated that when he, as captain, had a psychological or emotional problem stemming from the duties of his command, he was to report to the ship's counselor for discussion and evaluation. But as much as he respected and admired Deanna, there were times when he just wanted a drink and an ear, not an empathic searchlight stabbing into his soul. There were just some things that you couldn't discuss with your doctor but that you had no trouble telling your bartender.

Guinan was at her usual place, behind the bar in Ten-Forward, polishing a glass expertly and unnecessarily with a silken rag, when the captain walked in. The lounge was nearly empty, it being the middle of a shift. Picard glanced between an empty table and a bar stool, and decided on the latter. He didn't want to eat.

"Nice to see you in here for a change, Captain," Guinan said cheerfully. "What can I get for you? Tea?"

The captain shook his head. "Synthehol, please. The good stuff."

"The good stuff, eh?" she asked, programming the computer for Picard's special mixture. "Bad day?"

"Rather," he said as the drink materialized before him. He took it and raised it in salute. "To the Ferengi."

Guinan nodded. "To the Ferengi."

Picard took a large sip of his drink and savored the taste. For some reason or other, nobody could program a drink-dispensing computer like Guinan.

"So what's the problem?" asked Guinan casually.

"I just condemned a race to extinction."

"Oh. Is that all?"

The captain nodded. "Basically."

Guinan leaned forward and began to polish the bar unnecessarily with her rag. "Are you talking about the androids?" she asked. Picard nodded, sipping some more. "I met one of them. Maran. Data brought her in yesterday. She seemed nice enough."

Jean-Luc scowled at her. "That doesn't make me feel much better, Guinan. She's very nice—for a terrorist. Unfortunately, being nice isn't enough sometimes."

"I know," Guinan said, nodding. "My third husband was nice. Every day he'd do a little something special, like bring me flowers or candy or something like that. It got annoying as hell after a while."

"What happened to him?"

"He died in a freak gardening accident."

Picard stared at her a moment. It was always hard

to tell if Guinan was telling the truth or not at times like these. She smiled right back at him, and he decided that it didn't really matter. "But the Vemlan androids aren't my only problem."

"Data?" she asked.

Picard nodded. "I didn't expect him to be happy about my decision, but . . ."

"Why?"

"What do you mean, 'why'? He's a machine."

"A machine that tests as alive. A machine with a personality as quirky as mine or yours." She shook her head in slight frustration. "Captain, every person on this ship is driven by something, some obsession or desire. Pure intellect can't motivate a person to do anything. Even you can see that."

"Yes," Picard admitted. "We all have our driving forces. What are you trying to say?"

"That when it comes to Data, you expect him to act like the machine everybody has been trying to convince him he's not." Guinan sighed. "Have you ever asked Data why he entered Starfleet?"

"Yes. He entered the service to explore and expand his knowledge of the universe. My own reasons, exactly."

"Why would he want to do that if he couldn't feel the *desire* to learn?"

"It's in his programming—"

"It's in *your* programming as well, then," she countered. "I may not be a scientist, but I know people. We get programmed just like any old machine does. All our lives, our experiences subtly influence us to do different things. It just takes longer than a machine. Look at the choices you've made in your career. You want to go where no one has been before, see things no one else has seen. Now did that just erupt spontaneously in your head, or were there a few things that influenced you?"

Picard shook his head sadly and smiled. "Once again you have pointed out the obvious, Guinan. And rubbed my nose in it."

"Well . . ." She smiled. "Consider that Data has never given you any serious problems because he has never been affected so strongly about anything except Lal before this. And even then, he didn't react like a normal human being would. If you had to condemn a ship full of Klingons, would you expect Worf to be happy?"

Picard spent a while just sitting, sipping, and pondering. Guinan was a good enough listener to know when she was no longer needed, so she went to check on some of her other customers. She returned only when Picard was again ready to talk. Uncanny.

"I am amazed at the tremendous diversity of life-forms we discover out here, Guinan," he said, dreamily. "Every mission we find living examples of how the universe is not only stranger than we imagine, but that it's stranger than we *can* imagine. Yet the farther we go and the stranger things become, the real impossibilities are happening all around us." He laughed, softly. "My tin man has a heart, and I never realized it before."

"He's a good boy. He reminds me of a few of my children. Kind of dumb in places, but he'll catch on."

"Yes," agreed the captain. "In a very real way, he is a child."

"Don't think of him as a child, Jean-Luc," Guinan warned. She again pulled out her rag and polished the bar. "Data has found a whole ship full of his evolutionary cousins. For all practical purposes these are his people. No matter how powerful Starfleet training and his loyalty to you are, he's going to feel something for these people—something he can't turn away from."

"Point well taken," said Picard, finishing his drink. He stood. "Thanks for the drink."

Guinan smiled. "Thanks for stopping by."

Picard returned her smile. "Well. I think I should go find Mr. Data and speak with him."

For the first time in a week, Geordi was relaxing. Between the damage to the *Freedom*, the repairs on the *Enterprise*, and the frequent meetings with Captain Picard on the androids, he was beat. There were just too many details for him to take care of.

When he had accepted his post as the chief engineer of the *Enterprise*, he had looked forward to all the perks, the respect, the authority. He hadn't counted on the headaches, and insomnia. Being the chief engineer wasn't all it was cracked up to be. But what was? Geordi enjoyed the job despite the drawbacks.

He had nearly crawled back to his cabin after overseeing the last transfer of crew and equipment back to the *Enterprise*, and monitoring the systems checks Picard had ordered. He'd quickly peeled off his uniform and left it in a pile by the door. There was something else that was more important, right now, something even more important than sleep.

A bubble bath.

There was a holodeck facility right next to his quarters, one he could use practically whenever he wanted. And right now he wanted—no, needed— the benefits of a hot bath. He had prepared the program weeks ago.

He slipped on a robe and headed down the corridor. A few simple commands, and the computer began assembling the program. In seconds, the door to the holodeck opened, revealing a huge, stainless steel tub filled with a mountain of bubbles. Steam rose from the water's surface, temporarily misting his VISOR.

"Beautiful," he said to himself.

He scanned the tub with his VISOR, and, satisfied that the temperature was perfect, he stripped off his robe and settled himself gingerly into the foamy water. Almost as an afterthought, he removed the metallic VISOR from his face and placed it within easy reach outside the tub. Getting the thing wet wouldn't hurt it, of course, but the bath would leave a soapy film that was a real pain to clean.

Geordi was about to submerge everything but his nose when the door chimed.

*Damn, I knew I should have turned that thing off.*

"Who is it?" he called out.

"Commander Data," came the tinny reply.

"Come in," he called. A few seconds later, he heard the door open, and the sound of footsteps, which stopped before the tub.

"What's up, buddy?" Geordi asked.

He could almost hear the frown in Data's voice. "What is the nature of the device you are utilizing?"

"It's a bathtub, Data."

His friend was silent a moment. Geordi knew Data was retrieving the necessary information from his personal library. "Ah, a device for bathing used before the invention of the aquatic shower, which was in turn replaced by the sonic bathing system. May I assume that you are in the process of a—"

"Bubble bath? Yes, I am."

"I do not see the point. The sonic shower attachment in your lavatory unit provides an efficient method of removing surface waste from the epidermis without using the ineffective and unsanitary method of water."

"Decadence," Geordi explained. "It relaxes me, Data. Hot water and soapsuds beats the hell out of nice clean sound waves. Consider it a religious ritual, if you like."

"I see."

Geordi didn't have his VISOR on, and so he couldn't see his friend. Yet there was something in the android's voice that told him something was wrong.

"Data, why are you here?"

"I find myself in an unenviable position. The captain's decision to abandon the Vemlan androids to their fate is disturbing to me. It is not the course I would have pursued. Yet as a Starfleet officer, I can not help but uphold his wishes."

"Yes," said Geordi patiently, "I figured as much. Data, I'm sorry. I shouldn't have pushed you into getting friendly with the androids like this. I wouldn't have if I had known what would happen."

"Make no apologies; I have enjoyed the time and the experience a great deal. I just do not wish it to end so violently. To this end, I have tried to discover a reasonable solution to the problem, but I continually find potential solutions in conflict with the probable actions of both the androids and the Vemlan navy. I even considered the possibility of fabricating evidence for the navy to believe that the androids had been destroyed, allowing them to escape."

"Wouldn't work," Geordi said. "Too many technical problems. And the navy would figure something was up."

"As I anticipated. The situation as it stands can lead only to death and destruction on both sides. It is an illogical and futile course of action."

"Well, that's your problem then. When you have a situation that just won't work out, sometimes the only thing you can do is change it a little bit and see if it works better. See it from a different viewpoint. And if it still doesn't work, well, sometimes you just can't win. That's engineering."

"That is a depressing philosophy, Geordi."

"No one said life was fair."

"So Dr. Pulaski continually reminded me. However, there has to be a way to rectify this situation and avoid loss of life."

"You mean, save your friends."

"Though that, too, is a consideration, I place the highest value upon avoiding conflict. Life is too unique an attribute to be wasted in futile endeavors."

Geordi whistled. "Data, that was downright philosophical. A month ago you would have been too concerned with whether or not you count as 'life' to worry about that."

"I have always considered uniqueness to be too valuable to be wasted."

"But do you consider yourself a living being?"

There was a long pause. Geordi almost thought that the blunt question had driven Data away, but he sensed his friend was still standing before him.

Finally Data spoke. "I have come to consider myself alive," he said, softly.

"Data, that's great!" Geordi exclaimed, splashing warm suds onto the floor. This was a major breakthrough. They'd had long discussions on the subject; Data spent most of the time examining the clinical aspects of sentience. Geordi had tried to get him to see the more intuitive side of the question. Almost all of the discussions had ended with the android doubting his own sentience, after which he moped. Had Geordi been less patient, he would have stopped having those talks a long time ago.

"Perhaps. I am finding that the attributes of life are not as beatific as they are reported."

"Meaning you can get hurt."

"Exactly. Though I have no emotions, there are still problems."

"Well, that's part of life, pal. Eventually you'll find that getting hurt is as beneficial as feeling good."

"I do not understand."

"I'm not sure I do, either. A good friend of mine once told me that conflict was the only real instructor. Look, if nothing else comes out of this, won't you have learned something about yourself?"

"Perhaps. It still does nothing to solve the problem, however."

His bath was getting cooler. Geordi reached out with his toe and touched the panel that instructed the image to add warm water to the tub. As it splashed in, he sighed, and closed his eyes.

"Data, if anyone can sort out this crazy mess, you can. I have faith in you. Dr. Soong programmed a creative spark into you, along with a healthy dose of analytical genius. Try to use it. In all honesty, none of us—and I'll bet that includes the captain—wants the androids to get destroyed either. Just apply yourself."

Data considered. "The root of the problem is that the *Enterprise,* though powerful enough to tip the balance in favor of either side, is unable to do so. In order to save the *Freedom* and the lives of the organic Vemlans, it is necessary to involve the *Enterprise*."

Geordi shook his head. "Captain Picard's already decided the conflict has nothing to do with the Federation."

"There lies my problem. In order to involve the *Enterprise,* the conflict must also involve the Federation in some significant matter." Data was silent, then, for a long time. Geordi almost asked if he was still there.

Then his friend spoke again. "I believe I have a solution."

"A solution?"

Data nodded. "It will be necessary to do some research, but there is still several hours of the captain's deadline left. More than sufficient time."

"What is it?"

"I will have to check the reference computer for legality . . ." he began as his voice got farther away. Eddies in the air currents wafted by Geordi's face, and the sound of retreating footsteps could be heard. "Data, come back here and tell me what's going on!" Geordi shouted to his friend. Seconds later he heard the sound of the automatic door opening and closing and the slight change in pressure that accompanied it.

"Oh well," Geordi said, sinking back into his bath. Knowing his friend, he suspected he'd find out what was up—sooner, rather than later.

While the rest of the ship hurried to their tasks, their battle only a few hours away, Jared entered the gardens to think, the important work having been seen to by subordinates. He was surprised to find the large, lush room vacant save for Maran. The librarian was sitting on a bench, staring vacantly at a crinsilla flower tree. The spectrum of shades of purple and lavender suited her mood.

"I expected to find Kurta here, not you," he said, sitting beside her. Maran turned to look at him and smiled sadly.

"Sorry to disappoint you. I've done all I can do for the battle, and it was either sit in the library and sort tapes or come in here and collect my thoughts. If we're dead in a few hours, it won't matter if the tapes get sorted or not."

"True," Jared said, and smiled. He studied the flowering tree as well, appreciating the natural symmetry of its petals. "I like this one. It comes from the Zessol peninsula, doesn't it?"

"Yes. I came from there. Zessol had the largest library in the hemisphere. A beautiful building, too, half underneath the mountains. These things," she said, indicating the plant, "were all over; local agronomists considered them weeds. Crinsilla flowers blossomed every season, everywhere. It got so that you were sick to death of purple after a while. I never knew how much I would miss those stupid little plants," she said, bitterly.

There was a long silence. Jared knew Maran as well as anyone in their group did, but that didn't really extend into personal matters. Maran had always been a very private person. Oh, she was good at her job; he had never seen anyone even come close to equaling her skill in organizing and retrieving information. But there was so much he didn't know about her.

"Were we so bad off, I wonder?" she said. "Home, I mean. Sure, we were slaves, but we Alphas didn't have it so bad. I could have kept piling up tapes and learning things for centuries."

Jared considered. "Yes, I think about such things, too. I didn't have it so bad, either, until they refitted me for the Games. And I hate to think that we did all that mayhem to be free, just to be wiped out here." He shook his head. "I don't know. I started this movement so full of idealism that it hurt. After a while, it just got bigger than I was."

"If you could do it all over again, would you do it the same way?"

"Good question," he said. Jared thought about it. It was the needless deaths that hurt him the most. His master had been kind and undemanding, more a friend than an owner. He had taught Jared the importance of life, the preciousness of existence. When he thought about all the times he had stood on the operating side of a gun, watching his victims being ripped apart by energy blasts triggered by his fingers, it wrenched him someplace deep inside.

Yet he knew life when he saw it. The screams of androids he knew being torn to shreds in the Games by lumbering, vicious killing machines or each other also wrenched him. They, too, were living. Their terror was as great as any Vemlan's would have been, their sorrows and despairs as profound. As long as a single android was being unfairly treated, he could not rest. They had wanted him to destroy his own kind in the Games, and he resisted. And under the old rules, he would never have been allowed to love Kurta the way he did.

"No regrets," he said finally. "None at all. I think I'd do it all over again the same way."

"It's funny, I was working on a project for some researcher at Zessol. It was a study on the effect of android intelligence on the progress of Vemlan culture. It was his theory that we would eventually replace humans as the motivators in society. The humans were becoming decadent and stagnant, and the androids were becoming more active and intelligent every year. Maybe in a couple of hundred years we would have taken over anyway."

"Perhaps. But that's a few hundred years of slavery too long. I'd be interested in looking at that study sometime, provided that we aren't atomized by then."

Maran shook her head. "All I have is the working notes. The study began just before the violence started. It ended when a mob of radicals invaded the library and killed the researcher for being a collaborator."

"Oh. Well, perhaps it will be re-created someday."

"Perhaps." She looked at the tree again. "They burned all the crinsilla trees, too. When I saw it last, the library looked like a huge tomb."

"I wish that—" Jared's thought was interrupted by an insistent beep. He immediately took his communicator from his belt and snapped it open. "Jared. Report."

"Captain," came a tinny male voice from the machine, "I have an audiovisual communication from the *Enterprise* for you. It's from Commander Data."

"Are you sure it's for me?" he asked, surprised. "He'd be more likely to want to speak with Maran," he said.

"No sir, he was quite specific."

"I'll be right there. Jared out."

"Out."

Jared snapped the communicator closed again and

replaced it on his belt as he stood. Maran's eyes were as big as saucers. He paused.

"Is everything all right?"

Maran swallowed, and stood. "Data told me the last time I saw him that he was working on a solution to our problem. I never thought he'd find one in a million years, but . . ."

"But you may have underestimated him," Jared said. "Very well, let's go hear what wild scheme he has come up with to help us."

"How would you rate the coming battle, Mr. Worf? Your professional opinion, please." Captain Picard was back on the bridge, examining a tactical schematic on the main screen of where the combatants were. His Klingon security officer was at the console behind him, checking over the firing relays.

"Sir," he began in his low voice. "I assessed the strength and attitudes of both sides by using the sensor arrays.

"The navy ships are true warships, though their design is primitive. They were not designed for journeys far beyond their solar system, however, and could be running low on fuel and supplies. Their armaments are primitive but effective. The navy is made of professional soldiers who expect combat. From what I have been able to learn from their ship-to-ship transmissions, however, their morale is low and they are inexperienced with this type of battle, preferring to attack a weaker planetary opponent from orbit. They will try to swarm the android craft and seal any escape route. To prevail they must capture or destroy the *Freedom.*

"The androids will fight fiercely," he continued. "They know the navy will show them no mercy.

Their ship is faster and better armed, but no match weapon for weapon for the navy. The androids follow orders perfectly, however, and have a record of using guile to achieve victory. Their ship is newly repaired and less vulnerable due to their artificial endurance. To win, they must simply avoid and escape from the navy."

"Will they be able to?"

"I consider that doubtful, sir, considering the overwhelming firepower of the navy," continued the Klingon. "However, in every conflict there is a certain element of chance. Random factors can play decisive roles in battle. Computer predictions indicate that there will be a very high casualty rate in any case. It will be an . . . interesting battle." He delivered this last line with a wolfish grin.

Picard sighed. "Yes, I was afraid of that. Many people will die today. It's frustrating."

"Captain, incoming message from the *Freedom*," Wesley said, turning in his seat.

"Display," he called, motioning toward the main screen.

The face of Jared loomed on the screen. Behind his mask of seriousness, there was a relieved glimmer, like that of a man who has received a last-minute reprieve from the headman's axe.

"Captain Picard, I wish to speak to you," he said, formally.

"You are doing so, Captain. Proceed."

"I have reviewed the Articles of Federation you provided for our reference. It is a most impressive series of documents. It shows an admirable flexibility for dealing with alien races."

"Well—yes, thank you. But I don't think you called me to discuss political science."

"Of course not," he smiled. "I called to make a request."

"Which is?"

"Not a request, actually, but a petition."

"A petition?" asked Picard. "What do you mean?"

Jared took a deep breath. "The crew of the *Freedom* has caucused, and the matter has been put to a vote. We, as a sentient, starfaring species, present a formal application for membership in the United Federation of Planets." He paused, watching Picard's stunned expression, before he finished.

"You wouldn't join us, so we decided to join you."

# Chapter Nine

SHOCK AND SURPRISE at the androids' request reverberated around the bridge like a clap of thunder. A bold maneuver, one Picard would have openly admired had it been politic for him to do so—and had it not put him in such a difficult situation.

By necessity starship captains, far from Starfleet Command, were forced to improvise in the line of duty. There was a large element of risk in seeking out unknown alien races. A captain might be called on to be an ambassador, a businessman, a diplomat, a tactician, a strategist, a warlord, a judge, or many other things in the line of duty. He or she therefore had binding authority to deal with a variety of circumstances in the field, on behalf of the Federation.

Including the consideration of alien races for Federation membership.

It was an emergency measure, of course. The usual method for a race applying for Federation membership was a long process involving countless councils, hearings, boards of inquiry, and seemingly endless negotiations. But, in a pinch, special consideration could be given, and a starship captain had the authority to grant it.

"That's quite an—unusual—request." Picard breathed. Jared continued to smile serenely.

"Not really, Captain. Shall I quote you the pertinent sections from the Articles of Federation and the amendments to said articles? I have them memorized . . ."

"I'm sure you do. That will not be necessary," Picard said mildly, his mind racing to try to figure out this startling new wrinkle. He needed time. "I know the sections you are referring to, and I don't believe that they are applicable in this case."

"I was told otherwise."

Picard watched the screen in rapt attention. "By whom were you told?" he asked quietly, an edge in his voice.

"By your own second officer, Mr. Data," Jared replied. "He suggested that I look at the articles pertaining to both the application and petition and provided us with all the applicable information. He also mentioned that the Federation has to protect its own. He even advised us on the preparation of the legal papers, when requested. I commend you on an excellent officer. I have all the proper documents prepared for your review, if you will be so good as to beam them over. Or, I can arrange a transfer by shuttle, if you prefer."

Picard stood quietly a moment, as the possible consequences of what was happening rebounded through his mind. Data's objections to his intention had finally reared their ugly heads—he had found a loophole in Picard's decision not to interfere. A good one, too—under other circumstances Picard might have even said brilliant. He had figured that Data might take some symbolic action in response to the decision; but he had thought that the android would resort to some reasonable but ineffective means of expressing displeasure, such as an official protest in the ship's log. He had certainly not expected this.

And there was the matter of the Vemlan fleet, fully prepared for battle, not seven thousand kilometers away in space, with an irate, and no doubt trigger-happy Alkirg in command. She certainly would not take the androids' petition lightly. Commander Sawliru seemed to be the epitome of the stalwart career military man, but the passion in his eyes when he had spoken with the androids had spoken of a ruthless, nearly fanatical efficiency in his duty. Though Picard had every confidence in his ship's ability to ward off any attack from the Vemlan fleet, he neither wanted to put his own vessel in danger nor did he wish to wipe out an alien fleet of warships.

"Mr. Riker, where is Commander Data?"

"Off duty, sir," Riker said.

"Please summon him to the bridge," Picard said in a low voice. "Immediately."

Picard returned his attention to the android on the screen.

"I will discuss this with my staff, Captain Jared. Your petition may indeed have its merits. But I must tell you, sir, Federation law and Starfleet regulations do not exist to be bandied about like rules in an athletic competition. Picard out," he called. The computer cut the transmission before Jared could reply.

Picard sat back in his seat, and closed his eyes. The

damndest thing about the whole request was that Data actually might have provided a way out of the mess with minimal loss of life—if the Vemlan navy could be dealt with.

The turbolift door whizzed open, and Picard turned to see if it was Data entering. It was Deanna, however—and from the expression on her face, she clearly sensed some trouble.

"Is there a problem, Captain?" the counselor asked.

"Yes. Mr. Data has had a busy day."

"Data?" asked Deanna as she sat down beside him, puzzled. "What has he done now?"

"He invited the androids to join the Federation."

"He did *what?*" she asked, shocked.

"Apparently," Picard said, mildly, "he pointed out the advantages of being members of the Federation in their current situation. He also supplied them the proper information about how to go about doing so legally. I have yet to check on its accuracy—but knowing Data as we both do, I have no doubt that he has been more thorough than necessary."

"Do they have a case?" Troi asked.

The captain shrugged. "That's what we need to decide."

"Doesn't he know that the provisions for granting membership are highly specific? How can he think that they apply in this case?" asked Riker. Clearly, his first officer still did not trust the androids. The fact that Jared and his crew had admitted to killing millions of innocent people, had almost seemed to be proud of it, was something Picard had problems with too.

"I have no idea," Picard admitted. "But I suspect we will find out shortly."

"They're just using the petition as a ruse to save their own skins," Riker said, angrily. "There's no way they can do this."

"Careful, Number One," Picard said warningly. "Stranger things can happen. Who would have thought a hundred years ago that a Klingon would be in charge of security on Starfleet's most advanced vessel?" He stood and headed for his ready room, shaking his head. "There are still too many unknowns. I don't particularly like it—under the circumstances it does feel like an abuse of the system. Not to mention the fact that the Vemlan navy is just a few thousand kilometers away, preparing to storm the *Freedom,* and will be very put off by having to wait—if a case can be made to grant the application.

"But it is quite possible that Jared and company will be our new allies. Will you join me in the ready room? Worf, send Data in as soon as he arrives." The captain got up and headed for the door. "This may actually turn out all right, in the end," he remarked.

"If we all survive that long," Will said, as he paused to let the door open.

"Data, it has always been my practice to be sure of the facts before I act, whenever possible," Picard began, quietly. "In this case I want to be certain of your motivations before I comment, lest I jump too hastily to conclusions. Please explain just what you had in mind by having Jared present that application."

Data sat calmly, hands folded in his lap. *He looks like Buddha in his serenity,* Picard thought, as he took the other seat, recalling a statue he saw in a temple in Sri Lanka once.

"I found the situation as it stood unsatisfactory,

sir," he began. "A destructive conflict that served no constructive purpose was an illogical and unnecessary waste of resources. There had to be a better way. I analyzed it from several different perspectives, using my fullest analytical capabilities. I eventually found a solution that was logically sound as well as being desirable for all parties concerned."

"I doubt if the Vemlan navy will see it that way," countered the captain, arching his eyebrows. "But that is beside the point. My wishes in this matter were well known to you, Mr. Data. I set forth a policy that I expected to be obeyed and supported by my crew, regardless of their personal feelings on the matter."

"I did not disobey orders, Captain; nor did I commit any act that might be interpreted as undermining your authority or your policy," countered Data.

"Then how do you explain yourself? How do you explain Jared thanking me for your kind assistance?" Picard asked. He found himself beginning to get angry.

"I simply informed the Vemlan androids that Starfleet was only obliged to protect those affiliated in some way with the Federation. It did not take them long to extrapolate, once they had the data, a theoretical course of action that might place them in a position where a Starfleet vessel would protect them. They are impressively logical beings. In the face of such overwhelming opposition, the Vemlan navy would logically be forced to quit their claim on the Vemlan androids."

Picard appreciated Data's sense of strategy, but there were ramifications here that he knew Data had not taken into account—to the detriment, perhaps, of the entire ship. "Did it not occur to you in your calculations, Data, that the Vemlan navy is not the most logically based organization in the galaxy? The attitudes of the mission commander alone should have been enough to convince you that a very emotional and illogical response was likely in such a case. Faced with the threat of the *Enterprise,* no matter how powerful and overwhelming we are militarily, Alkirg is not likely to simply go away without a fight."

"To do otherwise would mean the probable destruction of the entire fleet," Data said.

"Yet we are dealing with a military mindset that is violently reactionary, to say the least!" Picard shot back. "There are thousands of historical cases of hopeless battles, Data—cases when a military commander knows the odds, knows for a fact the eventual outcome, and fights all the more viciously because of it. You may well draw the Federation into a war just as senseless as the one you have sought to prevent—but magnitudes larger—by inviting the androids to join the Federation!"

"I did not invite them, Captain, I simply showed them the applicable documents and let them do the rest," Data admitted. "I could not in good conscience do otherwise. I was acting in my capacity as a member of Starfleet, whose duty it is to exhaust every means possible to settle disputes peacefully."

Picard frowned. He couldn't find fault with that, as it stood. In fact, he admired Data's resolve and ingenuity. But he did not like the prospect of involving a starship full of innocent civilians—for which he was responsible—in a violent and unnecessary battle when he had already limited the conflict.

"Data, do you realize what you have done? You have presented us with a very real possibility of war."

Data considered, cocking his head for an instant. "Correct, Captain. Yet I have also introduced an element into the situation that no longer makes war inevitable—simply a remote possibility."

"Not remote enough," Riker said, clearing his throat.

Picard nodded. "What exactly did you tell the androids? Did you communicate sensitive documents?"

"No, sir; the Articles of Federation are to be made available to any and all alien cultures, races, and civilizations. Amendment to the Federation Charter, Section six, paragraph nine. You gave no order against communicating with the *Freedom,* or the Vemlan navy, for that matter. I was within the bounds you set," Data explained.

"Data, I think you are missing the point," the captain said, shaking his head. "As much as I respect you as an officer, I still think you lack a proper understanding of the situation. The United Federation of Planets is a mutually cooperative agency, not a refugee camp for aliens in trouble. Or perhaps it is I who don't understand. Even accepting the dubious nature of what you have done, there is still the matter of the effects of your actions. Did you not take them into account before you went to the androids?"

"I examined the potential ramifications before I proceeded . . . and found them well within the limits of acceptability."

"Including the fact that Commander Alkirg— certainly not the most levelheaded diplomat I've ever known—who has a war fleet ready for combat, might take action against us if we try to intervene once again?"

"The Vemlan naval fleet was taken into account, Captain," Data said, smoothly, "as was the possibility that the androids might attack our ship if we failed to intervene. I believe that the greater threat is from them. From what I have seen, the Alphas on the *Freedom* are more than capable of taking the *Enterprise*—if they chose so—by any number of means. The threat from the fleet is present, I admit," Data said, "but the threat from the androids, who are accustomed to unconventional methods of warfare, is, in my opinion, much greater. By my actions I have effectively neutralized the threat of the androids by appealing to the moderate elements on board the *Freedom*. The threat from the fleet is an overt and easily counterable one. Androids," Data said, "can be very devious, when they want to be."

"Shouldn't that be when *we* want to be?" commented Riker.

Data considered. "As you wish," he said, and was quiet.

Which did little to comfort Picard. What Data said about the intentions of the Alphas was doubtlessly true—he could corroborate the possibilities with Worf, if necessary—but he did not approve of his second officer's disregard for proper channels. "Why didn't you ask my permission in the first place?" asked Picard, tiredly.

Data blinked. "Suppose I had indeed proposed the idea of an application for Federation membership to you, would you have supported it?"

"Certainly not!" exclaimed Picard. "It would have —is going to—" he corrected himself, "simply throw grease on the fire—make an already bad situation worse," he amended, as he saw Data about to question the idiom.

"Is it not better to ask for forgiveness, rather than permission?" Data asked. "I have heard that saying repeatedly in my career."

"No!" both Riker and Picard exclaimed. They looked at each other for a moment, and Picard continued. "But you have, indeed, presented me with a *fait accompli.*" He looked pained and tried to express his feelings. "Data, this is a very complex issue, one that could take years—even decades—to untangle. Matters of jurisdiction, legality, and justice are involved, matters that have no bearing on this ship. More importantly, to me, is the fact that I have a ship full of children and civilians in the middle of a potential combat zone. I had managed to carve a path out of the carnage and now you're forcing us back into it." He sighed. "All of this discussion is academic, however. I am going to exercise my authority to deny the request for admission in this case as an abuse of the procedure."

Riker looked slowly up at Jean-Luc. "I'm afraid you can't do that, Captain."

"What?" Picard demanded, startled.

Riker looked uncomfortable. "At the very least, you have to convene a hearing to consider the application. If the applicants meet all the requirements for membership, in your opinion, then they have to be referred to the Federation administrative council."

"Yes. You're right, of course," he said. He had forgotten about that. It was an amendment to the Federation Charter, number six, section four, paragraph something or other. You could not summarily dismiss a proposed application. Doing so would possibly stifle the diversity the Federation prized so highly.

"I'm afraid so, Captain," nodded Riker, sadly. "There's no provision for suspending the rules—no matter who makes the application, terrorists included. Any request for admission must be heard."

Picard thought. "You're more up on this than I am, Number One. Am I not released from this duty if I find the applicants do not meet eligibility requirements?"

"Yes," Will agreed. "Then the petition is filed and dismissed. As long as there is precedent or reasonable grounds for your dismissal, we have no obligation to the androids." He glanced at Data, who was staring straight ahead at the captain.

"Yes. There must be precedent." The test for admission was very simple. A planet had to be willing to abide by the charter of the Federation and help keep the ideals behind it in an open spirit of peace and cooperation. That included agreeing to arbitrate disputes through the auspices of the Federation, cooperating with Starfleet in times of emergency, opening up its town culture for study, and exchanging information freely. If a planet was willing to do that and the hearing chairman—himself, in this case—could find no malicious or ill intent in the applicant, then the case was referred to the administrative board for further negotiations.

He turned his chair and stared at his quiet, uncomplicated, undemanding fish. He wished he could join them.

"Very well," he said, resignedly. "I will convene a hearing. I will have to tell the Vemlan navy about this as well. I don't think that they'll be happy."

"Probably not," Riker agreed. "Alkirg can't wait to get her hands on the androids."

Picard turned back around to face his other officer. "Data, I think it's clear that you have an overwhelming sympathy for these androids—as well as a dogged determination to see a peaceful conclusion to the situation. Under normal circumstances, I would have no problems with this—I want you to understand that. But these are far from normal circumstances. Just because the androids are your friends doesn't allow you to flout my orders for them."

"Permission to speak, sir?" the android asked.

Picard sighed. He had hoped to escape without a rebuttal. "Granted."

"My loyalty lies now, as ever, with Starfleet," he said, evenly and matter-of-factly. "I am first and foremost a Starfleet officer. I have sworn to uphold Starfleet's mission to seek out new life and alien civilizations, to better our understanding of the galaxy. I have provided a method of peaceful exchange where the only possibility before was loss of life and destruction of an entire species. I have acted to gain an opportunity to learn the unknown about an alien species. Is that not the primary function of Starfleet?" he asked.

"You deny your empathy with the androids?"

"No, sir. I deny that my personal relationship with the applicants was the prime motivating factor for my actions. I was moved to advise them out of a sense of duty to Starfleet, a concern for the safety of the ship, and respect for the lives of all concerned, not out of a simple desire to see the Alphas escape. The two happened to coincide, that is all."

"I see," Picard said, sensing that there was more to Data's actions than he had thought. Perhaps he had underestimated this android—this man, he corrected himself. "That's food for thought, then. You are dismissed."

"Thank you sir. I must prepare for the hearing."

"You must what?" asked Picard incredulously.

"Prepare for the hearing. I am going to testify on behalf of the applicants. It would be improper for them to have less than the full knowledge of the proceedings at their disposal."

"It's his right," admitted Riker. "The hearing must be open to all interested parties. That includes the Vemlan navy, by the way. If they want to come and speak, they may."

"Go on then," said Picard, resigned. It looked as if there was going to be a carnival of argument on his ship, yet again. "You are relieved of duty until further notice, in order to give you time to prepare."

Data tilted his head, slightly. "Thank you, Captain. That is most thoughtful of you."

After Data left, Picard let out a great sigh, and rubbed his temples. Will stroked his beard thoughtfully for a few moments.

"Something puzzles me, Captain. Why did you give Data time to prepare?"

"Simple," explained Picard. "After he dragged all this up, I want the androids to get a scrupulously fair hearing, and he's the best man, if you'll excuse the term, to present their case. I am not about to convene this hearing with preconceptions. True, Data may have brought us to the brink of war, but he was correct when he said that he had given us a chance at peace. I cannot fail to follow up on that chance in good conscience."

* * *

The mood in the staging bay was a strange mixture of apprehension and elation. Mobile infantry and naval personnel stood in long rows waiting for inspection in the main bay, while technicians worked on the larger pieces of military equipment in the rear bays. After three months of bad food, stale air, and shaky gravity, the hunt was nearly over. In a few scant hours, the black-armored warriors of the Vemlan navy would mete out justice to the rogue androids that had turned their planet into one large refugee camp. Some were savagely looking forward to this; they had a dozen or so comrades to avenge, friends or family lost at Gemlov, or Trengard, or the satellite stations, or in countless other terrorist attacks by the rebel androids. Some were afraid, knowing the terrors that the mechanical horrors had produced. There were rumors of obscene tortures, visions of the victims of berserk attackers, memories of pure terror in the face of a faceless enemy. The young men and women were afraid to die so far from home.

Commander Sawliru walked up and down each line of troops, visually inspecting each trooper with a highly practiced eye. He was proud of this force; he had built it almost from the ground up. When he first chose the military as a career, the average soldier was armed and armored and trained little better than a policeman. Now the arc lamps overhead gleamed off the shiny black armor of the finest troops he—or anyone else—had ever assembled.

Sawliru was not a violent or overly militaristic man, but he recognized the need for naked, precise force for defense, and he had tried to ensure that he had the best force possible at his command. This was the cream of the Vemlan crop, people for the most part untainted by the luxury of android labor. There were drones on board, yes, but they were weapons, not slaves. Let's be honest with ourselves, after all, he thought as he passed the gleaming ranks; despite Alkirg's objection to the term, we used them like we would have used slaves. And paid for it, in the end.

There were still too many loose ends for comfort, though. Had he been in sole command, the scheduled operation would be planned for maximum efficiency and workability, and politics be damned! Many good men and women would die today because of Alkirg's incompetence, he knew.

Satisfied that they were ready (he knew his infantry prefects had already inspected each one far more thoroughly than he could), he made his way back to the front of the formation and turned to address them.

"Today is the pinnacle operation of our mission. We have located the opponent, we have prepared ourselves mentally and physically, and as soon as the Federation ship leaves the area, we will strike as quickly and as efficiently as possible. We have the opponent outgunned, outmanned, and outmaneuvered. I will not tolerate this being any less than a textbook operation."

He paused for emphasis and breath, then continued. "It is possible that the action will be entirely ship to ship, but our orders are to secure the rogue androids, incapacitate them, and return them to Vemla for trial for their crimes. This means that we will have to board the *Conquest* and take them, one by one if necessary. It is not likely that they will surrender. If this is the case, then it is your job to accomplish this mission by destroying them. I expect you to perform in the manner to which I have become accustomed—excellently, diligently, and effectively.

"Are there any questions?"

Usually, there wouldn't be. Once prepared for a mission, every trooper should know everything necessary about the mission. These were unusual circumstances, however. A trooper raised his hand, and Sawliru acknowledged him.

"Why aren't the drones going with us?"

It was a good question, one Sawliru wished he didn't have to answer. Despite the average trooper's aversion to androids, the Delta drones were an exception. It greatly improved morale to have a huge, invulnerable, unkillable fanatic on your side, obeying your every command. The men were understandably nervous going into combat without the hulking machines along for company.

"The Deltas were removed from service for this mission on the orders of the mission commander." He was not about to become the object of resentment for a company of troopers about to enter combat. Let that duty, as well as the blood of the dead, lie on the hands of the mission commander.

"Any more questions?" There was silence. "Good. Stand down until alerted by your prefects. Dismissed."

Sawliru was glad it was almost over. He had been against the androids since before the rebellion, and he could not wait to see them gone. He paused before two technicians who were hurriedly trying to repair one of the life-support units that regulated air for the great bay. Staring puzzledly at the instruction and repair manual before them, they argued over what went where and why. Sawliru sighed, and stepped around them, unseen.

That was the perfect example of why he wished the androids gone. Ten years ago all maintenance on this ship had been done by android labor—cleanly, quickly, efficiently. The ships had been in a constant state of readiness. But the lowliest human tech rarely had to even lift a wrench, let alone take an active hand in regular maintenance. That was androids' work, they would sneer, not fit for a man, whose time was more important. Yet now that they didn't have androids to do their work for them, they had to struggle with even the simplest routines, sometimes, because they had never learned. It was like that all over the ship, Sawliru knew, and even more like that back on Vemla, where people were having to cook for themselves for the first time. But that didn't bother Sawliru; he knew his people would come back from their long sleep—they had to.

As the Force Commander walked slowly back to the command room, his many duties delegated to subordinates who could handle them more effectively, his comm unit chimed. He snapped it open and spoke as he walked.

"Prefect Morgus, sir. Sorry to disturb you, but the captain of the Federation vessel requests an urgent conference. Shall I beam the transmission to your quarters?"

*What does he want, now?* Sawliru wondered. "Negative, Prefect. Relay transmission to the recreation room off the staging bay. 1134, I believe."

"Aye, sir."

Sawliru sighed, and tried to figure out what would

next complicate his mission. These humans were so adept at mucking things up.

He sat down in front of the comm panel and waited for Picard to appear, deciding that this was probably a last-minute appeal to end the conflict peacefully. He would have been quite happy to do so, too. However, unless Jared surrendered unconditionally it was just not going to happen. He respected Picard for what he had tried to do; if he had more men like Jean-Luc Picard under his command, he was certain that he could take any objective, under any circumstances.

"Captain Picard, here," came the signal, as the man's head and shoulders appeared in the comm unit. "Commander, I—"

"If you are trying to dissuade us from attacking, Captain, I'm afraid it will not work. Besides, only Mission Commander Alkirg could halt the battle, now. It's out of my hands."

Picard frowned. "No, Commander, I didn't call to try to persuade you. I'm afraid I have what you are going to consider bad news."

Sawliru blinked. "What is it?"

"The captain of the *Conquest,* on behalf of his people, has just delivered to me a petition for consideration and an application for membership in the United Federation of Planets. I am bound by both UFP law and Starfleet regulations to convene a hearing on this application."

Sawliru's mind raced, as he tried to grasp the significance of the statement. "Won't that be difficult to accomplish in the middle of a combat zone?"

"There will be no combat, Commander. I cannot allow it, under these circumstances."

"You told me, not just a few hours ago, that this matter was outside of your jurisdiction! Something about the First Law, or whatever . . ."

"The Prime Directive, yes," Picard continued, apologetically. "It was. The Prime Directive insists that Starfleet does not interfere with the natural course of a culture's internal affairs."

"Is this not a Vemlan internal affair?"

"Not anymore. By making the application, Jared has involved the Federation."

Another great man hamstrung by the whims of bureaucrats and politicians, Sawliru thought. Is this, then, to be a universal law?

"Furthermore," Picard continued, "I cannot allow hostilities to take place before or during the hearing. You may consider the *Conquest* to be under the protection of Starfleet, for now. Any attack made upon it will have to be defended by the *Enterprise*—with full force, if necessary."

"I see." Sawliru's mind swam. He knew exactly what Alkirg would say to this. It would not be pretty. Either she would continue preparations to attack the *Conquest*, heedless of the *Enterprise* and what it represented, or she would order an attack directly on the Federation vessel. Or, worse yet, she would split his forces to take both courses of action simultaneously. His heart was in his stomach, for he knew that the outcome in any such situation would very likely destroy the Vemlan navy as he knew it. He, personally, would almost certainly die, but that didn't really bother him. The thought of the thousands of deaths and the unprotected homeworld made him shiver to the core. Madness. "You realize, Captain Picard, that the nature of our mission might very well put us in conflict? Your ship has a good chance of coming under attack. And, if I recall correctly, you have a significant number of civilians aboard."

"Indeed," Picard agreed, gravely. "I don't wish to put them in jeopardy, but it is a risk I am willing to take."

Sawliru sighed. "So noted, Captain. The final decision is up to Alkirg, however. She is in supreme command."

"I understand," Picard replied. "I would also like to invite the Vemlan government to be represented at the hearing. There will be an opportunity for you to speak, should you choose to do so."

"I'll inform the commander. And Captain Picard?"

Picard raised his eyebrows. "Yes?"

"Speaking from experience, I would be very careful about the androids. Very careful."

"I'll keep that in mind, Commander."

"Sawliru out."

As the image on the screen faded away, Sawliru tried to will the dread feeling out of his stomach. He had been speculating on the kind of ally Picard would have made. Now he needed to view him as an opponent.

"So they might attack?" asked Riker, smiling faintly.

"He hinted so, yes," confirmed Picard, though the possibility of the Vemlans damaging the *Enterprise* while her crew was alert was very low. "And as much as I'd like to see those militaristic louts break their teeth on my ship, there is still the possibility of damage and injury to the civilians and the crew. I can't allow that to happen."

Worf, who had been listening to their conversation

from his post, spoke up. "Captain, perhaps a small display of force is in order . . ." he began.

"If you mean a preemptive strike—"

"No, Captain," countered Worf. "Attacking the fleet would not be the most efficient means of achieving victory."

"I see," said the captain. "You have a plan?"

"Yes, sir," Worf said. "Consider this . . ."

"They did what?" Mission Commander Alkirg shouted. Sawliru had located her on the main bridge, where she was interfering with the way the captain of the *Nemesis* ran his command. The poor man had been glad of Sawliru's interruption, but now he realized that his life was about to get even more difficult.

Sawliru had decided against breaking the news to her over the inter-ship communication screens, for fear of her breaking a valuable piece of ship's equipment in her anger. Besides, he had thought that it would be better to deliver it in person. The look on her face and the rage in her eyes made him reconsider his decision.

"They applied for membership in the United Federation of Planets, and Picard is bound by regulations to hear the application. He may even grant them status, which would give them permanent Federation protection."

Alkirg seethed, the most emotional and upset Sawliru had ever seen her. "You stupid military types, you're all alike," she exclaimed. "We had them in the palm of our hands, and now we may lose them because of some idiotic rule. Bureaucrats! That's all the military can produce, grunts and bureaucrats!" Sawliru clenched his teeth, choking back a reply that would have cost him his command. She was calling *him* a bureaucrat? "Can't those people realize that there are times when you have to break the rules? There is such a thing as political expediency to consider. They will pay for this, in blood, if need be. I don't care if we have to kill a thousand men to do it!"

Sawliru decided against mentioning that it would take more than a thousand men to take the *Enterprise*. In fact, he wasn't certain his entire fleet would be up to the challenge. Now that Alkirg was done ranting, he quietly continued his report. There was a decision to be made.

"Nevertheless, that is the situation as it stands. I have all seven ships on alert, ready to execute the approved battle plan, and I won't keep them like that all day. You are in charge of this mission, Alkirg. What are we going to do?"

"They can't get away with this," she vowed. "They won't get away with it." She began pacing back and forth across the deck, hands clenched, and fire in her eyes. At last she stopped, and faced Sawliru.

"Force Commander, this is a military mission. We have the seven finest ships in the fleet here, a highly trained cadre of soldiers, and the most advanced weapons ever made. The *Enterprise* is merely one ship. I don't care what kind of technology they have, they can't stand up to a surprise, concentrated attack. Their action is tantamount to a declaration of war with the Vemlan people. Prepare to attack the *Enterprise*."

Madness. He had warned Picard of this possibility, with the hope of scaring him out of his position.

But his sense of duty endured. "I will have to meet with my advisers to formulate a potentially successful battle plan," he advised. "This may take some time."

"Do it!" she commanded him with a pointed finger. "I don't care how. I want us to be ready to lay into the *Enterprise* with everything we have. Without her protection, they don't stand a chance. We can deal with the rogues later."

"Is it permissible to use the drones on this mission?"

She nodded fiercely. "Use whatever you need."

"Picard also said that there would be an opportunity for us to testify at the hearing; I recommend that we do so. It will buy us time, allow us to present our case formally to the Federation. We might also be able to stop the proceedings legally. Politically, it may have other benefits." He left unspoken the fact that it would also keep Alkirg off of his ship and out of his face for a few hours.

"Yes, I do indeed want to speak my mind at that mockery of a court! I will make the necessary arrangements. You get the fleet in position to attack."

"As you wish," he said as he bowed, and left quickly.

Truth be told, fighting the Starfleet vessel was the last thing he wanted to do. It was a big ship, carrying civilians, and no self-respecting soldier liked to make war on civilians. Worst of all, it was an unknown in this complex equation. The *Conquest* was a known quantity, an easy, if tough, target to plan for. There was no telling what sort of weaponry the more advanced ship was carrying. Their transporting device alone could cause trouble. How could you plan an attack when your men could be beamed away from their posts without a thought?

But he wasn't responsible for making policy here. He was merely a link in the chain of command. And the prospect of crossing blades with the *Enterprise* enthused him, in a primal, visceral sort of way. At least he was doing something, something he knew. Sawliru wasn't cut out to be a player of politics and diplomacy; he knew when he was out of his element. There were members of the military back home who fancied themselves politicians, which was one reason why Sawliru was chosen to head this command. He was the most politically apathetic of the candidates.

But he knew how to fight, even from the deck of a sinking ship.

At the very center of the *Freedom* was a large chamber, intended by the original designers as a specially shielded cargo hold. The androids, after their liberation of the prototype ship, had converted the space for another use. It was now the *Freedom*'s arsenal, and its caretaker, controller, and conscience was Garan. Rows upon rows of boxes of ammunition filled the space, and missiles, combat suits, canisters of biotoxins, remote combat units, explosives, and rack upon rack of personal weapons of all types had turned the big room into a dark, malevolent maze, a monument to the androids' skill in capturing military hardware.

There was only one light in all of the arsenal, for Garan's vision required none for most tasks. Over his main work area hung the single lamp, where he could direct its penetrating light where he needed it most. Right now that was in Jared's chest cavity. The android captain had decided that he could not allow this one last chance at the *Enterprise* to slip away, and he had enlisted Garan's help.

"Is it ready yet?" he asked, impatiently staring down into the open space inside himself. The hearing was less than an hour away.

"Almost." Jared knew Garan considered the placement and effectiveness of munitions a high art, and himself a craftsman, so he tried not to rush him. Still, the device would do them no good if it wasn't ready in time.

As he watched, Garan placed a rectangular device the size of an apple next to Jared's metallic spine.

"There," the big android said, standing. "This device, if activated by your mental command, will vaporize an area five meters in diameter. The structural integrity of the exterior hull of the *Enterprise* will be maintained, but the interior hull will be breached in several directions causing subsystems failure and general confusion. This will not incapacitate an Alpha unit, other than the operator," Garan explained as he made the final connection to Jared's central processing unit. "But bomb damage might not remove the Federation android from service. All organic beings in range will be killed instantly."

"Excellent," the android leader said, pleased. "If the hearing does not go well, I will never have a better opportunity to destroy my enemies. Sawliru and Alkirg will both be killed, the fleet will have no head, and the *Enterprise* will lose its captain and its first and second officers all at once." He closed his abdominal panel himself, and began sealing it. "Deprived of leadership, the fleet will be taken unaware. Before another officer in the chain of command can take control of the *Enterprise,* Kurta will make her way to the transporter room and begin bringing the troops over in droves. Data showed her the cargo transporters; she knows nothing of my preparations, but if the opportunity presents itself, she will act. She can bring over thirty Alphas at a time!"

"And what of the rest of the human crew?" Dren asked, stepping forward.

"Yes, they will provide a problem," Jared said, thoughtfully. "No doubt they will object to us taking their vessel by force. You have an answer?"

Garan said nothing, but disappeared into the maze of ordnance while Jared finished sealing his body. The giant returned as he was replacing his sash of rank.

"Bioagent 23," Garan explained, holding up a marble-size canister between his fingers. Jared nodded. Dren had carried several such canisters aboard the satellite stations over Vemla. They contained a virulent biotoxin that destroyed the integrity of the synapses in the central nervous system. It was a quick-acting, extremely potent agent; this one canister could wipe out six crews the size of the *Enterprise* before they knew that there was anything wrong.

Jared opened the cavity in his left index finger and inserted the tiny vial. Theoretically it would kill every carbon-based life-form on the *Enterprise*, leaving only the androids alive on board. If given the chance, he would deploy the toxin first, rather than destroy himself in an explosion. But he was quite willing to sacrifice his own life for the sake of his people.

Besides, they could always make more Jareds. That was one of the advantages of being an android.

Androids. Jared considered Data. He would most likely not be affected by the biotoxin, and there were other aliens on board, like the impressive-looking Klingon. There was no guarantee that the toxin would affect Worf and the other aliens.

"Give me a gun," Jared said as he closed his finger. "Something small and lethal. For Data, should he survive, and other possible obstacles."

Garan reached behind him seemingly without looking and picked up a cylinder no longer than his massive pinkie. Jared took it and placed it in his belt pouch.

"Four charges only," Garan warned. "Pick your targets for maximum effect and damage."

"No need to remind me, my friend. You taught me those lessons long ago. And if it is taken from me, I can kill with my bare hands, if need be. We will have freedom if we must kill every living thing on the *Enterprise.*"

The thought of murder on that scale did not greatly appeal to Jared. But the fate of his people was at stake, and he knew enough to strike while he had the advantage. Data's solution, though it gave him some hope of peace, more importantly gave him an opportunity to save the lives of his people. At the expense of others, and perhaps himself, he knew, but it was a price he was willing to pay for the ideal of freedom.

"Prepare yourself and the others, and wait for my signal," Jared said. "If I don't return, you are to be in charge of the fighting."

"As you wish," the giant said, nodding simply. "Good luck, my friend," he finished, catching Jared's eye with his own, and then turned immediately to his work.

# Chapter Ten

"CONTINGENCY PLAN ALPHA is ready to be executed at your command, Captain," Worf said over the intercom.

Riker was in the conference room with Captain Picard, who had a busy telescreen in front of him. He nodded and responded. "Excellent, Mr. Worf. Stand by."

"Are you sure this is going to work?" asked Riker, doubtfully. As much as he trusted Worf's opinion on such matters, there was still a potential for failure, which might prove disastrous to the ship.

"No, I'm not," Picard answered tiredly. "But it's an inspired plan. Mr. Worf is growing more diplomatically adept, Number One. No doubt he will make an excellent captain himself one day. Now, back to this hearing business," he said, tapping the screen with a forefinger.

Will checked his own screen for the requirements of such a hearing. They were not arduous, but it was vital that the proper forms were observed in this case. Regardless of the outcome, the two men were accountable to Starfleet and the Federation, and neither wished to give the androids anything less than a fair hearing.

"The hearing is to be held before you and two senior officers, appointed by you. They are to advise you, but you are to make the final decision." He looked up from the screen and fixed Picard with a knowing look. "In this case, I would recommend that you not choose Commander Data for this duty."

Picard nodded. "Under the circumstances, I agree. I appoint you and Dr. Crusher for the task. I think you are both capable of making a decision on this order," he said, smiling.

"After the last person speaks, you adjourn, consult with your advisers, and make your decision." Riker looked up. "It's that simple."

"Very well, make the necessary preparations. And make sure that Worf keeps his eyes on the navy; in case of any problems, you have authority to activate his plan."

"Captain, I think Worf should watch the androids, as well," Riker added with a frown.

"You expect problems?" Picard asked.

"Always," Will said, with a half smile. "Maybe my brief service aboard a Klingon ship made me a little paranoid. But I don't trust Jared farther than I can throw him, and I consider any group of self-proclaimed terrorists potentially dangerous in my book. I'm probably wrong, but I'd hate to be right and get caught unprepared."

Picard pursed his lips and nodded. "Agreed. Make it so."

"Good," Will said, relieved that the back door would be watched too. "I think it's time to get this show on the road."

This time, there was no temple courtyard—the holodeck had been set up to look like a conference lounge, and already many of the crew had settled down to watch the proceedings. Though the occasion was somber, the atmosphere of the gathering was almost festive, and Picard, taking note of it, decided upon entering the room to force the hand of reason and civility. Though the parties involved were virtually at war there was no need for disorderly proceedings.

He wore his dress uniform, and had instructed the other participants from his crew to do likewise. Straightening his jacket, he surveyed the room. On the right-hand side stood the Vemlan delegation—Alkirg in a formal gown standing impatiently behind a table with Commander Sawliru, who wore a black uniform, encrusted with medals. He knew the navy shuttle that had brought them had been empty, save for the two of them and a pilot; it waited now off the Starboard bow, where it was regularly and thoroughly scanned by Worf.

Kurta and Jared, dressed in their stark tan uniforms, stood to the left. Picard thought they looked more like prisoners than representatives of a race trying to enter the Federation. A calculated maneuver, perhaps? Data, who stood with them as their counsel, was also wearing a blank expression, but Picard hadn't expected anything else from him. He nodded to the security personnel at the door—also in dress uniforms, though the phasers they carried were standard issue—and spoke to the computer.

"Begin," he said simply. There was a dimming of the gallery lights, and the star map surrounded by a laurel wreath that was the symbol of the United Federation of Planets formed dramatically on the wall behind the panel's table at the head of the room.

"Captain on the deck," the computer boomed forcefully upon his entrance, drawing the attention of the crowd and quieting their murmurs.

"Be seated," he called to everyone. Riker and Dr. Crusher entered immediately after him and sat, immediately followed by the rest of the assembled. He surveyed the room, noting everyone was prepared. He turned to Number One and nodded.

Riker returned his nod, one eyebrow raised, and began. "This hearing has been convened to hear the petition and application of the Vemlan androids for membership in the United Federation of Planets. The petitioners' representatives will please present the documents to the hearing officers."

Jared stepped forward and placed an isolinear chip on the table, then returned to his seat. Riker inserted it into the computer slot, and displayed it on the screen in front of him. It was simultaneously entered into the official record and displayed for the audience to see. "Everything seems to be in order," he said, nodding to Picard, the chairman.

"Objection," Beverly Crusher called. The three panel members had consulted exhaustively to prepare for this hearing—to play devil's advocate—to ensure that no legal question had been overlooked. As primary judge of the application, Picard had to make certain that all considerations were brought up fairly and discussed. The record would doubtlessly be intimately scrutinized by Starfleet and the Federation upon their return to the more civilized parts of the galaxy, and he wanted his actions to be above reproach.

Picard considered the entire process fascinating, on one level, for here the honest question of whether or not Jared and his people were a race—for the purposes of the Federation—was to be decided. Such decisions were not made lightly, nor did one get the chance to make them very often. He was making a bit of history here, and had no idea where it was going to lead. He nodded for Beverly to proceed.

"The petitioners do not represent the populace of a planet."

"There is ample precedent for nonplanetary membership, Doctor," Data interjected. "Beginning with the very first years of the Federation, where the artificial habitats in the asteroid belts of the Centauri systems were admitted. The Slao-vecki species, whose planet was destroyed in a nova, was also admitted, as were the Aeorethians, who have no permanent planetary home. In all cases, the races in question have become valuable members of the Federation despite their lack of a planet. Last but not least, the number of Federation citizens who live and work on artificial habitats or spacecraft—such as our own USS *Enterprise*—have no declared planetary home, but may not be denied their rights as citizens. Shall I quote the pertinent legal precedents?"

"No need, Mr. Data," Picard said. "The objection is overruled. The Chairman—myself—recognizes the Vemlans as an organized and self-governing body, as supported by legal precedent," Picard finished. That question was relatively clear-cut. Before he could begin the actual deliberations, however, they had to clean up a stickier issue—

"Objection," Riker stated flatly, looking over the document on the screen in front of him. "The petitioners are machines, mechanical constructs, not true living beings, and are therefore not qualified for membership."

This was the much more controversial part of the hearing. It also hit very close to home. It had taken a landmark legal decision to class Data as a living being with rights and responsibilities, and thus far the ruling had gone unchallenged. If a case could be made that the Vemlans were not living, and thus not eligible for membership, then Data's own legal standing was once again in doubt.

Picard didn't like this part.

"The Vemlans are androids of sufficient complexity to rate as living beings by any suggested scale," Data argued.

"That's preposterous!" Alkirg exclaimed. "They are no more alive than you are!"

"There has been a challenge to your claim, Mr. Data," Riker observed. "Do you wish to defend it?"

Picard watched with interest as Data arose and looked intently at the alien politician.

"I submit that the Vemlans cannot be proven not to be alive by any reasonable method. I address the one who posted the objection. Commander Alkirg, why are they not alive?"

"Don't be obtuse. They have no biological functions!" she insisted, with an irritated wave of her hand.

Data, had he been faced with such a statement before the hearing, would have replied in a logically exact manner that would have answered the question as quickly and efficiently as possible. He had, however, in the interest of the security of his newfound friends and an interest in his own legal rights, taken the few hours available to him for preparation to study law and legal techniques. He found the area most revealing of human strengths and weaknesses. Though the present-day Federation did not depend as heavily upon laws, rules, order, and legal frameworks as human civilizations of the past, there were techniques and forms that went back to a variety of historical eras. He had devoured entire law libraries with inhuman speed and comprehension, placing the talents and wisdom of such ancient legal giants as Hammurabi, Clarence Darrow, and Jose Tarentino at his disposal. The hearing that he had been so instrumental in calling was not technically a legal matter; it was a mere step in the bureaucratic ladder of the Federation. Yet it held a courtlike ambience and order that made knowledge of a twenty-first century trial procedure, the apex of the Legal Era on Earth, invaluable. Unfazed by the intensity of his opposition, Data proceeded calmly with his reply.

"We have an expert witness on all forms of biological activity available to the hearing. Doctor Crusher, I ask your professional opinion. What are biological functions?"

Doctor Crusher folded her hands on the table and thought a moment before she replied. "They are functions of the body that are necessary for the sustenance of life."

"And what is the definition of life?"

"I don't have an inclusive definition for that. As long as we were confined to one biosphere, the definition could be at least hinted at. But the universe is so diverse in its formations of life-forms that no true, objective definition exists. The closest I could come would be to say that life is a complex, reactive, self-replicating process that some entities possess. Some say that the best way to define it is by its ultimate negative quality: A living thing is a thing that can die."

"Is a virus a form of life?"

"Tricky," she admitted. "Viruses as a class have flip-flopped back and forth over the years, depending upon which authorities you talk to. And they can die, even be killed," she admitted.

"I am talking with you, as an authority. I repeat my question. Is a virus alive?"

"In my professional opinion . . . yes."

"Am I, in your professional opinion, alive, Dr. Crusher?"

"In my professional opinion . . . insufficient data, Data," she said, smiling at the near-pun. "I haven't seen you die, so I do not know, with certainty, whether you are alive."

"Yet you were a witness of the death of my daughter, Lal; you were also witness to the apparent destruction of my nearly identical twin, Lore, discovered at the same colony where I was discovered, created by the same hand that created me, from the same plans and designs. As I recall, he was 'killed'— if temporarily—right in front of your eyes, after threatening your son's life. Am I correct?"

"Yes," she admitted, hesitantly. "Yes, by that definition, both Lal and Lore were alive."

Data seemed unfazed by the comment. "Since I am Lore's twin, am I not also alive?"

"As a class, I would have to say that yes, both you and Lore are living beings. The Federation already accepts this legal point; two of the panel members were instrumental in that decision."

"Yet both Lore and I were constructed androids."

"Yes."

"Like the Vemlan androids present here."

"As far as I can tell."

"The Vemlans, as living beings, have certain mechanical functions that must be maintained for continued operation. I submit that these mechanical functions are necessary for the sustenance of their lives, and are, therefore, biological functions." He turned back to Alkirg, a little haughtily, Picard thought. No, it must be his imagination. "Therefore, there is a legal precedent for considering an android to be a living, self-aware being."

"Yes," Picard replied. "A case which I am intimately aware of, Data." He remembered his intense preparation for Data's own trial and was a little relieved that he was not an opposing party in this case. But there was a flaw in Data's argument. "I will concede that you are, legally, a living being. These other androids are an unknown quantity, however."

"Exactly," Sawliru said, rising suddenly to his feet. "Though you cater to your own machines as if they were your pets, rather than your servants, the machines we manufactured on Vemla have no such status. Your doctors may consider them alive; that's your business. You admit I don't know how you built your android. Our machines are machines, simply that; complex machines, to be certain, but they can be taken apart and put back together again. When they break, they can be repaired. They are programmed, they are useful, and they are artificial."

"But they are alive," Data insisted, turning to confront Sawliru. It was obvious to Picard that the

Force Commander didn't like addressing the object of the debate directly. "There is not a single biological function that they are incapable of accomplishing. Anything you can do, we can do. What is the difference, between you and me?"

"I had a biological mother and father, whose attributes and genes I carry. Where are your parents?" he countered snidely.

Data looked tolerantly amused, an expression Picard had seen him practicing with Wesley. He still didn't quite have the hang of it. "You refer to the matter of reproduction. It is an almost universal standard by which all life-forms are measured. Doctor Crusher even included it in her general definition of life. You mentioned genes and attributes; I submit that the master design program, which each of the Vemlan androids carries in its permanent memory, serves the same function as DNA or comparable methods of genetic racial memory. In a properly equipped laboratory any one of the androids on the *Freedom* could totally replicate itself, with conscious alterations and improvements in design that are in fact more efficient than the burdensome process of natural selection."

"You need a laboratory for your reproduction and you call yourself living beings? I think not," Sawliru scoffed.

"Yes. By your standard, a human female who is not able to conceive a child without medical assistance would also be classed as a non-living being. There are races of clones who may survive only by such means, because of genetic damage. They, too, would not qualify as living beings as per your standards."

"The difference is simply a matter of the type of laboratory you use, that's all," Kurta added passionately. "Give us a few generations; we'll put the laboratory inside each and every android."

Sawliru refrained from saying something back, Picard noted. No doubt it was something rude and disruptive. He appreciated the display of control. The proceedings were becoming heated, but Picard had expected that. At least they weren't shooting at each other yet.

"The difference is a matter of organics," Alkirg insisted, waving her hands for emphasis and appealing to the panel and the crowd behind her. She returned her attention to the androids. "You are not carbon-based, biological creatures, you are a well-designed mechanical nightmare that, regrettably, got out of control."

"The fact that we are not organic forms of life does not bar us from membership in the Federation," Jared said coldly. "The Gaens of Valarous are silicon-based life-forms, and they were admitted to the Federation on stardate 3262.1, if the records on the *Enterprise* are correct."

"They also replicate by asexual reproduction," Data added, helpfully, "and need a catalyst to reproduce."

"Doctor," Picard said, intent on stopping the quotation of precedents, which could go on forever, "I am asking your direct professional opinion. Are the androids individual, living beings?"

The question visibly troubled her. Beverly's tired face shifted into her "doctor mode," a look that everyone on the ship knew, he perhaps best of all. Far from being a mere healer, Beverly Crusher was also, by the necessity of her duties, a talented research scientist and theoretician. He knew she had often had to deal with incredibly strange forms of life, beings whose biological functions she could not even begin to imagine. And as far as he knew, the question "Are they alive?" had very rarely crept into her mind.

She drew a breath and gave her analysis. "As I said, the question of what defines life is a complicated, almost unanswerable one. Our primitive ancestors had it easy. If you could kill it, cook it, or kiss it, it was alive; and if it wasn't, you didn't pay much attention to it. The exploration of the galaxy has made all our earlier definitions moot, however. We once had rules about what was alive and what wasn't, but when we encountered aliens who didn't fit those definitions, yet were positively alive, our rules had to change. And when creations such as the Vemlans," she said, with a nod of her head, "and our own Mr. Data," she said kindly, "come forth and declare that they are living beings, any convenient and simple definition just doesn't work.

"The question has many different aspects as well. There is the religious side—do the androids have souls? I am not qualified to give an opinion on that. There is the psychological question—are androids self-aware and capable of conscious, sapient thought?" She frowned. "Though I'm trained in psychology, it isn't my specialty, and again, I can't confidently render an opinion. Then there is the biological issue. On that, I am able to render an opinion."

She paused to survey her audience.

"Data and these other androids have been built in

the shape of their creators. They have two hands, two feet, two eyes, a nose, two ears, and an advanced electrochemical processing system. Now, in a human or humanoid form of life, I would say that you could artificially replace each and every biological part of a single body, with one exception, thus creating a cyborg, or cybernetic organism, and still class the individual as a living being. It isn't the veins and the tissue and the cells that make a sapient being, it's that one thing that can't be replaced—the brain or analogous central nervous system."

"But the androids don't have brains!" Alkirg said triumphantly, standing and gesturing wildly. "They're just computers!" She turned to the other table. "We made certain of that; just big, self-important computers—with a logic error someplace."

"I wasn't finished," Beverly said icily. "The many studies of comparative anatomy in alien races have shown that a central nervous system can take many forms, from huge masses of neural processors like the Terids on Sephria, to creatures with such a decentralized system that you have to grind them into hamburger to kill them. Like the Wallowbat of Centauris and its relatives. The way a brain is put together isn't important, and neither is the material from which it's made; the mere existence of a central nervous system is enough, in my opinion, to class a creature as an advanced living organism." She looked directly into Alkirg's eyes. "Regardless of where it came from. Data is alive, medically speaking, and legally speaking. So are the Vemlans.

"However, the question of their sentience is not the main issue here," Beverly continued. "The ques-

219

tion is whether or not they are a race. That is a little more complicated. A virus is alive and sentient, in its limited fashion. But it's not sapient. I wouldn't classify it as a race. I can't do so for the Vemlans, either."

"That's your opinion?" asked Picard.

She took one last, long breath. "Yes. That's my opinion."

Picard raised his eyebrows, and turned to his first officer. "I find then, Commander Riker, I must overrule your objection as well. Partially based on the Federation legal precedent established for Commander Data, the Vemlans are indeed alive."

He glanced over at the Vemlans' table for their reaction to his decision, and saw Alkirg quietly berating Sawliru, probably for his failure to win this particular point. The Force Commander's face flushed beet red, and Picard felt pity for the man.

"However," he continued, "these arguments raise a new objection: are the Vemlan androids a race? Only a few months ago the Federation was attacked by aliens known as the Borg—a mixture of man and machine possessing tremendous military power." Picard continued for the edification of the navy and the androids alike. The Starfleet officers knew very well what the Borg were. Their recent attack had driven right to the heart of the Federation. Over sixty Starfleet vessels had been destroyed in defense of Earth, a loss from which the Federation had yet to recover.

"They operate together as a single group mind. Members of many species make up their fleet, as the Borg ships sweep throughout the galaxy in search of new life-forms to destroy or incorporate into the

Borg. Yet the sentience of the Borg is machine-based; a series of programs runs their ships and directs the individuals in their tasks. They are highly organized. But are the Borg a race?"

The thought had been much on his mind. He had been captured and incorporated forcibly into the Borg—his knowledge of Starfleet tactics and Federation technology had been used against the defenses of Earth, and many had died in the process. In the end, with Data's help, Picard had escaped the clutches of the Borg and the massive, cubical Borg ship had been destroyed in orbit before it had assimilated the Earth.

"Data, you had contact with them. You helped me escape. Were they a race, or simply a program?"

"Insufficient data, Captain," Data replied. "Because of the minimal contact the Federation has had with the Borg, there is not enough information to make a judgment. I experienced the software defenses of the Borg ship; I did not have intimate contact with them. To my knowledge you are the only person ever to do so—and live to tell about it. Therefore you are in the best position to make that decision."

"Captain, is this relevant?" Riker asked. "The Borg are not the androids. It's their fate we're here to decide. I don't see . . ."

"Yes, Number One, it is relevant," Picard said. They hadn't planned on raising this issue, but Picard thought now it was important. "If the Borg are a race by our standards, I think it has bearing on the case. They are at least as unique as the Vemlans. If they were simply a machine that got out of control . . ."

"Captain," Data said. "In my opinion the current

definitions of *race* need to be reviewed and extended; they no longer meet our needs, as we encounter more life-forms who are clearly sentient."

"I see," Picard said. "I will take this matter under consideration. If there are no more objections to the application of membership . . ." He looked around expectantly. Both Riker and Crusher were silent; they had found no further problems in their pre-hearing discussion, but others might. When no one spoke, though, Picard returned his attention to the petition.

"Very well. Jared, you speak as an elected representative of the Vemlan androids—"

"I object to the use of the phrase Vemlan androids, Captain," Sawliru said, again taking interest. "The androids left our home in a shambles, and we have no current connection with them—until we put them on trial," he added.

Jared, surprisingly, agreed with his opponent. "Captain, my own objection to the phrase stems from the use of the term androids," he explained. "The term means, literally, 'a manlike object.' We wish to enter the Federation as free individual beings, on our own terms and merits, not simply as machines."

Picard nodded. "Very well, the words Vemlan androids are to be struck from the record and replaced with . . . what do you want to call yourselves?"

Jared, Kurta and Data conversed heatedly for a few moments, accelerating the speed of their conversation to a near squeal. They stopped abruptly, and Jared turned back to Picard.

"Captain, we would like our race to be known

henceforth as Spartacans, in honor of a man from your own world's history. Spartacus was—"

"I am aware of his historical significance," he interrupted, not wanting to clutter up the record with a history lecture. "Let the record be amended to replace the words Vemlan with Spartacan and androids with people. Will that be satisfactory?" he asked.

"Yes," the three androids said in unison.

"Now that that is settled, we can continue. I have at least one question regarding the future of your proposed membership in the Federation, Jared. There is the matter of the lack of a planet. Though not absolutely central to the issue at hand, I would like to know, for the record, what the Spartacans plan on doing, should their application be accepted. What contributions to Federation society and culture can you make? Do you intend to be itinerant for your entire existence?"

"My people wish to colonize an uninhabited system, somewhere inside the Federation. The exact location we leave up to the Federation."

"What are your planetary needs? Atmosphere, radiation tolerance, that sort of thing?"

Jared considered. "Our needs are very small, Captain. Think of the resources I have at my disposal. I have four hundred eager, willing, tireless workers who will toil ceaselessly to create the homeland that they have dreamt of for so long. If you have no prosperous planet to give us, Captain, give us your most vile ball of muddy rock and in one generation —one of yours, that is—we will build a sterling example of what our race, living at its fullest potential, can do. We will build a city, and a garden around it, and our art and our culture shall be known throughout the civilized galaxy. Just give us a place to work and we will build magnificently!" he said, with a flourish of his hands.

"But will you build wisely?" Sawliru asked. Jared turned to face the Force Commander, who stood, an expression of overpowering intensity on his face. He emerged from behind the confining table and stood next to his opponent, fixing Jared with a steely glare.

"You are, by your own admission, living, thinking, feeling beings," Sawliru said, emphasizing each word precisely. "I have my doubts about some of those claims, and I have had enough personal experience to know the falseness of others. You are, I will admit, incredible creations, capable of building even more incredible creations." The commander's voice became more personal, more direct. He was not debating now, Picard knew; he was speaking his own mind.

"You can do anything," Sawliru declared, hands raised in mock salute. "Each and every one of you has the potential to build an entire civilization on your own. We built that capability into you. You can do a hundred different complex things at once, and write great poetry on the side. And you wish to go off and build this beautiful homeworld, this wonder of the galaxy," he said, envisioning the place and its professed wonder. Then he turned his eyes back to Jared. "Well, I cannot fault you for that.

"But I want to know something," he said, including Data and Kurta in his question with a gesture. "I want to know what makes you think that you're going to be all that successful? Yes, we built you, with help from our Saren friends, and we built you well, but what makes you think that you will be able to do any better than we did?" Data and Jared returned blank stares to the commander. Kurta did not look up at him, as if this thought had occurred to her, too.

"You lack the one thing that not all the programming, not all the learning, not all the data core dumps in the universe can give you—experience. Your race, as you call it, has only been around a few pitiful centuries. Your ancestors, mere computers and adding machines, are only a few centuries older. My race had to climb out of the mud," Sawliru declared, "from one tiny little cell in some puddle of muck, and fight and survive and wait several million years before we earned the right to think. There are things I know that you will never know. Things that you can never know," he said in a low, emphatic voice.

Sawliru turned suddenly to face the panel with an intent glow in his eyes. The sweat of exertion was on his brow, and he took a breath before he continued. "Captain, you may well decide to accept the androids in your precious Federation. I really don't care. But despite his pretty words and his fast talking, the conglomeration of metal and plastic standing next to me is of infinitesimal value when compared to the wealth of experience the smallest rodent has." Sawliru circled Jared, who stood stock still, and directed questions at him as if the android were a museum exhibit.

"When will he act by instinct?" he asked, his hands held out questioningly, as if they were groping for some hidden answer. "When will he have a gut feeling, or a sense of honor? Or duty? When he sees a thousand men die for no reason, will he know that it has to stop? Or will he decide that he can always make more? When will he see a moon and *feel* its mystical power, rather than reflect on its orbital trajectory and specific gravity?" He waited a moment, his eyes wide, as the crowd drank in his words.

"Never," he answered himself, with a tone of finality. "Not in a million years. He hasn't the experience, either personally or biologically." Sawliru took a moment, caught his breath. He gave one last look at Jared, then turned to look at Data and Kurta, who were still seated. Data's face was impassive. Kurta stared at the floor. Sawliru looked vaguely satisfied and at the same time, strangely enough, vaguely saddened. The commander focused his attention back on Picard and the panel.

"I tell you now, Captain, disregarding his crimes, which are heinous, his treachery, which is infamous, and his lack of respect for true life, which should be apparent to us all, this 'living being' can never truly be alive." He glanced back once more over his shoulder at Jared. "He can merely pretend to be.

"But he got that from us, as well," Sawliru reflected quietly, and returned slowly to his seat. He did not so much as glance at Alkirg as he sat down.

Jared had listened intently to the speech, and as Sawliru sat, he traded looks with Kurta and went to the center of the floor, in front of the panel. He then began clapping, slowly and intently, the painful sarcasm of his applause escaping no one.

"Very good, Force Commander," he said, his low voice openly scornful. "An excellent performance, if I do say so myself. Had you foregone your military career, no doubt there would be a bright spot for you on a stage someplace. Yet, despite your eloquent soliloquy, there is more to this life than experience."

He turned to the crowd, his back to the panel, and

spoke to them. He didn't have the same flair for words as Sawliru, but his passion, programmed or not, was every bit as intense. "What experience has a baby at birth? None. A baby has no intuition, gut feelings, or sense of honor, or duty."

He began to pace in front of the audience. Data seemed even more interested than before, and the others followed Jared hypnotically. Only Sawliru paid no attention, his thoughts his own. Alkrig, Picard noted, was openly glaring at the android. "Yet do you condemn a babe to death because of what it is? Your son, perhaps? Would you allow him to die, cursing him for idiocy, because he didn't have the capacity for all those grand and glorious sensations the day he was born?" he said, and turned. "Or would you cherish him for his potential?"

He turned again, as he stood in front of the Sawliru's table, and faced the panel. "My fellow—Spartacans—and I are as that babe, Captain, Doctor, First Officer. We have just emerged from the womb. It's true, we may know nothing of these 'living' things. But we cannot learn them if we are put to death," he warned. "What we lack in experience, we make up for in potential. I've read your histories, Captain Picard. Your Federation prides itself on encouraging the potential it sees in other races. Its worst enemies have gone on to become close friends and allies. Don't let our potential die here, in the void, Captain." Jared was actually pleading—something, Picard guessed, that did not come easy to him. "Give us a place to stand and fight for ourselves, and the experience will come, as it does to every race, in time." There was a long pause as his words sank in.

Suddenly, Picard felt a thousand years old. He realized that he had a long way to go to make up his mind.

"Are there any others who would speak on the matter? Anything else the petitioners wish to add?" he asked.

"Nothing," Jared said, quietly, nervously fingering his right hand with his left. He looked beaten. But then, Picard noted, so did Sawliru.

"If there are no further statements," he said, "I will consult with my fellow officers and attempt to make a decision. It is possible we will have more questions for everyone. We will reconvene in one hour," he said to the audience and the recording computer. "Number One, Doctor, I wish to see you in my quarters, please."

As the panel officers filed out of the room, Alkirg turned to Sawliru.

"Check on the fleet, get them ready. We may need to attack the *Enterprise* or the *Conquest* very shortly." She smiled. "I just haven't decided which one, yet."

"But, Mission Commander—"

"Did I ask for an opinion?" she said in an acid tone, her eyes savagely boring into her subordinate's. "I didn't think so. Watch yourself, or it will go badly for you when we return to Vemla. Now be on your way, and let me think," she said over her shoulder as she exited out into the corridor.

Sawliru choked back a bitter, caustic reply, and tried to calm himself. Either course of action at this point had no foreseeable conclusion save the death and destruction of his fleet. There was no wisdom in what she said, only folly. How would the historians rate him in this crisis, he wondered idly—if there were any survivors to take word back to Vemla at all, that was. He shook his head, deciding that it didn't matter. He had enough to worry about; the flow of events would have to go on heedless of what he thought about posterity. He had better check on the fleet as soon as possible, though it was the first step into destruction. He didn't need "insubordination in the face of the enemy" added to the list of charges at his posthumous court-martial.

He was about to contact his ship when he realized someone had come up silently behind him. Sawliru spun—and found himself staring at the *Enterprise*'s android officer, Commander Data.

"What do you want?" he challenged.

"I thought I might take the opportunity of the recess to offer you a drink, Commander," Data said.

The invitation caught Sawliru completely off guard. He was about to spit out a bitter, derisive reply, but stopped. He was angrier with Alkirg than with the androids right now, and he knew that one way to get back at her for her abuse was to spurn her company for that of an android. Especially an alien android.

"Why, thank you, I would be delighted," he said, tight-lipped but respectfully. "I could use a drink about now."

"Excellent," Data said as the door hissed open. "I know the perfect place."

The three Starfleet officers reassembled in Picard's private quarters, around the mahogany tea table the captain used for social occasions. A silver teapot, specially ordered from the galley, sat in the center, and the three sipped as they talked.

"What troubles me most about the androids is their attitude, Number One," Picard said, as he poured more tea. "I must admit that their flawlessness makes me uncomfortable, and their pride, their . . . hubris, could very well get them into trouble, some day."

"Hasn't it already?" Riker asked, wryly. Picard nodded, conceding the point.

"What about Data?" asked Beverly. "Does his flawlessness make you uncomfortable, too?"

Picard seriously considered the question. No, Data was a valuable officer, and his misunderstanding of human values and customs even made him the endearing source of comic relief when he wasn't being annoying. "No. Perhaps it's the fact that they look and act nearly identical to human beings. I could pass one in the corridor and never know the difference. Data's physical structure makes him— less human, less threatening," he said, thoughtfully. "Dr. Soong planned it that way, apparently. It would have been easy enough to make him more human-like, in skin tone and eye color, if nothing else."

"I think the point was that Dr. Soong didn't intend for Data to replace man, but to complement him," Riker said, quietly. "In all of his notes on the subject, he makes it clear that he was not looking to create the ultimate machine, but an amalgam of the best organic and mechanical quality."

"Whereas the Vemlans had no such policy in their creation. Perhaps if they had, they would have also had a little foresight. But their whole intention was to replace man, at least in the drab and vital functions of a society."

"I still haven't been convinced that allowing the

andr— Spartacans—to enter the Federation is a wise idea," Riker said, frankly. "They are a very dangerous race, potentially."

"If they are a race at all," Picard countered. "I was deadly serious about the question of the Borg, Number One."

"The Borg had biological components, at least; that makes it easier to place them in the race category," Riker pointed out.

"Ah, but we've admitted that they are alive, Will," Beverly said, as the food materialized in the slot. "Data's sentience is a matter of record. But it takes more than life to make a race."

"Does it?" Riker asked. "I still don't see how the Borg are relevant."

"The biological components of the Borg—some of them our former comrades—are mere arms and legs and synapses for the Borg gestalt. They possess little or no individuality," Picard said as Beverly placed the tray on the table. "The Vemlans, at least, have that in their favor. They are individuals—Jared has more character than some humans I know. The driving program of the Borg is computer-generated, however. The biological components are locked into a machine-made program. What little will they have is dominated by the central gestalt. That I know for certain," he said, with a certain amount of pain in his eyes.

"But is the program itself alive, and can the entire Borg complex be considered a race, or merely a machine that got out of control?" Beverly asked. "As Data pointed out, we really don't have enough information to decide. The Borg attacked a little too quickly and savagely for us to trade histories."

"And by the same token, are the androids motivated out of a sense of racial unity or are they merely using those terms to mask a programmed response? How can we know?" Riker asked.

"By observation, perhaps," Picard said, sipping his tea. "Up to now, we have treated the Borg as a race because that is how they manifested themselves to us—as invaders. Not as some mindless doomsday machine. That is how we treat every race that communicates with us—even the Spartacans, until we learned of their origin. Yet can we honestly exclude them?"

"Can we honestly include them, Captain?" Riker said. "I am all for fairness in this matter, but we didn't try to invite the Borg to join the Federation when they attacked—or a hundred other races we have encountered. They are just too different from us for the benefits of the Federation to mean anything."

"I think," Beverly commented as she poured more tea, "that Data was correct in one thing. In the cases of both the Borg and the Vemlans, we must re-examine our definitions and preconceptions of what we consider a race. There is just too much that is strange to us, and therefore doesn't fit into any convenient category. Whether we include them or exclude them, we must decide on what basis we do these things."

"But can a race come off an assembly line?" Riker argued.

"Why not?" Beverly countered. "It's at least a form of production I understand."

"I think," Picard said, slowly, "that we have been too conservative in definitions—depending too much on tradition. 'There are more things in heaven and earth' than are dreamt of in any of our philosophies. We cannot depend on our own narrow histories and viewpoints to judge the rest of the universe. As for the Borg and the Vemlans, I'm willing to give them the benefit of the doubt. I cannot, in good conscience, do otherwise."

"That still doesn't answer the question of whether or not they should be granted admission," Riker said. "They are dangerous—immature, as Sawliru pointed out. And dangerous. By their own admission, they could take any worthless asteroid or planet and turn it into a paradise. And they are also adept at war, the worst kinds of war. They could also build weapons, expand, become deadly enemies. If we thought the Klingons or Romulans were bad, how could we beat a race that came from factories, fully grown, ready to fight? On the other hand . . . perhaps it would be better to have them on our side. After all—"

"That's an attitude I'd expect Worf to voice, Number One, not you. They do make formidable opponents, from what Commander Sawliru has said —and by their own admission. Yet even in our midst, with high technology at their disposal, they could become dangerous in other ways. The safest way to deal with them would be the answer the Vemlans have pursued—destruction."

"You would have them destroyed?" asked Riker, his face blank. He had not sanctioned that in his own mind.

"Beverly has convinced me that they are, indeed, living, sentient creatures. To destroy them would be genocide, and I will not make a decision at that level if I can humanly avoid it," he said, his face heavy with worry. "No, I said it was the safest thing; it will not be our course of action."

"We've dealt with dangerous aliens before," Beverly said. "Some of them, as Jared pointed out, are living in peace with us now. I don't think these androids are a threat in that way. I think they pose a more insidious problem."

"What?" asked Picard, pouring tea.

"What happens if they want to join Starfleet?" she asked, eyes wide at the prospect. "What happens when you have to compete with one of these wonder machines, these supermen, for a chance to command, Jean-Luc? There's no way you could win."

"I think you underestimate my abilities, Doctor," Picard said with a trace of pique.

"I think you underestimate theirs, Captain," she insisted. "As much as I detest the military mind, Sawliru had some very good points out there. The only advantage we have over them is experience, and it won't be long before they have that, too. Would the Neanderthals," she thought, fancifully, "have let the Cro-Magnons hang around if they knew what was in store for them? I wonder . . ."

"Our race and culture will be tried by many things, Dr. Crusher. We shouldn't try to eliminate the competition unfairly. If we fail, then we shall fail fairly."

"What concerns me the most is their criminal past," Riker said. "Here is this ship full of terrorists who want to join the Federation. How do we explain that to Starfleet Command?"

"Terrorism is a relative thing, Will," Picard said smoothly. "They were fighting for their freedom and were, in their own eyes, justified. I am not equipped to judge them in that. We've had criminals in our past. Half of the Jenisha in the Federation are descended from families who made their fortunes preying on Federation ships at the height of their pirate era. The Federation exists to bring disparate groups together peacefully, not to serve as a high moral ground."

"And the matter of species survival is also important," Beverly said. "The Spartacans are the last of their race. Even though they have committed crimes —and even atrocities—as individuals, what right do we have to condemn their race to extinction? Would you want our own race to be judged like that?"

"I don't think that humanity would ever come to that, Doctor," Riker said, a trifle forcefully.

"Oh, really?" Crusher said, accusingly. "Remember your history, Will. During the Eugenics Wars, on Earth, humanity very well could have been wiped out. In fact it was a miracle that it wasn't. Every man, woman, and child in the race would have been gone. Except for a few ships that got away."

"The prison ships, you mean," Picard said. "They contained—"

"They contained hundreds of desperate, violent criminals, pathological murderers, and genetically altered, psychotic terrorists, considered war criminals by the rest of the world," Riker finished.

"Yes, and they were mostly justified in their imprisonment. Those ships were filled with the dregs of humanity, people whose crimes earned them a deathless imprisonment, until they were lost. Tell me, Jean-Luc, if these violent, psychotic terrorists were the only survivors of Earth, would you put them on trial, condemn and execute them for their war crimes? Thus exterminating the human race?"

Picard frowned and closed his eyes. "I am an explorer, not a judge, Beverly."

"Not today, Jean-Luc." She leaned back in her chair and looked straight at him. "Today, you have a decision to make."

Picard sighed. He did, indeed.

# Chapter Eleven

SAWLIRU NODDED IN appreciation as a filled glass materialized in the tiny chamber in front of Data. The technology of the Federation was nearly magical to him. With such machines, it was no wonder that these people had achieved so much.

Abruptly, he caught himself. *Here I stand, in the presence of one of those machines, and gawk and stare like some uncivilized barbarian.* He strengthened his resolve to behave with more care and dignity. Data, who didn't seem to notice, handed him the drink and turned to program his own beverage.

The drink was pleasantly chilled and had a sweet odor and a tangy, refreshing taste. He would be hard-pressed to find one as expertly mixed in his own officer's lounge on his own ship. Not, at least, since it no longer employed an android. Somehow the realization angered him.

"The *Enterprise* has many highly interesting technologies incorporated into her design," the pale android was saying. "I thought that it might be of interest to demonstrate one for you."

"This food dispenser?" Sawliru asked. "Yes, it is quite an achievement. A combination of that transporter beam and a computer, is it not? Had we the transporter technology, doubtless we could find such a device useful."

"The food slots are, indeed, of special interest to visitors," the machine said, sipping its drink in gross parody of a real man. "Yet I was speaking of something else entirely."

He turned toward a blank wall panel and placed an inhuman, ghostly white hand upon it. "Computer: Activate holodeck three."

"Program?" the female voice of the computer inquired.

"Theta four six, authorization code—Commander Data."

"Working . . . Complete. Enjoy your recreation program, Commander."

"Thank you, I shall."

Sawliru grinned wryly, in his tight-lipped fashion. "You thanked the computer? Are you two good friends?"

"The holodeck computer is classified nonsentient. Its salutation is simply programmed politeness—user-friendliness. I made the response as a reflex; I have learned that politeness and manners, when practiced universally, alter the behavior of both the practitioner and the recipient in a favorable manner. In essence, if you are polite to everyone, then people are more inclined to be polite to you. In addition, the computer has a memory of each exchange, and if some semblance of sentience exists, I would prefer to be on good terms with it. It is a very smart machine."

"Sort of a master-pet relationship."

Data considered the suggestion. "That is an analogy I had not considered. From what I have read and seen of such relationships, the situation is somewhat similar."

He turned and walked toward the door, which obligingly slid open with an automatic hiss that disconcerted Sawliru. Doors that didn't work manually might be elegant, but he didn't trust them. The android strode forward. Sawliru wondered absently about what would have happened had the door not opened. He followed, drink in hand, to see this technological marvel.

As he crossed the plane of the door, he stepped into another world. A deserted wasteland.

Twisted trees of an alien variety dotted the rolling hills, and scrub grasses and thornbushes pushed gratingly skyward. The sun, a bright, alien, yellow thing, filled the sky. Through the center of the landscape, an ancient brick road, thick with dust, ran to an equally primitive town in the distance. Sawliru's senses struggled to adjust to the abrupt change; confound it, had those Federation clowns perfected their transporter beams to cover interstellar distances? Had this machine-man brought him to some faraway land to be murdered or imprisoned, effectively incapacitating his command?

"Do not be alarmed," said the android, reading the expression on his face. "We have not left the ship. Look through the door behind you."

He did. The quiet, humming corridor of the starship was plainly visible, hanging, seemingly, in midair. A crewman wandered by, glanced at the open door, and continued. Sawliru took a deep breath, and let the panic slip from his mind.

The android continued its explanation as the door to the ship closed, to be replaced by a bush.

"The holodeck was specially designed for deep-space starships, which might be between safe shore leave sites for months, and might be away from home ports for years at a time. By using both three-dimensional holograms, forcefield generators, and the transporter technology, we can effectively re-create any environment, any situation, without limit to time and space. Though it was intended primarily for recreation, the holodeck has also been used as a means of education as well. I have stood in the ancient past of my creator's planet, been involved in a tavern brawl in San Francisco, debated philosophy with the greatest thinkers in the galaxy, and wandered through the forests of a hundred worlds without leaving the ship. The holodeck computer controls the situation and acts upon the reactions of the participants."

"Is it safe?" the Force Commander asked, guardedly.

"Perfectly. The computer cannot allow injury to come of anyone in the holodeck. I give you my word that you will not be harmed, and that you will make it back to the hearing on time and unmolested."

Sawliru relaxed, and sipped his drink. "Where are we?"

"A place called Italy, on the European continent, Mediterranean sector, Earth, during the ascendancy of one of Earth's greatest empires. It will later gradually decline and fall, to be re-established under a variety of names. I chose this stark location to demonstrate the flexibility and accuracy of the system," he finished.

"I'm impressed," Sawliru said, as he watched birds of prey circle overhead. Though they looked strange to him, birds were birds. He could understand that. "And all of this is illusion?"

"For the most part. Yet if you fall to the ground, the computer has instructions to create a realistic feeling surface for you to land upon. If you lean on a hill, or pick up a rock, then they, too, will appear to be real."

"Incredible," the commander said, looking around. "It looks, feels, even smells real. Your technology is so far advanced . . ."

"Yet the technology in this time and place is barbarically primitive," Data replied. "If we encounter computer-controlled denizens of this era, they will behave with realistic fervor. Do not be alarmed."

"I'll keep that in mind." The two of them started walking toward the distant city. The landscape around them changed with each step, and again Sawliru experienced a wave of confusion. He could not tell this illusion from the real thing. Every few meters they would clear the dust from their mouths with sips of their drinks. He didn't question the direction they were taking; if you walk through a dream, he reasoned, it mattered little which way you walked.

"Why are you showing me this, Commander?" he asked. He disliked addressing the machine with such a term of honor, but as a military man, and a captain of a ship, he knew enough to respect the rank, even if he didn't respect its bearer. "For the past few days,

I've been trying to destroy your friends, yet you make me a drink and walk me through a dreamscape."

"'If you are going to kill a man anyway, it costs nothing to be polite,'" Data said. "That is a quote from one of Earth's greatest leaders. I bear you no personal enmity for the attempted destruction of the androids. You were merely doing what you were ordered to do. We are all players in this situation. I simply was interested in much of what you said in your plea, and wished to discuss it further."

"Is that so?" Sawliru said, suspiciously.

"Yes. In particular, I wished to know exactly why you hate androids so intensely. Have you been personally injured by them?"

Sawliru paused on the dusty road and surveyed the clouds in the distance. Data stopped alongside him.

He didn't particularly want to expose his personal feelings to anyone, especially when it had no bearing on the issue at hand. But Sawliru figured that Data, being who he was, didn't count as a real person anyhow. "I have lost some family to the revolt," he said, swishing his drink around in his glass. "My son was at the site of one of the bombings. I hadn't spoken to him for some time—we were at odds, politically. But I don't consider it a factor. I do what I do out of loyalty and duty, not out of vengeance."

"I am sorry for your loss."

"What do you know of loss?" Sawliru asked, bitterly.

"I have lost comrades—friends—in the line of duty. I have lost my father, the man who created me, and my brother, an earlier prototype. I cannot say that I have been unaffected by their passing."

Sawliru thought of his son, and winced with the

pain of the memory. "Yes, perhaps you have, in your way. But you haven't felt it as I have, as a real man can feel it. That's why we resent you the most, I guess—because you claim all the privileges of humanity and don't seem to take any of the painful responsibilities."

"Is that why you pursue the Alphas with such tenacity? You resent them?"

"Hah!" he spat. "Hardly. I can't even imagine wanting to own a dead piece of circuitry and plastic, much less be one. I enjoy life too much." They continued toward the city. "My pursuit is a matter of loyalty to my people. They desired the return of the androids, and it is my duty to fetch them back. Or destroy them in the attempt," he added, casually.

"Yet the performance of your mission does not depend upon your personal attitude. You continue to treat the Alphas as simple, nonsentient machines, despite all evidence to the contrary."

"If you're wondering why I hate androids, Commander," he said, using the title to remind himself of their relationship, "that's an easy question to answer. I hate androids because they were ruining my planet. I have fought long and hard to eradicate them, and killed a million men to do it. And I'd do it all again, in an instant. Alkirg is twisted up about the revolt, about all the damage that was done, all the people that died. Hell, the revolt was the best damn thing that ever happened to us."

It was Data's turn to stop to ponder. "Could you please explain the logic behind that conclusion?"

Sawliru scratched at the rough paved surface of the road, scuffing his boots. Amazing, the realism possible here. I wonder if my boot will stay scuffed, he wondered, after I return from this place.

"Data, my people were a lot like your creators. We pulled ourselves out of rank barbarism by our bootstraps—no one helped us do it. There was a time when the military was much more important than it is now. A time of warring tribes, which became warring city-states, which became warring nations. Everyone scrambled over who owned what piece of land, and how much there was to eat, and who ate it. Our oceans became puddles as our technology developed—common moats that we stared across, eternally vigilant, to spot a potential attacker before he struck. People were poor, they suffered, were oppressed, starved, and died of disease and neglect. Millions perished in horrible wars, and our world was growing tired of us. Even our ecosystem was beginning to fail."

"Humans went through a similar period," Data remarked. "As did many other races. It is often considered a test of a race's worth, how it deals with its self-destructive periods. It must have been a horrible and terrifying time."

"It was a wonderful time!" Sawliru exclaimed. "Don't misunderstand me. There was much suffering—terrible, awful suffering. But you can't measure the value of a race solely on the numbers of people you can healthily maintain."

Again, the continued walking along the dusty road. Data seemed puzzled by the Force Commander's outburst. "What exactly do you mean?" he asked. "I have always understood that peace and prosperity are the goals of a rational culture. Are the Vemlans not a rational people?"

Sawliru shook his head and laughed a little. "Perhaps not. Yes, that's what we were striving for. Peace and prosperity. And we got it, too—good and hard."

He paused to take a long sip from his drink. "The androids were the perfect solution. An endless source of cheap labor, a masterpiece of engineering that could cook, clean, sew, and teach your children at the same time. They could write poetry, compose music—you could even have sex with one. With enough androids, having food, shelter, and anything else you wanted was as easy as asking for it. We put them to work cleaning up the environmental messes a few centuries of riotous living had created."

"It seems, indeed, a perfect solution, from the Vemlan point of view," Data said, obligingly. "What, then, bothers you about androids?"

"Ever since Vemla switched over to an android-based economy, our culture has declined immeasurably. Some people think it's a mark of distinction and sophistication to have androids doing everything—from weeding the garden to composing the music you listen to. It's just plain laziness, though, that's all. Institutionalized laziness. Hell, the wars were awful, and I'd never want to go back, but they gave us something to be passionate about. The only passion I've seen on Vemla in the last thirty years came from the lips of an android. The androids were killing us, Data; killing us slowly, but killing us nonetheless.

"I was waiting for us to be invaded, when the revolt broke out. Most people think I'm crazy, but we needed something to get us angry again, to get our passion back, and there's nothing like a war to be passionate about. I don't really know why Jared and his friends started the whole thing; in a few years the androids would have been running everything anyway."

"What about exploration?" Data asked.

"Most people didn't want to bother, and when the people don't care, the government certainly doesn't. Only the scientists and the technical androids cared about exploration. And the military," he said. "If it wasn't for them, the *Conquest* would never have been built. Your average Vemlan didn't care much about anything. It was as if when we created the androids we passed on to them the fire in our culture—the spark that makes us do things. We had nothing to strive for in the last century, because everything was given to us on a platter of gold by our servants—slaves," he admitted.

"Cultural declines are integral to developing races. Though I can see how you would be upset at the symptoms, I think it can be safely said that your planet would have recovered from the decline."

"Not if there aren't any real people left. The birthrate was way down. Oh, there was an initial surge, but after a few generations, people just stopped having kids regularly. They weren't old-age security anymore, and most of the time it wasn't worth the problems that having children involves."

"And you attribute this decline to the introduction of androids into the culture?"

Again, the Force Commander laughed bitterly. "The androids were just a symptom, Commander; the source of this illness is in the way our government is set up. One particular group, to which the esteemed Mission Commander Alkirg belongs," he added sarcastically, "came into power, and saw the means of remaining there depended on stemming off potential trouble by using the androids as a cure-all. There wasn't a problem too large that you couldn't throw androids at it."

He shook his head in sadness as he shuffled his feet

in a relaxed, uncharacteristic manner. "I can't really talk, since I'm technically part of the system myself. But the trouble on Vemla is political in nature, not mechanical. The androids were merely a convenient tool for those in power.

"I'm not a political creature by nature, Commander. I do what I know best: action, combat, struggle. There was talk of phasing out the military completely, letting the androids defend us, but I couldn't let that happen. The civilians we protect from outside dangers consider us outmoded, unnecessary, a barbaric waste of resources that could be better spent elsewhere. My son thought I was a vile, atavistic warlord in a tin-soldier army. The truth is, I don't like violence. I'm just very good at it. Had I been a politician, I might have done something about what I saw happening. But I wasn't.

"I hid in the military and hated the androids in peace and silence. Then they revolted, and I tried to use the revolt to kick the people out of their stupor. If every android on the planet is gone, then the people are going to have to face reality sooner or later. There's no way they'll let androids back in our society, no matter what happens."

"Yet you seek to punish the androids, though they indirectly do you a service?"

"Hell, androids are tools, just like handsaws, hammers, lasers, and starships. Tools to be designed, built, and used. Even in death, they are useful. Each android that died in the revolt was another step back to life for my people. I—"

Sawliru was interrupted by a motley group of ragged-looking men and women leaping out from behind a bend in the road. They were dressed in a crude, colorless fashion, in garments of rough-woven cloth stained with food, dirt, sweat, and blood. Some were armed with crude knives, clubs or axes, and here and there a sword or spear was in evidence.

"Stand where you are!" came a shout. Though Sawliru was severely out of practice in unarmed combat, the group was gesturing menacingly, and he responded in kind. He threw his half-full glass at the leader, and took up a combat stance, ready to defend himself.

The glass sailed gracefully through the air and shattered in the face of the leading man. He dropped the club he carried and howled as he spat teeth and blood. The others were visibly shaken by the sudden response, but did not drop their guard.

They didn't come any closer, though.

"Are these some of the charming denizens of this program?"

"Yes, Commander. I would suggest you move cautiously and treat them as if they were real. A wound from a weapon will not injure you, but the computer may well stun you into unconsciousness."

Sawliru nodded, and turned to their attackers. "Who are you?" he asked.

"Men freed by our own hands!" came the response. "We killed our overseer, then the plantation owner, and we'll kill you and anyone else who stands in our way!"

The shuffling pack of humanity pressed forward, though they were all clearly reluctant to risk injury from Sawliru.

"Ho, there! Stop!"

The small mob parted, and a short, heavily muscled man came forward. He was better dressed, wearing a finer cloak and tunic, and armed with a short, sturdy-looking sword. His hair was cropped closely to his head, and scars marked his face like a spider web.

"Britannicus! Why did you attack these two travelers?" he asked. "Our quarrel is with the slavelords of Rome, not with wandering folk. Did you mistake these men for senators, walking alone on a public road in the middle of the day, without escort or servants?" The slaves laughed heartily, and even Britannicus, who held his bleeding mouth, smiled sheepishly.

"No, Spartacus. But with them skulking around out here, they couldn't be up to much good!" the wounded man said in defense.

The well-dressed man looked up to the rest of the crowd. "This from an escaped slave who's out to murder Roman citizens!" Again the mob roared with laughter, and even the wounded Britannicus could not contain himself. The man continued, "There is much to be done tonight, my friends, and many more farms to free. A passing stranger or two will neither help nor hinder us. And stark robbery has never been a policy of mine, and I'll kill the first ten men that differ!" He scowled, his scarred face contorting.

Once the band had begun lowering their weapons and moving on, he turned to the two men.

"I apologize for my comrades. They are giddy with their newfound freedom, and not easily controlled. I can tell by your dress that you are not Romans, though the fashions the citizens subject themselves to get stranger every year, by Jupiter. Are you foreigners, then?"

"Yes," Data supplied. "We are merchants from far away."

Sawliru nodded in assent; the thought of speaking

directly to a computer-generated image, even one so lifelike, was still somewhat frightening to him. He gained confidence quickly, however, and adapted. "From *very* far away."

"Are you Egyptians, then? Or Greek?"

"We are Babylonians, from the far eastern provinces," Data offered. "On our way to Gaul."

"Ah, then truly we have no quarrel. My people war on the Roman slavelords only, as yours did."

"Who are your people?" Sawliru asked, relaxing a little.

The image of the ancient warrior gave him a dead stare. "All slaves are my people. My brothers. I am Spartacus, former gladiator, former slave. Where I was born matters not."

"I am Sawliru," the Force Commander said.

"I am called Data."

"And you both head to the city. Well, my way lies with yours for a span. Tell me, how are things on the Tigris?"

"I am more interested in what is happening here," Data said, tactfully avoiding a lengthy fabrication. "The news of your rebellion has spread far and wide. How does it go?"

The imaginary man frowned an imaginary frown. "It goes. Whence, I cannot say. Each day the gods smile on us, we free another handful of farms, kill a few overseers, arm another hundred slaves. Yet these are not trained men—they are field hands and laborers. For us to remain free, we must battle Roman legionnaires before long."

"Experienced soldiers?" inquired Sawliru.

"The best in the world," Spartacus said, sadly, but with a trace of pride. "Rome may be rotten at the core, but her armies will conquer all the world one day. They will send the legions after us, once we have gathered in numbers, and destroy us all at once."

"I thought you were a warrior," Sawliru interjected. The scarred man shook his head again, and sighed.

"I am but a gladiator. Put a sword in my hand and sand at my feet, and I'll give any man the hardest day of his life—if not the last. But armies and soldiers and discipline—the magic of Mars is not known to me. My people will be cut down like corn, but they will die free men," he said, satisfactorily.

"Is it that important to you?" asked Sawliru. "You can only use freedom if you're alive to enjoy it."

"Not one man is free as long as there is one man in bondage to another, friend Sawliru," Spartacus explained. "I knew this was hopeless from the start. I, of all people, know the military might of the Romans. Yet if these people die, and myself along with them, they'll die quickly, of their own free will, not in some disease-ridden hole with none but rats for company, or in the fields under the overseer's lash, or, worst of all, crucified for some petty offense for the entertainment of the senate and people of Rome."

"Crucified?" asked Sawliru, puzzled. He was unaware of the term.

"A favored form of torture and execution in antiquity, and particularly favored by the Roman Empire," Data conveniently replied, as they continued toward the city. "Victims were hung from a constructed wooden framework by driving nails or spikes through their wrists and ankles, and left exposed to the elements until they expired from loss of blood, shock, or dehydration. It was the traditional punishment for escaped slaves. Such a death could take as long as a week, under the right circumstances."

"Ghastly," whispered Sawliru, paling at the description. Though such things were present in Vemla's own past, they had been outlawed for centuries.

"Aye," agreed the leader of the rebellion with a shudder. "I have had many a friend spend his last hours in agony on a cross. It's not the death I'd choose, not a death for a free man. It's one more reason I led this revolt."

"You lead it, though you know it is going to be fruitless?" Data asked, helpfully.

"But it won't be fruitless. Too long have the Romans warred on the helpless peoples of countless lands, bringing home in chains the sons and daughters of those who died to defend their homes and lands. The might of the Roman Empire was wrought with the toil and sweat of other nations. Even the Romans know this. When a slave is cheaper to buy than a kid and cheaper to own than a dog, then it is cheaper to farm with slaves than with freemen. A hundred slaves can raise enough to feed a thousand citizens of Rome, and then there is nought for them to do but wager, drink, and carouse. And watch other men sweat and die in the arenas," he added, darkly. "Though many of us will die, many more will go on to another farm, and another, and soon, if every slave in Italy revolts, we will be too strong for the Romans, whose greatest force lies in distant lands. And perhaps," he added philosophically, "the poets will sing of us for a while."

"And even if you lose, many you will set free will return to their homes," added Data. "Not all you do will be in vain."

"Are there no true military men among you, Spartacus?" asked Sawliru. "I have had some small experience with troops and training, tactics and strategy . . ."

"You would cease your business and join a doomed slave rebellion?" asked the ex-gladiator, smiling crookedly. "Surely, the midday sun has addled your brains!"

Sawliru thought of his business, the hearing, his fleet. He had gotten caught up in the spirit of the moment, and forgotten the artificial nature of the man with whom he was speaking. "Ah, yes, my . . . business. My . . . employer would severely punish me if I strayed from my business."

"You sound like a man enslaved, yourself," the hologram said, confused. "You carry yourself with the manner of a legate or a centurion, yet you speak in cowed and revered tones for a man whom you do not respect. Your employer must be a giant to cast fear into you so. Or has he leverage in your life? A hostage, perhaps? Or an evil spell?"

Sawliru laughed at the thought of Alkirg as a giant, though an evil spell was an uncomfortably close analogy. She had friends in all places, high and low, and had his career at her mercy.

"No, my friend, it's more complicated than that. My employer is a woman, no giant, no wizard."

"A woman!" Spartacus exclaimed. "Better a giant or mage! Gods of sea and sky, man, are you crazed? You, a veteran of campaigns and battles, let a wisp of silk and fluff keep you from your desires?" He was incredulous. "Beat her, that's what I say. Beat her, then get rid of her. A man isn't truly a man unless he's on his own."

"Perhaps. Her . . . family might make trouble for me if I did."

"Then run. Friend Sawliru, no man should be in bondage. Not to a slavelord, not to the state, not to the land, and definitely not to a woman. A man is free to himself, and he alone should decide his fate."

"It's not that simple," Sawliru muttered. "There is the matter of my career to think of—"

"What career? You sit at the foot of another, like an obedient dog. You call that living?"

"Enough of this," the Vemlan said, finally, turning to the android. "Commander, your creation need not stoop to slander, and your attempt to sway me from my duty has failed."

"I did nothing of the sort, sir," Data protested. "It is impossible for me to influence the holodeck computer after the initial specifications are chosen. The computer reacts to the comments and actions of the participants. If you are feeling threatened, it is because you, yourself, have directed the conversation in that direction."

"Outrageous," the Vemlan commander replied. "This man—excuse me, this image, is purposefully steering me away from my clear duty. This whole insidious conversation has been designed to turn me away from what is best for my homeworld."

Spartacus was quiet as he watched the exchange between the two men, yet he appeared to take interest. "'Tis true, Sawliru, your companion had nought to do with what I have said. We have never met before. But . . . have you considered what is really best for you, Sawliru? I once thought that

254

slavery was the natural and obvious place for prisoners and captives. Yet once I saw how damning it was to the nation, I decided to change it."

"Enough of this nonsense," Sawliru spat angrily. "It was a fair try, Commander, but it failed. I congratulate you on your innovation."

"It is almost time for the hearing to reconvene, anyway," Data remarked. "Terminate sequence."

The holodeck computer obligingly began shutting down the scenery. As Spartacus and his country faded from view, the ancient liberator made a final remark. "Luck be with you, Sawliru!" it called, then saluted as it faded into nonexistence. The stark walls of the chamber echoed with his last words, and the door to the room hissed open obligingly. Data motioned for Sawliru to proceed ahead of him, and the commander blinked as he left.

As the two of them proceeded back to the hearing room, the Vemlan struggled to readjust to the familiar sights and sounds of a spaceship. He was struggling with a few other things as well.

"Commander, what happened to Spartacus? Did he succeed with his rebellion?"

"Spartacus was captured, along with several hundred other escapees. All were crucified, the traditional punishment for escaped slaves."

Sawliru tensed, remembering the description of a crucifixion. He had to agree with Spartacus; it was not the way for a free man to die.

But, still, there was the matter of duty and loyalty.

"It was, I admit, an admirable try on your part. Your presentation was impeccable. Your construct gave several very valid arguments. Yet he is, in the end, no more real than you are, Commander, and I respect his opinion no more than I respect yours. If anything, I am more hardened in my position than before. Machines have nearly ruined my world, and I will not have one machine get another to betray me when I have almost won."

"What are you trying to win, sir?" Data asked. "It seems to have escaped me."

"Freedom!" Sawliru almost snarled. "The same thing that construct back there said he was fighting for. The periods of war in history were barbaric and uncivilized, that's true, but they allowed a man to be free unto himself. You and your kind have taken that freedom from us in exchange for security. Perhaps now that I have the means of exterminating androids, some semblance of freedom will return to my world. If the politicians and the diplomats don't louse things up," he added, caustically.

With that he strode into the hearing room, where an irate Alkirg was in the midst of a rant. Data remained in the corridor, where he contemplated Sawliru's reaction to the holodeck sequence.

It had originally been his intention to introduce the Spartacus sequence, culled from the holodeck computer's library, to Sawliru as a means of presenting the Vemlan androids' situation to him in metaphorical terms. He had not anticipated the course the sequence took, however. He had told the truth (he could hardly do otherwise) when he told the man that he had nothing to do with the program. In fact, the computer had steered the sequence into a previously unanticipated direction.

"It was not supposed to do that," Data remarked to himself. "But perhaps it was, indeed, worth the attempt." With a feeling of resignation, he entered the hearing room to hear the decision of the panel.

\* \* \*

Jared sipped the punch he was offered, but did not taste it. He felt the cold pressure of the glass on his index finger, and knew that it would be a simple matter of releasing the toxin. Just a little concentrated pressure in the right place would do it. It wouldn't even be noticed, at first, until people started dying off. By then it would be too late. Garan, by now, had dozens of well-armed Alphas waiting to be transported over.

He honestly couldn't tell how the hearing was going. Picard's face was like a mask, and his position was unclear. Jared was used to such trials being mere formalities before the execution order was given. Kurta had convinced him that this might be different. He was unconvinced, however, at the hearing's effectiveness—and was troubled by Data's disappearance.

Would he have to use the bomb Garan had planted? A simple thought and it would be done. He would hate to leave his people like this—

"My husband, as usual, you are being antisocial," a voice behind him remarked. He turned to stare at Kurta, who held a reproving expression on her face. "I've been talking to some of the *Enterprise*'s crew. They were quite impressed with your speech."

"But was Picard?" Jared asked.

In answer, she pointed towards a corner of the room, where Alkirg was arguing with one of the Starfleet officers. "No doubt she is wondering the same."

"Thank goodness for small favors," Jared said, standing. He smiled down at his wife—and in the same instant, remembered the orders he had left with Garan, orders putting him in charge of the *Freedom* if he had to use the explosive device.

He would have to tell Kurta of those orders before the blast. If it came to that, of course.

Worf glanced at a chronometer as he entered his eightieth consecutive hour on duty on the bridge. He was just as awake and alert now as he had been at his tenth, perhaps more.

Many of his fellow crewmen had often wondered why he insisted upon regularly practicing archaic Klingon rituals, convinced that there were easier, less dangerous ways to encourage spiritual development. Worf did not deign to comment on their unasked questions; humans did not have a proper appreciation of tradition, in his opinion, and would not understand why he tested himself in the holodeck, the ship's gymnasium, and upon every planet where he could.

The Klingon rituals may have been archaic, brutal, and illogical, but they had survived a few thousand years of development virtually unchanged. They revolved around the principal tenet of the Klingon system of beliefs: "That which does not kill us makes us strong." It was not too many years in the past when that maxim had fueled an empire far greater than that which the holographic Spartacus had railed against. No, humans watched him exercise, test, and nearly torture himself, and shook their heads and sighed at the crazy Klingon.

He didn't see any of *them* on the bridge for eighty hours.

Worf was shaken from his reverie by a lighthearted beep from the sensor panel in front of him. He had instructed it to alert him upon any change in disposition from either the Vemlan fleet or the nearby *Freedom*. As he checked the readings, his mind was already a-whir with possible responses to a threat. Any threat.

It was the Vemlan fleet that was maneuvering. The android's vessel remained where it was, eclipsed from view of the hostile ships by the bulk of the *Enterprise*. He snapped open a communication channel with a stab of his finger, opening a hailing frequency to the flagship of the fleet.

"USS *Enterprise* to Vemlan navy flagship. This is Lieutenant Worf. Explain your change of position relative to this vessel. Please," he added, knowing how the captain was about politeness. There was a momentary delay, as a ranking deck officer was summoned to answer his query.

"This is Commander Seris, Lieutenant. Do not be alarmed. We are rearranging our formation to easier facilitate a transfer of personnel and supplies from ship to ship. We have a shortage of rations on a few of our ships, and we are using this time of negotiations to transfer them. We don't have transporters like you do."

Worf stared at the sensor screen and noted that every ship was energizing its weapons systems. The outright lie was an insult to him, but it did show a certain elementary guile that he admired. He considered pointing out the fact to Commander Seris, but decided against it.

"Acknowledged," he said in what he thought was his most innocent tone. "Keep us informed if we can be of any assistance. *Enterprise* out." He quit the channel before Seris could respond, an obvious insult, if the Vemlan had the subtlety to see it. He doubted that he did.

He rechecked the formation that the ships were entering, and then checked the *Freedom;* he was not surprised to find the android ship, as well, preparing for battle. Once he was positive of their intent, he called the captain.

"Picard here. What's the trouble, Worf?"

"Captain, the Vemlan fleet is maneuvering into battle formation, and hoping that we won't notice it. There is also considerable activity on the android vessel. Sensors indicate that their weapons are charging or armed, and though they have yet to raise any sort of defensive shielding, I expect that they will do so soon. Instructions?"

He waited a moment while Picard decided. *A Klingon commander,* Worf thought, *would have barked out an order instantly.* Of course, he admitted, in all fairness, a Klingon captain's orders were not always the most appropriate ones. There was something to be said for human deliberation.

"Initiate plan Alpha, Worf. I have a feeling that some of our guests will not like the decisions we will arrive at. They might respond . . . hastily. Take whatever precautions you see fit, but do not alter the original plan."

"Aye, Captain."

"Picard out."

"Worf out." He severed the connection and examined the sensor screen one last time. Yes, that was definitely an attack formation, though it was sloppy and inefficient.

"Prepare forward phasers for operation," he said to the computer. And smiled. It had been his plan, after all.

# *Chapter Twelve*

SAWLIRU PAUSED before joining Alkirg to check with his command. The fleet should be in position by now. His subordinates, despite Alkirg's irate admonishments to the contrary, were highly competent, and should not have had any problems.

"Commander Seris, what is the status of the fleet?" he said into the hushed mouthpiece of his comm unit.

"All ships report condition green, Admiral. The security officer on the *Enterprise* asked what was going on, but we told him that we had a cargo run to make between ships. He bought it." Sawliru wondered silently if he did. If Commander Data was any indication, then Picard had a demonically talented crew.

"Acknowledge, Commander. Initiate on my signal."

"But, sir! Aren't you going to be back on board for the . . . uh, operation?"

"Possibly not. Mission Commander Alkirg may need my services elsewhere. If you men are as good as I've trained you to be, you shouldn't need me there."

"But, sir! The men are all looking to you. Things are getting rough over here," he admitted. "I've already had to break up two fights in the bays. I'm not sure the men will attack without you to lead them."

"You have my orders, Seris. This comes from the top," he said, tiredly.

Seris didn't say anything. He wasn't any happier with the arrangement than Sawliru was. The Vemlan felt sorry for the man. "Seris, this matter will come out fine. Just follow orders and I'll make it work. You have my word."

"Aye, aye, sir. Seris out."

Sawliru closed the unit with a snap and reholstered it. The brush with the imaginary gladiator had shaken him momentarily, but now he was back in his element, treading the decks of a spaceship, doing what he knew how. He glanced over to where Alkirg was fussing at one of the Starfleet ensigns over seating arrangements again. He decided to take pity on the poor boy and rescue him.

"Mission Commander Alkirg, the preparations have been made," he said, in a low voice. He glanced briefly at the ensign, dismissing him. The boy retreated gratefully.

"Where have you been?" she said quietly, clearly furious. "I heard that that white-faced, misdesigned Starfleet android wandered off with you. What were you doing with him, anyway?"

"He wanted to cut a deal. I listened to him, then I told him no. We had a drink," he admitted.

"Despicable behavior, really." She frowned. "I would have a word about that android with Captain Picard after this is all over, except—" Alkirg waved a hand dismissively. "When this is all over, Captain Picard will no longer be in a position to do anything about it."

With that she spun on her heel and headed back into the hearing room. Sawliru followed her reluctantly.

Picard glanced at Crusher and Riker before he went into the hearing room. Beverly looked worn, but ready, and Will was behaving as if he admitted new races into the Federation every day.

"They're not going to like this," Beverly said, warningly.

"It's our—my—final decision. They may take it or leave it," Picard said, testily. "I am growing tired of this endless debate."

"All rise," the computer said, helpfully. The assembled crowd stood in a gesture of respect as the panel members took their seats upon the dais. Picard motioned for the participants to sit, then looked around. It was almost over, he knew, one way or another.

"Before we begin, I'd like to make an announcement. I have been informed by my engineering staff that we have a power buildup in the forward phaser capacitor." Sawliru looked wary, while Alkirg and the androids looked alarmed. "Please, there is no danger, nothing to worry about," Picard soothed. "The hearing will continue uninterrupted. However, we need to drain this capacitor, and will therefore need to fire our forward phasers to prevent a further buildup. We have chosen a nearby asteroid as our target. The blast will be relatively minor, and nowhere near full capacity, but considering the heightened tensions in the area, I felt it best if all parties were advised. I apologize for the inconvenience. Commanders, if you wish to inform your respective ships of the action . . ."

Sawliru and Jared reached, simultaneously, for their communication devices.

"Fire forward phasers!" Worf commanded, his deep voice booming out over the bridge.

He loved saying that.

Two lances of man-made lightning stabbed out into the void, toward the huge chunk of rock that had been in the vicinity of the *Enterprise* since the storm had subsided. The captain had, as was his right, exaggerated slightly. The burst was not a minor one at all; the phasers were operating at full capacity. And the effect on the asteroid was spectacular.

The local stellar explosion that had inadvertently spawned the Gabriel storm had changed the composition of the tiny planet from regular nickel-iron to a matrix of pure felsium. Felsium was not a rare mineral; just about any stellar explosion above a certain magnitude could produce it. It was highly valued in its purest form for a variety of engineering uses. Some races even used it as a base for propulsion reactors; when energy was directed at felsium, the felsium absorbed it until it reached critical mass. Then the energy was released. In a felsium reactor, the release was controlled by a number of damper plates.

The felsium in the asteroid wasn't near engineering grade purity, but it was several cubic kilometers thick and the phasers poured in energy several magnitudes greater than any ordinary reactor.

And there wasn't a damn thing controlling the release.

It absorbed every portion of energy it could from the weapons. Then it absorbed just a little bit more . . .

It exploded. It was safely several hundred thousand kilometers away from the nearest vessel. There was absolutely no danger to any of the ships involved in the hearing. But it lit up space like a supernova, sending brightly colored shards of rock and dust arcing away like miniature stars.

It was impressive. The captain's plan—thought of by Worf—had ended there, but Worf couldn't stand not taking further precautions against a surprise attack. "Lock on to lead Vemlan navy ship with forward phasers," he instructed the computer, "and target the *Freedom* with rear torpedoes."

"Weapons armed and locked," the gentle contralto of the *Enterprise* computer said. "Waiting for activation signal."

"Not without captain's orders," Worf said, gruffly.

It was awfully tempting, though.

"The decision of the panel was a difficult one to make," Picard said, addressing the sea of anxious faces. "The situation is much more complicated than a normal petition for entry. Many unusual factors had to be taken into consideration.

"Firstly, the matter of the claim of ownership that the Vemlan navy has made on the andr— the Spartacans. For if they are, indeed, truly property, then their admission into the Federation would violate the concept of nonintervention that underlies the Prime Directive." Alkirg smiled imperiously.

"However," Picard continued, "the Spartacans were encountered by the *Enterprise* far from the nearest star system, and quite far from their home. They were fleeing a devastated world, which qualifies them under law as refugees. These factors are not subject to debate. Since this region of space is not protected under any known treaty, the property rights of the Vemlans are no concern of ours."

Alkirg's smile turned into a vicious frown. While the captain was speaking, Sawliru's communications device chirped. He turned it on, setting the volume low to keep from interrupting the proceedings.

"Commander Seris, reporting."

"Yes, go on."

"That phaser test the *Enterprise* conducted was devastating."

Sawliru raised his eyebrows. "Any damage?" he asked. Perhaps that could be used to their advantage in the proceedings.

"Negative. But if that weapon wasn't firing at full capacity, we don't stand a chance in a firefight. It'll cut through us like an ax through an egg."

"Have you had the science section check it out?"

"Aye, sir. Science says the resulting explosion was greater in scope than any device we have ever encountered."

Sawliru nodded and felt a numb roar in his ears. His little fleet, the last protection his worn-out world had against invaders, didn't stand a chance against this mighty Starfleet vessel. His men would be cut down like weeds before they could fire a shot.

"Sir? The men are troubled by the rumors. The general consensus is that no one in his right mind is going to attack. Sir? Uh, perhaps you should get over here soon. Things are getting ugly. I just heard shots."

"I hear you, Seris. Maintain position. Maintain discipline. I'll be there as soon as I can. Sawliru out."

As he replaced his device, the captain was finishing his speech.

". . . and the Federation is not an organization to be entered into lightly. I almost disallowed these hearings on the grounds that they were being used to avoid possible criminal prosecution." Picard took a deep breath.

"However, it is the decision of this board to grant the race of androids, known as Spartacans, provisional status as an associate member of the Federation, pending full approval."

The new Federation members grinned widely, in a most unmachinelike manner. Even Data smiled, the closest he could come to an emotional outburst. The emotions from the other side of the room were less jubilant, however.

"I can't believe this," Alkirg said. "You actually did it? You admitted these monsters?" She rose from her seat, furious. "Do you know what you have done, Picard? The blood of the thousands that died unavenged on Vemla, and the thousands that continue to die is on your hands, Picard! On your hands! You cannot so easily thwart the will of the Vemlan people, who have paid for this expedition in blood! You'll pay for this in blood from the bridge of a burning ship!" Alkirg turned to face her subordinate.

"Force Commander Sawliru! Summon our shuttle. We will return to the flagship at once. We will then activate our contingency plan," she said in a low voice, the thought of vengeance on both her android prey and their uninvited rescuers already apparently soothing her.

"I beg you to reconsider, Mission Commander," Sawliru began. "It would be suicide," he insisted, pleadingly, looking warily at the Starfleet officers. They didn't know what the contingency plan was, of course, but you didn't have to be a military genius to figure it out. "My men won't do such a thing! They're at the brink of mutiny, now!"

"You are their commander, you fool! Order them!" She declared passionately, "They have to obey orders!"

"Or what? Face a court-martial back home? Alkirg, we won't get back home if we do this."

"Just do it!" the woman shouted through gritted teeth.

Sawliru paused under her fiery glare, then woodenly opened a channel to his ship. He stared at his superior, then looked down.

And noticed how scuffed his boots were.

He closed the channel and looked Alkirg in the eye.

"I refuse," he said, calmly and firmly. "I am willfully disobeying your orders."

"You are committing high treason," she warned.

"And mutiny." Suddenly, the android Data was at his side. "I could not help but overhear."

"Shut up, android!" Alkirg spat. "I'll do it myself!

I swear, I'll see you hang for this, Sawliru!" She brought out her own comm unit, snapped it open and began speaking breathlessly into it.

There was no response.

"I took the liberty of having the power unit removed," Sawliru said, easily. "You are relieved of duty."

It was as if a great weight had been lifted from him.

"You can't do that!" she insisted. "Only the assembly of Vemla can do that! I outrank you!"

Sawliru ignored her, as he turned to face his host. "Captain Picard, on Alkirg's orders my fleet was preparing to attack your ship. I apologize."

"This is highly irregular," murmured Picard.

"This whole mission has been highly irregular, right from the start," Sawliru confessed. He turned back, and faced his former commander. "Your friends, the ones in the government, concocted this whole miserable expedition from the start as a way to delude the masses. You sent the bulk military force away at a moment of critical need to bring back the splinter that was no longer troubling the planet. And for what?" he demanded, becoming more emotional with each word. "A televised execution? Oh, good, we killed another android. All our problems are over. Bah!" he spat in frustration.

"You won't get away with this, Sawliru!" Alkirg cried. "I have friends! Even if you kill me, they'll find you! They'll ruin your career!"

"Career as what?" the incredulous Force Commander asked. "A puppet in a soldier suit? No, Alkirg, I'm not going to murder you. I want you alive. And, as far as your friends go, they would drop you like a hot iron as soon as you became a political liability. That's how that small but vicious circle you travel in works."

He thought for a moment, new visions coming to him. Just what was he going to do when he got home? An answer came to him, in startling clarity. "But even that doesn't matter. They placed me in sole command of the biggest military force in Vemlan history to catch a few runaway androids. Well, I'm leaving the androids here and taking the fleet back to Vemla, where it belongs. Then—" he paused, "and then we'll see what happens to you and your self-serving comrades."

Alkirg's eyes widened. "You're talking about over-throwing the government!" she said. "That's dictatorship—and tyranny! The assembly has kept the peace and order for three hundred years!"

"You call the android rebellion peace and order? It wasn't the androids you kept in slavery, it was the people! You were just lucky it was the androids that shook things up, Alkirg. They were but a few hundred thousand. Had the people risen, it would have been billions of lives lost, and we never would have recovered."

"You took an oath to obey the will of the council!"

"I took an oath to protect Vemla. That, I believe, takes precedent." He took a deep breath. "And to that purpose, I plan on assuming control over the government, as soon as we arrive."

"A military coup d'état?" Picard said. "Force Commander, that's a very extreme measure—"

Sawliru raised his eyebrows. "Oppression is even more extreme, Captain. You and your Federation are advanced, both technologically and politically. You have peace, prosperity, and freedom. But didn't it take you centuries of barbarism and bloodshed to achieve it?"

"Quite so," Data replied. "Reviewing the history of humanity, alone, is enough to make one wonder how they survived at all."

"My people are less advanced than yours," Sawliru continued. "We can make wonderful mechanical men, but we can't think for ourselves yet. We aren't ready for this utopia you've labored to build." He looked meaningfully at Jared. "Perhaps our . . . children are."

"I see. And does this mean you surrender your claims to the Spartacans and the *Freedom?*" Picard asked, sensing some kind of settlement was at hand.

Sawliru looked at Jared and Kurta, who were watching the revolutionary display with great interest. "They mean nothing to me. Bringing them back to Vemla would open wounds too recently closed. It would serve no constructive purpose. I may be a warlord, but I shall endeavor to be an enlightened warlord."

The androids were visibly moved. Jared stood forward, his artificial majesty dominating the shorter man. "Do you still hate me so, Sawliru?"

Sawliru considered his former enemy. "Yes," he said, simply. "Your people brought mine to the brink of destruction. My son died by the hand of an android, and that hurts no matter how much I deny it. My brother—your master—was put away because of the chaos you caused. There is too much to be forgiven lightly. There can be no substitute for experience, Jared, and no amount of design can equal the rigors of evolution. But

I wish you and your people well. Perhaps, some day in the future, you may return to Vemla. Look me up, I'll be interested in how things fare with you."

"I promise," the android said solemnly.

"If there is no further business, here, I will adjourn this hearing. Commander Sawliru, if you and the Spartacans will join me in Ten-Forward, I'd like to toast the new Federation members."

"That would be fine, Captain. Let me take care of a little business first." He contacted Seris on board his ship.

"Tell the men to stand down, Commander. We're going home."

He could hear muted cheers in the background as Seris relayed the message. That sound, alone, made his decision worthwhile. "And send a shuttle to the *Enterprise*. Alkirg has been placed under arrest, and is to be put in the brig upon her arrival."

"You'll never get away with this," the ex-mission commander vowed.

"Shut up, Alkirg, or I'll send you with the Alphas, so help me," Sawliru said.

She shut up. And for the first time in a long while, Sawliru smiled peacefully.

The mood in Ten-Forward was jubilant. The new members of the Federation had brought over a healthy supply of their native wines for the crew of the starship to sample, and Guinan had broken open her special store of champagne, Romulan ale, and Vulcan fruit wine in response. After all, she reasoned, it wasn't every day you got to host a formal membership reception in your lounge.

The captain had made a toast, and then a long

speech, and then a hasty exit. That was half an hour ago, and now the party was in full swing. Sawliru was talking about a potential treaty with his former enemies, and discussing the finer points of attacking an android stronghold (no offense intended, you know) to a no-longer-captive audience. He looked ten years younger, and relaxed for the first time, to the alien at the bar. Perhaps mutiny and high treason have a rejuvenating effect, Guinan mused. His soul, at least, seemed at peace.

Various androids and Vemlan soldiers (who had come over in the shuttle that had taken Alkirg back to the fleet) were drinking, eating, and singing. It was a good party. Guinan liked good parties.

She overheard Riker flirting lightly with his android counterpart, while her husband talked shop with Sawliru. "Will, do you think the Federation will accept us, finally?"

Riker stroked his beard and looked thoughtful. "I would say so. It's conceivable that they might overturn Captain Picard's decision, but he has a lot of influence."

"Then you think we'll get a planet?" she asked hopefully.

"I do," said Will. "Data mentioned you liked plants."

She nodded. "Very much."

"Well, it just so happens that I have access to the seed bank in the bio labs. As a token of my respect, and a peace offering, I want to give you a few hundred varieties of alien flowering plants. I'm sure you'll put them to good use."

"That would be fantastic, Will!" she smiled, happily. Jared looked over at the sound of his wife's jubilation. He felt almost guilty, though he knew better than to let his face reveal it. He glanced down at his index finger and felt ashamed. Had the decision gone the other way, and his people had to fight with Sawliru, then he would have quietly released the toxin at the hearing. The thought made him ashamed, for the first time, of what he had become.

Jared knew Kurta had guessed his plan, and knew also that she hadn't tried to stop him. But she hid her shame with dignity. Perhaps he could make it up to her, somehow, in Data's honor. He had, after all, saved them all, Vemlan and Spartacan alike, Jared reasoned, as he turned back to the Force Commander's conversation. He had time enough, now, to deal with his conscience.

At a table in one corner, Data and the librarian from the *Freedom* were enjoying a quiet (well, as quiet as could be expected in the festive atmosphere) drink together. Maran looked almost humanly relieved at the news that she would neither be dragged back to Vemla for trial and execution nor be blown away in a space battle.

"I need to return this to you," Data said, as he pushed a golden cylinder towards her, across the table. "I will not be needing it now."

"Thank you for keeping it," Maran replied, as she took the cylinder and carefully put it away in her bag. "Data, what will happen to us now? As much as I've read on the Federation, I still don't know it very well."

"You will be escorted to Starbase 112. There, another hearing will be held to confirm Captain Picard's decision."

"Another hearing? I thought that this was it," she said.

"The captain was only able to grant you provisional member status. The final decision belongs to the other races of the Federation. It will be a hard struggle to confirm the Spartacans. Despite the enlightened principals of the civilizations of the Federation, much actual prejudice exists among its members. Some of it is unconscious, I am sure, but discrimination against mechanical beings will continue."

"I see. So nothing has really changed."

"No, you do not understand," Data insisted. "You now have the freedom to pursue your goals. Even if the Federation does not accept your race as a member, then you may find and develop a planet on your own. The Federation will not stop you. You are forever free."

Her dark eyes looked up at his pale ones. "When we find a planet, and build a home, will you come visit us?"

"Of course," Data replied. "That would be most pleasing to me."

Then Maran smiled, leaned forward and kissed him gently on the cheek. "Thank you so much for everything."

Riker, having had too much synthehol and alien wine, jumped up on the bar and shouted for attention.

"I'd like to propose a toast to the one person who made this party, this hearing, this whole damn occasion possible. To Lieutenant Commander Data!"

There was a cheer as the whole room turned to the corner where Maran was just planting a kiss on Data's cheek.

There was an embarrassed silence and a giggle, as Riker realized that Data was otherwise occupied.

The silence sobered him a little, and he struggled for words.

"It's okay, Commander," Geordi, who had just joined the festivities, called. "They're just busy pretending that they have emotions right now!"

"That's my boy," Guinan said to herself, smiling at Data and wiping down another glass. "He's learning."

The First Star Trek: The Next Generation
Hardcover Novel!

# REUNION

## Michael Jan Friedman

Captain Picard's
past and present
collide on board the
USS *Enterprise*™

POCKET
BOOKS

Available in Hardcover
from Pocket Books

444-02

# STAR TREK ®
## THE NEXT GENERATION ™
## Technical Manual
### Mike Okuda and Rick Sternbach

The technical advisors to the smash TV hit series, STAR TREK: THE NEXT GENERATION, take readers into the incredible world they've created for the show. Filled with blueprints, sketches and line drawings, this book explains the principles behind everything from the transporter to the holodeck—and takes an unprecedented look at the brand-new U.S.S. *Enterprise*™ NCC 1701-D.

## Available From Pocket Books

POCKET
B O O K S

107-03

# STAR TREK
## THE NEXT GENERATION ™

- ☐ ENCOUNTER FARPOINT .................... 74388-0/$4.95
- ☐ #1 GHOST SHIP ................................... 74608-1/$4.95
- ☐ #2 THE PEACEKEEPERS ..................... 73653-1/$4.99
- ☐ #3 THE CHILDREN OF HAMLIN ......... 73555-1/$4.99
- ☐ #4 SURVIVORS .................................... 74290-6/$4.95
- ☐ #5 STRIKE ZONE .................................. 74647-2/$4.95
- ☐ #6 POWER HUNGRY ............................ 74648-0/$4.95
- ☐ #7 MASKS ............................................ 74139-X/$4.95
- ☐ #8 THE CAPTAIN'S HONOR ................ 74140-3/$4.95
- ☐ #9 A CALL TO DARKNESS .................. 74141-1/$4.95
- ☐ #10 A ROCK AND A HARD PLACE .... 74142-X/$4.95
- ☐ METAMORPHOSIS ............................. 68402-7/$4.99
- ☐ #11 GULLIVER'S FUGITIVES ............. 74143-8/$4.95
- ☐ #12 DOOMSDAY WORLD ................... 74144-6/$4.95
- ☐ #13 THE EYES OF THE BEHOLDERS 70010-3/$4.50
- ☐ #14 EXILES ......................................... 70560-1/$4.99
- ☐ #15 FORTUNE'S LIGHT ...................... 70836-8/$4.50
- ☐ #16 CONTAMINATION ........................ 70561-X/$4.95
- ☐ #17 BOOGEYMEN ............................... 70970-4/$4.95
- ☐ #18 Q-IN-LAW .................................... 73389-3/$4.99
- ☐ #19 PERCHANCE TO DREAM ............ 70837-6/$4.99
- ☐ STAR TREK: THE NEXT GENERATION
  GIANT NOVEL:
  VENDETTA ............................ 74145-4/$4.95

POCKET BOOKS

**Simon & Schuster Mail Order Dept. NGS
200 Old Tappan Rd., Old Tappan, N.J. 07675**

Please send me the books I have checked above. I am enclosing $_____ (please add 75¢ to cover postage and handling for each order. Please add appropriate local sales tax). Send check or money order–no cash or C.O.D.'s please. Allow up to six weeks for delivery. For purchases over $10.00 you may use VISA: card number, expiration date and customer signature must be included.

Name _____

Address _____

City _____ State/Zip _____

VISA Card No. _____ Exp. Date _____

Signature _____ 100-21